W9-BUP-542

Her secrets only make her more alluring. . . .

It was disconcerting to be examined at such close quarters.

She was in Michael's lap, her face so close to his that if she leaned forward even the slightest bit, their lips would touch.

The thought sent tremors of— Was it amazement? Trepidation? Uncertainty? Whatever it was, it was uncomfortable, to say the least. Jane wiggled, trying to loosen his hold.

"Stop that." Michael's voice was so strained that Jane instantly froze. His eyes were now closed, his brows lowered, and he bit into his bottom lip as if in pain.

"I'm sorry. Did I hurt you?" she asked.

Michael's swallow was audible over the coach's creaking. "No. But you shouldn't squirm like that."

"Why not— Oh! Your—" Her cheeks heated. "I didn't mean to—"

"I'm sure you didn't."

She was instantly aware of how his voice rumbled in his chest and thus against her arm when he spoke.

He met her gaze now, as bold as ever. "If you don't stay still, I won't be responsible for my reactions."

Turn the page for rave reviews of
Karen Hawkins and the Hurst Amulet series . . .

Praise for
Scandal in Scotland

"An entertaining romantic battle of wits . . . [a] humor-rich historical."

—*Chicago Tribune*

"A humorous, fast-paced dramatic story that's filled with sensual tension. Hawkins' passionate, intelligent characters make it impossible to put down."

—*RT Book Reviews* (4½ stars, Top Pick)

"Rollicking good fun from beginning to end! Pure, vintage Hawkins!"

—Romance and More

One Night in Scotland

"Known for her quick-moving, humorous, and poignant stories, Hawkins begins the Hurst Amulet series with a keeper. Readers will be delighted by the perfect pacing, the humorous dialogue, and the sizzling sensual romance."

—*RT Book Reviews* (4½ stars, Top Pick)

"A lively romp, the perfect beginning to [Hawkins's] new series."

—*Booklist*

"Couldn't put it down. . . . Ms. Hawkins is one of the most talented historical romance writers out there."

—Romance Junkies (5 stars)

"Charming and witty."

—*Publishers Weekly*

"An adventurous romance filled with laughter, passion, and emotion . . . mystery, threats, and plenty of sexual tension, plus an engaging premise which will keep you thoroughly entertained during each highly captivating scene. . . . *One Night in Scotland* holds your attention from beginning to end."

—Single Titles

"With its creative writing, interesting characters, and well-crafted situations and dialogue, *One Night in Scotland* is an excellent read. Be assured it lives up to all the virtues one has learned to expect from this talented writer."

—Romance Reviews Today

and Karen Hawkins

"Fast, fun, and sexy stories that are a perfect read for a rainy day, a sunny day, or any day at all!"

—bestselling author Christina Dodd

"Hawkins always delivers delightfully humorous, poignant, and highly satisfying novels."

—*RT Book Reviews*

"Humor, folklore, and sizzling love scenes."

—*Winter Haven News Chief*

"Always funny and sexy, a Karen Hawkins book is a sure delight!"

—bestselling author Victoria Alexander

"Delightful in every way."

—Reader to Reader

"Romance at its best!"

—Romance and More

ALSO BY KAREN HAWKINS

Available from Pocket Books

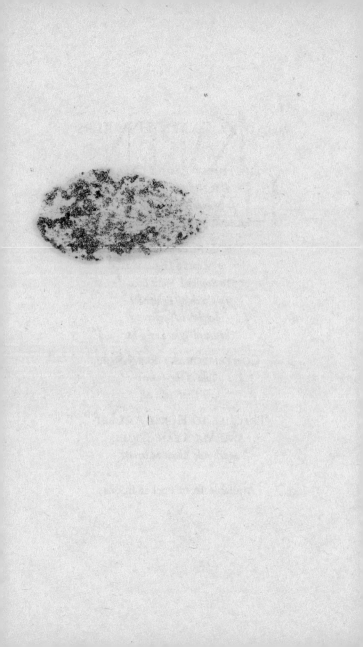

KAREN HAW

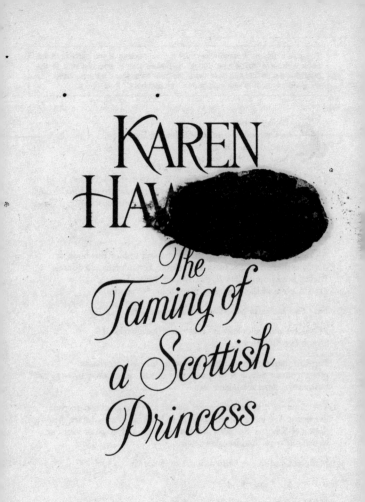

The Taming of a Scottish Princess

Pocket Books

New York   London   Toronto   Sydney   New Delhi

The sale of this book without its cover is unauthorized. If you purchased this book without a cover, you should be aware that it was reported to the publisher as "unsold and destroyed." Neither the author nor the publisher has received payment for the sale of this "stripped book."

Pocket Books
A Division of Simon & Schuster, Inc.
1230 Avenue of the Americas
New York, NY 10020

This book is a work of fiction. Names, characters, places, and incidents either are products of the author's imagination or are used fictitiously. Any resemblance to actual events or locales or persons, living or dead, is entirely coincidental.

Copyright © 2012 by Karen Hawkins

All rights reserved, including the right to reproduce this book or portions thereof in any form whatsoever. For information address Pocket Books Subsidiary Rights Department,
1230 Avenue of the Americas, New York, NY 10020.

First Pocket Books paperback edition June 2012

POCKET and colophon are registered trademarks of Simon & Schuster, Inc.

For information about special discounts for bulk purchases, please contact Simon & Schuster Special Sales at 1-866-506-1949 or business@simonandschuster.com.

The Simon & Schuster Speakers Bureau can bring authors to your live event. For more information or to book an event contact the Simon & Schuster Speakers Bureau at 1-866-248-3049 or visit our website at www.simonspeakers.com.

Manufactured in the United States of America

10 9 8 7 6 5 4 3 2 1

ISBN 978-1-4391-7595-8
ISBN 978-1-4391-7603-0 (ebook)

To my sister, Robin
February 8, 1962–October 3, 2011
I miss you.

The
Taming of
a Scottish
Princess

CHAPTER I

From the diary of Michael Hurst, famous explorer and Egyptologist:

Finally, I have the entire treasure map in my possession—the one that will lead us to the lost Hurst Amulet, which was taken from my family so many centuries ago. I was certain the map revealed the final clue to the amulet's location and I was ready to proceed thus. Or I was until my blasted assistant, the redoubtable Miss Jane Smythe-Haughton, made a completely unrequested observation that I was "anything but well versed in this particular form of cartography" and I should have an expert examine the bloody thing.

Her distrust in my knowledge is as large as it is abiding. However, I'm now forced to prove myself, so I'm having the map reviewed by a renowned expert. Once I receive confirmation that my theory is correct, we will begin the final quest for the amulet. After, of course, I finish mocking Jane to hell and back for her disbelief in my profound and infallible map-reading abilities.

London, England
October 12, 1822

Michael Hurst ignored the stir of excitement that flowed across the ballroom at his entrance. "Damn fools," he muttered, tugging on his cravat.

His sister Mary sent him an exasperated glance. "Leave that alone."

"It's choking me."

"It's fashionable and you must look presentable." At his annoyed glare, she added in an earnest tone, "Michael, this ballroom is full of potential investors for your expeditions."

Potential *headaches* were what they were. "I'm here, aren't I?" he asked irritably. "Where's that damned refreshment table? If I'm going to face these monkeys, I'll need a drink."

"They're not monkeys, but lovely women who—" She caught his expression and grimaced. "Perhaps a drink will improve your spirits. Lady Bellforth usually sets the refreshment table by the library doors."

He nodded and stepped in that direction. As if in answer to that one step, fans and lashes fluttered, seemingly hoping to trap him in a gossamer hold. "For the love of Ra," he said through gritted teeth, "don't they have anything better to do than stare?"

"You're famous," Mary said calmly.

"I don't wish to be famous."

"But you are, so you'll just have to live with it." She placed a hand on his arm. "Just smile and nod and we'll make our way through this crowd in no time at all."

"Smiling won't work, but *this* will." He scowled instead, noticing with glee that several of the flowery fans stopped fluttering.

"Michael, you can't—"

He placed his hand firmly under her elbow and led her into the crowd, scowling at first one hopeful-looking miss and then another. They blushed, then sagged, as if he'd stabbed their empty little hearts.

Mary made an impatient noise and then said in a low voice, "We'll never get another sponsor if you keep that up. These women are the daughters and sisters of wealthy men who could aid your expeditions greatly!"

"They are cotton-headed bits of fluff, and I refuse to pander to them." He almost stopped when one of them boldly winked at him. "Good God, what happened to female modesty while I was in the wilds of Egypt?"

"More to the point, what happened to gentlemanly manners?"

"I left those worthless skills on the reedy shores of the Nile," he retorted. "Good riddance, too."

She gave him a sour look. "Our brothers are right: you have turned into a barbarian."

"Why? Because I do and say what must be said?"

"No, because you barrel through life and never stop to consider the consequences of your words and actions. I—"

A young woman stepped into their path, almost thrust into place by the girls who circled behind her.

Tall, with a large nose and auburn curls, decorated with pearl pins, she appeared to be all of seventeen. "Mr. Hurst! How nice to see you again." She dipped a grand curtsy, her smirk letting him know that she expected a welcome greeting.

Michael lifted a brow but said nothing.

Her cheeks bloomed red, her lips pressed in swift irritation, though she hid it almost immediately behind a forced smile. "I'm Miss Lydia Latham. We met at Lady MacLean's soiree."

Michael stared as Miss Latham held out her hand expectantly.

"*Ooof!*" He rubbed his side and glared at his sister, who'd just elbowed him. "*Must* you?"

"Yes." She leaned closer and said through her gritted smile in a voice only he could hear, "I will stomp on your foot right here and now, in front of the entire world, if you don't take her hand and at least *pretend* you are a gentleman."

Michael suddenly remembered when, as a child, Mary'd once tossed him head over heels into an icy pond for nothing more than laughing at her new hairstyle. Of course, she'd been younger then, and less prone to care what others thought of her public deportment. He wondered for a bare second if she would really cause a scene, but the icy gleam in her eye made him think better of finding out.

With a grimace, Michael turned to the waiting girl, took her proffered hand, and held it the minimal time required by politeness before releasing it. "Miss Latham," he intoned with as little enthusiasm as possible.

Miss Latham beamed as if he'd just conferred a cask of gold coins upon her. "I *knew* you'd remember me. We spoke at length about the Rosetta stone."

"Did we?" he asked in a bored tone.

"Oh, yes! I've read every word you've ever written."

"I doubt that, unless you've managed to sneak into my bedchamber and procure my diaries. I'm fairly sure no one has read those but me."

Mary murmured a protest under her breath, but he ignored her.

Miss Latham's face turned several shades pinker and she tittered nervously. "Oh, no! I would never, ever sneak into a man's bedchamber."

"More's the pit—"

"*Michael,*" Mary interjected hurriedly, shooting him a dagger glance before she offered a kind smile to the sublimely unaware Miss Latham. "What my brother means to say is that *The Morning Post* serial is but a small portion of his writings. He's the author of many scientific treatises on various artifacts and ruins that he's unearthed, and—"

"My diaries," he said smoothly.

One of the other girls—they could hardly be called women, as they were gazing at him as if he were a sweet cake and they were ready to devour him—clasped her hands together and said in a soulful tone, "I've never known a *man* to keep a diary."

"And just how many men do you know?" Michael asked, irritated to be placed upon a pedestal for the most mundane of things.

Mary glared at him as if she were fighting the urge to toss him back into a pond. She said under her breath, "No one will invite you anywhere if you continue like that."

"Nonsense," he assured her *en sotto*. "They are too silly to know any better."

As if to prove his point, yet another girl, this one with brown hair and a protruding chin, said brazenly, as if every word were a challenge that he wouldn't be able to resist, "Mr. Hurst, I daresay our petty little parties bore you to death."

"Yes, they do."

Not realizing he found their party boring because of inane comments like hers, she sent her companions a triumphant glance. "I knew it! A ball is too tame for him after wrestling crocodiles and—"

"Hold!" Michael frowned. "Did you say 'wrestling crocodiles'?"

"Why, yes." When his brow creased, she added in a helpful tone, "You wrote about it in the *The Morning Post* just last month."

Mary's hand slipped from where it had been resting on his arm.

"Pray excuse me for just one moment," Michael told the vapid ingénue before he turned.

His sister was two steps away, looking for a way to escape, but the crowd—trying to get closer to hear him speak—pressed too closely.

He grasped her elbow and pulled her back to his side. "There's never a trapdoor about when you most need one, is there?"

Face red, she glanced at their interested audience. With obvious effort, she fixed a frozen smile on her face. "Pardon me, but my poor brother is famished and needs nourishment." With that, she locked her arm through his, turned on her heel, put down her head, and burrowed her way through the crowd.

Michael allowed her to tug him along, glad to be rid of the pests in laces who stared after them.

They reached the refreshment table, where Mary

quickly selected two half-filled cups and grabbed a small plate upon which sat a tiny piece of stale cake. Then, with an air of determination, she found an alcove hidden from prying eyes. Once there, she let out a huge sigh and dropped wearily upon the small settee provided for those fatigued from dancing.

"A crocodile?" Michael asked. "What—"

"Shush!" She gestured for him to take a cup. "Give me a moment to rest before you quiz me. I vow but I was holding my breath during that entire conversation. I just *knew* you'd be rude and ruin all of our efforts."

Michael sniffed his cup and then took an exploratory sip. He choked. "Bloody hell, what *is* this stuff?"

"Orgeat, which you'd know if you'd throw your mind back to the few dances Mother and I dragged you to as a youth."

"It's vile." Michael dumped the contents of his cup into a nearby plant, and then reached into his pocket and pulled out a small silver flask.

Mary paused, her own cup halfway to her lips. "Scotch?"

"Yes. And damned good Scotch, too. Our beloved brother-in-law Hugh sent it to me." Michael filled his cup from his flask. "I admired the MacLean stock while visiting Hugh and our sister Triona several years ago, and he sent me a case. I'm almost to the end of it, so I may need to visit them again."

"Perhaps *I* need to visit them." Mary wistfully eyed his cup. "Triona was sad not to join us here in London."

Michael paused in taking a drink. "I'm surprised she hasn't yet been to town."

"Mam told her not to."

"What's our grandmother to do with Triona's travel plans?"

"Triona's hoping to have a child and Mam specifically told her she should stay home just now and—"

"Hold. Triona's following Mam's advice?"

"Our grandmother is a healer. A *noted* healer."

"Noted by a village full of uneducated fools."

Mary's gaze narrowed. "She's helped many people."

"Many people *think* she's helped them."

"Isn't that the same?"

"No. Mam's tendencies toward the flamboyant would have served her well upon the stage but do little to recommend her as a healer. If Triona and Hugh wish for a child, they would do better to come to London and see a physician."

"Triona's already been to every physician in London *and* Edinburgh. She and Hugh even went to Italy to see someone and—" Mary frowned. "I've already told you all of this in my letters. Didn't you read them?"

"Of course I did."

"Then what did I say about Triona and Hugh's efforts to have a child?"

He swirled the whiskey in his cup.

"You didn't read a single one of my letters, did you?"

"I read them all; I just didn't read them *closely*."

"Michael!" From where she sat on the low settee, Mary stomped her foot, her skirts fluttering. "You're a— I can't believe you— *Oh!*"

"I can't read every damn word of every letter I get! I have *five* brothers and sisters, and then there's Father, who cannot let a day go by without sending me some preachy epistle, *and* Mother, who is determined to discover who I'm to wed before I even know it myself. I didn't yet mention Mam, who writes such damned cryptic stuff that it's harder to slog through than a stone scratched over with hieroglyphs, and—"

"Stop complaining. You enjoy our letters and we know it."

She was right. Though he may not have read the letters from his family closely each and every time he received one, he loved getting the missives. He traveled so much that they connected him to his home and kept him grounded.

Truth be told, he owed his siblings a lot. If not for their efforts, he would still be trapped in a sulfi's prison. He shrugged and then smiled at Mary. "You're right; there were days your letters were my only light." *More than you'll ever know.*

Mary eyed his flask. "I don't suppose you're thankful enough to share a sip, are you?"

He handed her the flask, noting how she eagerly poured a liberal splash into her own cup. "Now, that's the sister I know and love," he said with fondness as he replaced the flask in his pocket.

She took a sip and then sighed blissfully. "It's wonderful. But you, Michael, are not. If you'd read my letters you'd know that Triona agreed to drink Mam's potions for one year, and if there is no child by that time, then Triona'll give up."

Michael curled his lip. "Potions. There is no such thing as magic."

"Then why are you so determined to get your hands on the Hurst Amulet? You've seen written accounts that say it's magical."

"I've also seen written accounts vowing that the earth is flat."

Mary held out her empty cup and gestured for Michael to refill it. "There's no harm in our sister drinking Mam's potions. They give Triona hope."

"False hope."

"Which is better than none," Mary replied in a spritely tone, pointing at her waiting cup.

Michael removed the flask from his pocket, unscrewed the top, and tipped it over her cup, before saying in a resigned tone, "But I suppose Triona wouldn't listen to anyone else. Plus, there are benefits to keeping Mam preoccupied, for she'll be far too busy with our sister's business to interfere in our lives."

Mary frowned. "You've become very self-absorbed. Robert says it comes from being in charge of so many people for so long, and having your every wish seen to."

"Our brother is a fool. He makes it sound as if I had servant girls following me around, waving palm fronds and feeding me grapes."

Mary's eyes widened. "Michael, you didn't—"

"No, I didn't. Bloody hell, I've been on an expedition, not a holiday. Instead of nattering on about something he knows nothing about, Robert should accompany me on my next expedition to Egypt. I'd like to see his soft, lace-bedecked self sleeping upon a pallet under a mosquito net, working from dawn to sundown in stifling heat, and digging in the dirt for hours upon end."

"I thought you hired men to dig for you."

"I can't let them dig without supervision. Besides, if it's a rich find, it's better to dig myself so that fewer artifacts are broken by careless shovels and picks." He cocked a brow at her. "Speaking of carelessness . . ." Michael tossed back the rest of his whiskey and refilled his cup. "We really should discuss this crocodile I supposedly wrestled. You've been wielding your pen far too artfully in 'my' serial for *The Morning Post*."

"You asked me to write the serial for you," she protested halfheartedly.

"Only because I didn't have the time to do it myself, not because I wished someone to fabricate stories that make me appear ridiculous."

She bit her lip, though she peeped at him through her lashes. "I let you win."

"Thank you," he returned sarcastically. "When I first arrived in town, people spoke enthusiastically about my expeditions and I mistakenly thought they were beginning to warm to true scientific discovery. Now I see that they were merely amazed at your preposterous tales."

"People *are* interested in your research. Just last week Lord Harken-Styles said he wishes to invest even more in your adventures."

"Lord Harken-Styles waylaid me in White's last night and asked if he could see the arrowhead from the savage who shot me through the neck."

Mary bit her lip again. "Oh. That."

"Yes, *that*. The real indignity was that he believed me to be such a sapskull as to keep the arrowhead tied about my neck as a good luck talisman."

Her lips twitched. "I thought that was a very romantic touch."

"And thoroughly untruthful," he replied sternly, wondering at the depth of his sister's imagination. He shuddered to think of what other stories she'd concocted.

"I'm surprised Lord Harken-Styles didn't offer to purchase it; he's a notorious gambler and could use a lucky talisman."

"I would have sold him an arrowhead had I one on my person, which—not being forewarned—I did not.

I meant to ask about that tale in the coach on the way here, but I was distracted by this damned cravat, which is about to throttle me even now." He tugged at the cravat again. "I shall burn this damned thing the second I'm able."

"You're just not used to it. Once you've been home for a few more weeks, you'll hardly notice it."

"I won't be here that long."

Mary's mouth dropped open. "But . . . we only just rescued you!"

"For which I'm eternally grateful. But that does not turn me from my original intent of finding the Hurst Amulet, a feat that cannot be accomplished in London." Excitement warmed him even now at the thought of his next adventure. For years he'd pursued a number of ancient artifacts, but only one object had kept his interest—their lost family heirloom, the elusive Hurst Amulet.

It was supposedly quite a beautiful piece, made of amber and precious metals. But, of more interest, the amulet held a mystery. It had been lost from their family hundreds of years before, given to Queen Elizabeth, who—from the references he'd found—had grown to fear it for some reason, and so had gifted it to a foreign emissary. The trouble was, they didn't know which emissary or which foreign land.

Finally, after years of following every lead he could find, the amulet was nearly within his grasp. "If all goes well, I'll have that damned amulet before the month's out."

Mary sighed. "Robert said you were about to fly, but you've only been here a week. Surely you can wait until—"

"I can't wait. I have the map, and now I must finish this quest."

"But you need more funds to proceed! You must either court support from the wealthier members of the *ton*, or"—her gaze narrowed on him—"accept funding from others."

Michael frowned. "I am not taking Erroll's money."

"Why not? It's not as if my husband doesn't have the money! It's rude to admit it, but he is fabulously wealthy."

"I don't care. I won't have my own brother-in-law interfering with my work."

"He wouldn't interfere."

"Fustian. I knew Erroll for years before you did, sister-mine. He would interfere, and you know it."

She hesitated, then sighed. "Fine. He might interfere a *little*, but no more than that. He's opinionated, as are you."

"Which is why I won't have him as a partner." At her stubborn look, Michael added in a milder tone, "Erroll's a good man and I'm very happy for the both of you. But we're too much the same. Besides, it's bad to mix family and business."

"And yet you allow me to write your articles, and our brothers to assist you even more. Robert sells your artifacts here in London, while William's ships ferry you and your expeditions all over the world."

"*Hiring* your relatives is different from *borrowing* from them."

"No one said anything about a loan. Erroll and I would expect a return, so it's more of an investment."

"Which is even worse. When I hire my relatives, the situation is based on services rendered, which is simple and straightforward. An investment, meanwhile, is based upon the luck of the venture, over which I have no control."

She sniffed. "Fine. Then get used to wearing a cravat and attending every ball and soiree in London as you groom your next investor."

"Mary, don't get in a miff. Erroll didn't seem upset when I turned him down, so why should you?"

"I thought it would be a way to help."

"You've helped enough as it is, perhaps too much. Are there any other surprise adventures that I supposedly participated in other than wrestling a crocodile? A long-lost civilization found at the bottom of a dry lake? A duel over an Arabian princess in the desert? A fall from a cliff into an icy sea? Any missing limbs I should know about?"

She ruined any appearance of contrition by giggling. "It is all your fault, you know. You are such a horrid correspondent that I was forced to make up things. If you would write more often, I wouldn't need to resort to such stratagems."

"Nonsense. I've written home plenty of times."

"To issue orders like a general, but you never *tell* us anything. One letter from you was only two sentences long and was merely a request to find a book you'd left at Mother's and send it to you as soon as possible."

"Unlike others in my family, I only write when I have something to say."

"You only write when you need something. Worse, when you *do* drop hints about your adventures, you scatter them here and there like a bread crumb trail. You'll send a brief letter to Robert one month, a short note to Caitlyn the next month, and on it goes. None of us would know anything about you at all if we didn't share what few crumbs of information you toss us."

"If I didn't have so damn many siblings, you'd get more letters from me. But my lack of correspondence doesn't give you permission to fictionalize my expeditions. Really, Mary—an arrow through the neck?"

She bit her lip, though her eyes danced merrily. "That was a bit dramatic, wasn't it?"

"Very. Had I known Jane back then, I would have had her write those damn articles instead of you. She wouldn't have made such a romanticized botch of it."

"Jane? Do you mean Miss Smythe-Haughton, your assistant?"

"Who the hell else would I mean?" He disliked the interested note in his sister's voice. "Jane is her name; what else should I call her?"

"I would think you'd call her Miss Smythe-Haughton."

"My tongue would be exhausted if I had to say that every time I needed a fresh pair of socks or couldn't find one of my notebooks. Speaking of which"—he frowned and pulled out his pocket watch, flicking it open with his thumb—"she should be here by now."

"Miss Smythe-Haughton is coming *here*? But—" Mary blinked. "Michael, she wasn't included on our invitation."

"Which is why I wrote our hostess a letter this afternoon and asked her to send another invitation for Jane."

"You didn't! Michael, you're hopeless! You can't ask a hostess to include another guest—someone she doesn't even know—at the last minute like that. It's unheard-of."

"Why not? It worked. Our hostess sent the invitation, and I passed it on to Jane, who sent word that she'd be here. Though she said it would be before ten and here it is, fifteen after, and—"

A commotion roiled across the ballroom like a hot wind blowing through a field of wheat.

Mary hopped to her feet, lifted on her tiptoes, and craned her neck. "Has the king arrived? Blast it, I cannot see a thing. Michael, you're taller. Look for me, please. Is it the king? They said he might come."

Michael shrugged, uninterested. "I don't know. Everyone has turned toward the door and— Ah! It's not the king at all, but Jane."

Mary dropped back on her heels and frowned at her brother. "Why would Miss Smythe-Haughton's arrival cause such a stir? No one knows her, do they?"

Michael had already turned his attention back to his cup of Scotch. "I can't imagine they would."

Mary waited, but her brother offered no more. Impatient, she snapped, "Well? Is Miss Smythe-Haughton from London?"

"No." He took a drink. "At least, I don't think so. I've never asked her."

Mary closed her eyes and counted to ten. When Michael had first returned from his imprisonment, she'd been so happy to see him that she'd thought she'd never feel angry or upset with him again. That had lasted less than a week. Her brother was a brilliant explorer and historian. His essays and treatises were prized the world over, and he was beyond intelligent in a number of areas.

But his skills in dealing with society had greatly deteriorated from years of living abroad in the wildest and most untamed circumstances. "Michael, who *is* Miss Smythe-Haughton? She must be *someone* to cause such interest."

The wave of excited murmurs wafted closer.

Mary leaned this way and that, trying to peer through the crowd. "I can't imagine people are so excited over Miss Smythe-Haughton's arrival that—" The crowd parted and Mary was afforded a direct view of her brother's assistant.

Mary's eyes widened.

She looked once.

Then twice.

Then she clapped a hand over her eyes and fell back upon the settee with a groan. "Oh, Michael, what have you *done?*"

CHAPTER 2

From the diary of Michael Hurst:

One good thing that comes from living the nomadic life demanded by an expedition is that one sheds the fake skin donned from living too closely among society. For those of us who live for the freedom of such a lifestyle, that skin is dry and itchy and ill fitting.

From my observances, that skin is much like a callus caused by the pure irritation of being forced to spend so much time with one's fellow man. Thank God I am spared such nonsense.

$\mathcal{M}$ ichael frowned at his sister. "What the devil's wrong with you?"

"Miss Smythe-Haughton! Oh, Michael, you should have had me speak with her before she appeared. Her gown—and that hat—and who is the servant with her? He looks as if he could murder someone!"

Michael looked over his shoulder to where the servant could be seen, towering over all present. "There's not the slightest bit of harm in Ammon."

"But he's huge!"

"Almost seven feet, in fact. He's a good man and I trust him with my life. I've done just that on several different occasions."

"But his face—it's so scarred and— Oh, dear! I believe the Duchess of York just fainted as he walked past her."

"The last time I was in town, the Duchess of York fainted when Pemmeroy's poodle jumped upon her skirts."

"She is a bit theatrical, but you can't deny that this time she has a point." Mary pressed a hand to her forehead. "Oh, dear!"

"Nonsense. Ammon's perfectly civilized. The man's been with me for twelve years, after my fifth English valet quit on me. The weakling had the temerity to cite the heat and discomfort of our expeditions as an excuse for his abject laziness."

"You've had Ammon for twelve years? But you've never mentioned him once."

"Why would I? He's the son of a guide I once used, a marvelous fellow in his own right. I've never had a more meticulous or capable servant—well-read, too."

Mary's eyes widened. "Well-read?"

"Yes, in several languages. He's going through some French Restoration plays right now. I lent him the books myself."

"So he's harmless, then."

"I wouldn't say that, exactly."

"No?"

"I wouldn't slip up behind him with a knife, for he might retaliate." Michael shrugged. "But that's to be expected. He kills only when necessary."

Mary covered her face with her hands and moaned.

Michael frowned down at her bent head, her blond curls falling about her covered face. It was a pity, but sometime during the last few years while he'd been abroad, his youngest sister had become annoyingly missish. He wasn't used to such theatrics, and they made him appreciate Jane's calm practicality all the more.

Jane had been his assistant for four years now, and he couldn't remember his life before she'd swept in and begun arranging things. Since her arrival, his clothes were where they should be, his pen nibs sharpened just so, his scientific equipment always ready, his travel arrangements flawless and comfortable. In a word, she was efficient, unassuming, and for a woman, relatively undemanding. He rarely, if ever, had to think of her.

Better yet, she spoke several languages fluently and was a crack cryptographer. While he supposed that, if forced, he could replace her, he suspected he would have to add three or four additional people to his retinue to do so, and the last thing he wanted about him was more people.

It was fortunate he'd taken a chance on hiring her as his assistant; there weren't many women who were qualified to do such a complex job, and even fewer who did it so well.

He looked over the crowd and saw Jane standing on her tiptoes in the center of the room, looking for him, no doubt. At her shoulder stood Ammon, looking dark and impassive, ignoring the faint panic spreading across the sea of pasty-faced Englishmen who surrounded him.

Michael lifted his arm and let out a shrill whistle.

Everyone looked startled except Jane, whose eyes, framed by her spectacles, crinkled with a sudden smile. She waved back, slapped a hand upon her hat, and dove into the crowd, pushing a direct line in his direction. Her large hat marked her way so that she looked like a yellow lily pad swimming across a pond filled with reeds, Ammon doggedly paddling behind her.

"It's about blasted time she arrived. She said she'd be here at—" Michael frowned as he saw that his sister was holding her hand over her eyes. "What's wrong? Do you have a headache?"

She dropped her hand. "Michael, you cannot whistle for the poor girl as if she were a dog."

"I didn't. When I whistle for a dog, I do it like this." He whistled two short whistles. "When I whistle for Jane, I do it like—"

"*Don't!* I already heard it and once was enough." Mary scowled at him. "I can't believe Miss Smythe-Haughton allows you to whistle for her like that."

"Why should she care? It was an efficient way to let her know where we were. Besides, Jane is in my employ. If I wish to whistle for her, I shall do so."

"And if she protests?"

Michael frowned. "I don't know. She's never protested before, so I assume that she doesn't care, either."

Mary threw up her hands. "Perhaps the two of you deserve one another, then. I must admit that I've quite misjudged your relationship with Miss Smythe-Haughton. We all have."

"What does that mean? You didn't—" He narrowed his gaze. "Surely you didn't think I was romantically involved with Jane?"

"You write about her in almost every letter," Mary answered in a defensive tone, her face pink.

"Probably to complain. Jane is my assistant and nothing more. When you meet her, you'll understand."

"Oh. Is she very plain?"

"I don't know. She's just . . . Jane." If he'd been asked to describe her, he probably would have said that she was small, quick, brown, and rather wrenlike. But it was one thing to describe Jane's physicality and yet another to explain her presence. She always *seemed* bigger than her size, more visible than other women, and infinitely more capable. "I can't describe her, but you'll see how she is when you meet her."

Michael wished his sister would leave well enough alone. He and Jane had a very comfortable, established relationship, one he had no wish to change.

"Michael, I could kill you." Mary stood and smoothed her skirts. "You didn't bother to tell me Miss Smythe-Haughton was coming, and then, when she does appear, she's dressed like—I don't know what! Plus, she has a dangerous-looking character with her and—"

"Ammon's not dangerous unless you—"

"Yes, yes. Unless I sneak up on him with a knife. That's not very reassuring."

"You don't even own a knife—not the kind you don't butter bread with, anyway—so you're perfectly safe around him."

Mary ignored him. "And *then* you whistled for Miss

Smythe-Haughton in a *most* undignified way. If she should decide to snub you for that, I am sure no one in this room would blame her."

"Nonsense. If I hadn't whistled, she'd have spent an hour wandering through this crowd of overjeweled fools looking for us."

"It was rude."

"Not to Jane," he replied comfortably. He watched as she made her way past the final few dancers, looking about her with her usual bright interest.

Jane's hat was a wide yellow confection and not any larger than the hats he'd seen parading about Hyde Park this afternoon. It also seemed to have quite a few big feathers. Very large feathers. Feathers so large that when Jane turned her head, the feathers slapped some silly bumpkin in a ridiculous orange waistcoat.

Michael smiled. "I like that hat."

"You would," his sister sniffed.

Michael noted that no one else seemed to be wearing a hat. "Perhaps Jane should have left her hat with a footman in the vestibule."

"If only she had," Mary replied fervently. "I should have known that Miss Smythe-Haughton was unconventional, since she's been shepherding you through the wilds of Africa for the last three years; but I thought she might understand society's rules a little better."

"It's been four years, and I don't need a shepherd. She's my assistant, nothing more and nothing less. She organizes our travel arrangements and makes certain we are all fed, and writes up our schedules and catalogues the finds and all of that sort of thing." He waved a hand to indicate that he couldn't remember all of her numerous duties.

"Whatever she does, someone needs to take her to a good modiste. That gown is painfully out of fashion."

Michael eyed Jane's gown, which was like all of her gowns. It was gray and didn't have all of the silly furbelows that other women seemed determined to plaster all over themselves. It was also high cut at the neck and long at the wrists, which provided her with excellent cover while they were on expedition. "I don't see anything objectionable about that gown."

"How can you say that? It looks like a *sack*!"

"Which is why I like it." Ignoring Mary's startled look, Michael noted that Jane had paused by the silly bumpkin who had received the face-slap from her feathered hat. She spoke to him for a moment, laughing at something he replied in return.

The man no longer appeared upset, either. In fact, he was regarding Jane with sudden interest.

Michael frowned. When he and Jane had been abroad, naturally she'd attracted attention because she was often the only white woman present. As such, she was an oddity.

Here there was no such excuse, and yet . . . he looked about the room and noted with vague surprise that

several men were watching her, some with very pronounced interest, even with Ammon scowling over her
shoulder.

That's certainly odd. His explorer's soul stirred a bit,
and in an attempt to understand this mystery better, he
decided to list the evidence at hand. For the first time
since he'd hired her, Michael looked at Jane critically,
trying to see her with unknown eyes. With a man's eyes.

She wasn't a beauty, though he had to admit that
she wasn't ugly, either. She was a small woman, with a
slender figure. She had plain brown hair, brown eyes,
and because of her years in hotter climes, brown skin.
Though she looked a bit of a hoyden because of her
coloring, she was still unmistakably feminine. Her face
was piquant and delicately cast, with high cheekbones,
a straight nose that barely held up her spectacles, and
a stubborn little chin. In fact, everything about her
was small—her feet, her hands, everything except
her thickly fringed brown eyes and her wide, mobile
mouth.

Those two items seemed overlarge for her slender
face yet oddly balanced one another.

He rubbed his chin, finding this mystery—like all
mysteries—intriguing.

Perhaps it is her mouth that attracts such attention . . . He narrowed his gaze. Something about her mouth made her
appear sensual. He'd never noticed that before, though
now that he thought about it, the sulfi who'd held him

prisoner had been most vocal in his admiration for the no-nonsense Miss Smythe-Haughton and her lush mouth.

In fact, the man had been a positive idiot about the matter, even writing a poem. "A *poem*," Michael muttered.

"Pardon?" Mary asked.

"Nothing."

"Michael . . . is she wearing *boots*?" Mary's voice sounded strangled.

"It's what she wears when we're on expedition."

"But you're not on expedition here. She's in *town*."

"What does it matter how she dresses? No one is funding *her*." He was a little envious of Jane's freedom, truth be told.

Mary gave a puff of indignation. "Because she will be laughed at, of course. Surely you don't want that!"

His jaw tightened. "I *dare* anyone to laugh at her."

Mary's eyes widened.

Michael ignored her. He hadn't meant to become angry, but—blast it—Jane wasn't like other women, who had to don silly finery to prove their worth. She already *had* worth in making his life go as smoothly as possible. *Damn it, I wish I hadn't invited Jane to this blasted ball.* But it was too late. She had finally broken free from the bumpkin who'd tried to monopolize her, though the idiot was gazing after her as if longing for something more. As he passed, Ammon sent the man a withering gaze, which dealt with the situation well enough.

Michael muttered "Fool!" under his breath. *Jane would never be interested in such a man. Thank Ra she's not a ninny like so many other women who—*

Jane finally broke from the crowd and was now standing before him, Ammon behind her. Michael looked at his pocket watch. "You're late and Mary says your hat—"

"Michael," Mary interrupted hastily. "Please introduce us."

"Oh, no," Jane said, "there's no need to bother Mr. Hurst with an introduction; he's spoken of you so often that I feel as if I know you." She dipped a curtsy that even the biggest stickler of society couldn't fault. As she rose, she held out her hand to Mary and smiled warmly. "Lady Erroll, it's delightful to finally meet you! I've enjoyed the newspaper serial so much, though I'm several issues behind."

Mary looked pleased. "Thank you. Not many people know I write it."

"Which is a great pity and means you're denied the glory that is your due." Jane leaned forward and said in an undertone that carried quite clearly, "I've been telling Hurst he should come clean about that and announce you the authoress, but he's far too lazy to do it."

Mary sent a startled glance at Michael, who scowled at them.

Jane merely laughed. "Oh, never mind Hurst. He is always in a mood when he's forced to wear society clothing. But have no fear; those who work for him never take his dark moods to heart, do we, Ammon?"

The servant inclined his head from his incredible height.

Mary looked at him with interest.

Jane introduced the servant. "Lady Erroll, I have been remiss! This is Ammon, Hurst's valet and aide-de-camp."

"Speaking of which," Michael broke in, "Ammon, why are you here? I didn't expect to see you."

"I met Ammon on the stoop outside," Jane said. "The butler wouldn't allow him to enter, so I took matters into my own hands and, well, here we are."

Ammon reached into the folds of his tunic and produced a small, tightly folded missive. "The missive you were waiting on arrived, sir. As you instructed, I brought it directly here."

"Excellent!" Michael withdrew his spectacles from an inner pocket and slipped them on. Then he opened the letter and scanned it. "Interesting."

Jane tried to peep around the letter to see it, but he swiftly folded it and tucked the letter and his spectacles into his pocket.

She frowned. "Being secretive, Hurst?"

He didn't usually bother with such silliness, but he was irritated with Jane, though he couldn't exactly say why. "I'll explain it to you tomorrow."

For a moment, it looked as if she might argue, but after a second, she shrugged. "Fine. I'll wait."

"*I won't!*" Mary pinned her stern gaze on Michael. "What's in that missive that you couldn't have waited to read it after the ball?"

"Nothing that concerns you," he retorted instantly.

"Lady Erroll, I'm sure Ammon didn't mind the trip here," Jane said in a soothing tone. "He's from a nomadic tribe, you know. I've often wondered how he can stand to remain in one place for so long as it is."

Mary blinked up at Ammon. "You . . . you're from a *tribe?*"

He bowed his head. "Yes, my lady."

She eyed his turban with interest. Seeing her expression, Jane launched into a humorous story about how she'd attempted to wear a turban but it had come unwound at an unpropitious time and had gotten caught in the wheels of a passing cart and sent her spinning.

Within moments Mary was laughing heartily, and though he didn't smile, even Ammon's stern visage had relaxed.

Michael regarded them all with a growing sense of satisfaction. His sister was in the hands of a master. That was one of Jane's gifts; no matter where they were, in the wilds of Africa or a sulfi's palace or even the treacherous ballrooms of London, she knew just what to say and how to say it.

It was that particular ability to understand others and to blend into whatever society she was in that made his many expeditions so profitable. Where another explorer might be greeted with distrust, after a few deft words from Jane, Michael and his party were almost always welcomed and charged far less for services than others.

Jane continued to draw out Mary. Soon, Jane's clothing and hat were forgotten, and the two women were talking quite animatedly about marriages and children and other frivolous topics that Michael knew Jane cared nothing for.

She must have read his thoughts, for though she continued to chat with his sister, Jane sent him a laughing look beneath her lashes, which he answered with faintly raised brows and a mocking smile.

After several more moments of listening to female chatter, Michael yawned.

Ammon immediately stated, "It is time to retire."

"He can't leave," Mary exclaimed. "He hasn't spoken to a single potential sponsor yet."

"I'm not going to, either," he said. "This damned cravat is too tight and I wish to go home."

"Then we shall go home," Ammon announced.

Jane tsked. "Ammon, Mr. Hurst cannot leave yet. He has a chore he must complete first."

Michael scowled. "Not this evening."

"Hurst, think about it. You must speak to at least *one* potential sponsor before you retire from this evening, because if you don't, you will have wasted the time you've already spent wearing that atrocious cravat."

He'd been tugging on the damned thing when she said that, which made him stop. "Atrocious?"

"Oh, yes. Quite atrocious. Made all the more so, since you've been tugging on it. If you don't find a sponsor tonight, you'll just have to wear it again and again and again—"

He made a disgusted noise.

Jane continued as if she hadn't heard it, still speaking in an annoyingly perky tone: "—and again and again until you *do*. If I were you, I'd refuse to leave this ball until I'd found a sponsor."

He scowled. "I hate it when you speak of something that I dislike in such a bloody *happy* tone."

Her eyes twinkled. "I know. Which is why I do it as often as I can."

"Oh, look!" Mary nodded toward the refreshment table. "There's Devonshire! His grace expressly asked to meet you."

"Who?"

"The Duke of Devonshire," Mary said impatiently. "I told you in the carriage on the way over that we were to speak to him here. Weren't you lis— No. Of course you weren't."

"Devonshire might support more than one expedition," Jane said, looking as pleased as if she'd discovered a reference to a new tomb. "He's dreadfully wealthy."

Michael sighed. "Stop your blathering, you nagging wench!" He ignored both Jane's grin and Mary's scowl.

"I'll do it. I just wish I'd brought a bigger flask." He squinted at the refreshment table. "Which asinine fop is Devonshire? Please tell me it's not the man in puce who looks like a fool. I can't— Bloody hell, are those diamonds upon the lace at his wrists?"

"He may be a fop, but he's a very well-heeled fop," Mary said. "And he's already stated to several people that he's interested in sponsoring the great Michael Hurst; Devonshire's an avid follower of the newspaper serial."

Michael sighed again. "Which means he thinks I wrestle crocodiles by the dozen."

Jane choked, and even Ammon looked as if he might break into a sudden grin. "I beg your pardon," Jane said, "but . . . crocodiles? Oh, dear. I *do* need to catch up with the newspaper serial."

Michael eyed her sourly, even more unhappy when Mary looked as if she might join in the laughter. "Blast you both! I wish these fools would just mail me a cheque and leave me the hell be."

"So do I," Jane said in a soothing tone. With a deft touch, she smoothed his lapels and tucked a corner of his cravat back into his waistcoat. "But fools that they are, they seem to think they'll enjoy speaking to you. I'm sure that if they knew you as I do, they'd never wish to speak to you at all."

"Thank you," he snapped.

"You're welcome. But that's what happens when you allow a nice person to write a newspaper serial for you; now the world thinks *you're* nice, too, which is silly in the extreme. Sadly, it's a burden that you must bear."

"Hold it. If I have to speak to that fool, you do, too."

"No, I don't. I now realize that though I'm wearing my best gown and my favorite hat, I'm woefully underdressed and so must leave before I damage your prospects. I shall take Ammon with me, too."

Michael was about to answer with a strong "You'll do no such thing!" when Mary added, "Miss Smythe-Haughton, since you're leaving, I'll escort my brother to meet the duke."

"A perfect plan." Jane's brown eyes shimmered with mockery as she met his gaze. "I'm *so* disappointed not to meet the duke, but you know how it is."

"Fainthearted twit."

"Cravated grump."

"Saucy, foul wench."

"Ham-fisted curmudgeon."

"Shrill shrew—"

"Please!" Mary interjected. "*Both* of you!"

Michael kept his gaze locked on Jane. "Admit it: you have no more wish to talk to that fop than I."

"Oh, no," she returned gravely. "It's my dearest wish, *especially* as you'll be answering questions about how many crocodiles you've wrestled."

"Damn it, it's a blasted false story, and—" He realized that Jane's eyes were once again alight with laughter. "You're a pain in the rear."

Mary moaned. "Oh, Michael, pray attempt to be less rude!"

But Jane just twinkled up at him. "Hurst, need I remind you that I will not work for you if you don't have the funds for my very considerable wage?"

"No, you don't. You're already far too fond of reminding me of that fact."

"Because it's true. So you'd best find a sponsor, and soon. You'd find it very inconvenient if I were to leave your employ. Who would make certain your favorite pillow is in your tent each night?"

"I don't have a favorite pillow."

"Yes, you do; you just don't know it. You also like your meals on time, your notebooks stowed in a particular order, certain foods upon your table, and clean socks at every stage of the journey."

He couldn't refute that, so he just glowered.

She didn't seem the least bit upset by it. "If you wish those things to continue, then you'd best set about wooing a sponsor . . . or ten, if need be."

Damn it, he hated it when she was right. He searched for a scorching response but had to be satisfied with "It would serve you right if I dismissed you."

"Which you won't do, because no matter what you say, you *do* like having your favorite pillow with you when you travel and I cannot, for the life of me, see you washing your own socks."

Does she wash my socks, too? He couldn't remember ever seeing her do so, but he had to admit that he'd never faced a dirty pair on any of their long sojourns.

Jane turned to Mary. "He pays me quite well, you know, but I'm worth every penny."

"I don't doubt it," Mary said fervently.

Jane held out her hand. "Lady Erroll, it was lovely finally meeting you."

Mary clasped Jane's hand warmly. "It was lovely finally meeting you as well! I can see that Michael is in good hands when he's on expedition."

"I do my best. Now, if you'll excuse us, Ammon and I will slip out the terrace doors. Hurst, I'll stop by your town house tomorrow afternoon and we can plan our expedition to pursue the Hurst Amulet."

"No," Michael said, seeing a way to exact vengeance upon his dulcet companion. "There's been a slight change of plans."

"Oh?"

"Yes. I'll tell you about them tomorrow. We'll leave at six." He waited for that to register before he added, *"In the morning."* He grinned at her frown.

Her gaze narrowed, but she didn't balk. "Fine. I'll be ready. At *six*." She dropped a stiff curtsy. "Good evening, Mr. Hurst." Jane delivered a much friendlier and more graceful curtsy to his sister. "Good evening, Lady

Erroll. I hope to see you again soon." After again clasping Mary's hand, Jane turned and made her way to the terrace doors, her large hat wreaking havoc as she went.

Michael grinned until he noticed that the bumpkin who'd so eagerly spoken to Jane on her way in was already pressing through the crush, trying to reach her once again. *The blasted fool had better not importune her.* Michael would deal with such an impertinence swiftly and without pity.

Fortunately for them all, Jane slipped through the terrace doors, her yellow hat and Ammon's tall, dark figure disappearing from sight. Her would-be admirer was left trapped in the middle of the crowded room, looking disappointed.

"Serves the fool right," Michael said.

"What fool?" Mary asked.

"Never mind." He patted his neckcloth again and then left it to its fate. "Now, where's this duke of yours? Jane's right about one thing: I'll be damned if I wash my own socks on my next expedition."

CHAPTER 3

From the diary of Michael Hurst:

I never feel more alive than when I'm standing at a newly opened tomb or vault, on the precipice of a new discovery. It's the pure excitement of the find combined with the golden possibilities of what-may-be; one of bated breath, thundering heart, damp palms, and trembling limbs; a mixture of excruciating hope and the painfully exquisite fear of disappointment.

It's a feeling that only another adventurer can truly understand.

$\mathcal{P}$ardon me, sir, but you must arise." The deep, faintly accented voice intruded into Michael's sleep.

He opened one eye, fighting off an absurd dream in which Jane sat upon a large silk pillow while dozens of love-struck men danced waltzes in her honor.

"It is time, sir." Ammon stood by the bed, holding Michael's robe, a single lantern the only light in the otherwise dark room.

Irritated at being awakened and from such a silly dream, Michael growled, "What time is it?"

"Almost six, sir." Ammon shook the robe invitingly. "I warmed the robe by the fire."

Michael closed his eyes. "The bed is warmer."

"I have coffee waiting, too."

That was tempting, but the lure of the comfortable bed was stronger. "I'm sleeping."

Ammon sighed. "Sir, I do not wish to alarm you, but Miss Jane is awaiting us downstairs."

Jane? Downstairs? Why— "Oh, yes. I told her to come." *What the hell was I thinking?* "It's still dark."

"Yes, sir. Miss Jane had the coaches ready to travel a half hour ago. It is only by my hand that she has not marched into this room and awakened you yourself."

Michael had only said such an early hour to tease her, but he'd promptly forgotten to inform her that he wasn't serious. Last night had been too filled with triumph after Devonshire had promised to support Michael's next three expeditions.

Three expeditions, he thought, gloating once more. *No more starched cravats for three entire years.*

Downstairs, the sound of a strong feminine voice could be heard delivering a string of instructions.

Michael rubbed his face. "I suppose Jane has the whole damn army ready?"

Ammon dipped his turbaned head. "If by 'army' you mean myself and the other servants, yes. We are all ready. Everyone is ready except you."

"I don't plan on being ready until I've had a leisurely breakfast, so you're all just going to have to wait."

"Miss Jane says that if you are not downstairs in ten minutes, then she is coming up to fetch you herself." Ammon's voice held grudging respect. "She is standing before the great clock, watching the minutes."

"Damn that woman. I've never met a ruder, more demanding witch of a—"

Ammon shook out the silk robe, the rustle sounding like a quiet rebuke, which it probably was. Jane always said that the Egyptian culture was subtle, but forceful. Michael was inclined to agree with her.

Scowling, he pushed himself up on one elbow and

brushed his hair from his eyes. "Give me one bloody good reason why I should drag myself from this bed."

"Miss Jane will descend upon us like the locusts in only eight minutes. I do not want that." Ammon's dark gaze met Michael's. "*You* do not want that."

"You said I had ten minutes."

"I was downstairs when she said ten. I had to come upstairs, set your breakfast tray upon the table, and—"

"Fine, fine. I'm getting up, blast you." He sat upright, groggily running a hand through his hair. "Miss Jane is becoming more and more impertinent and high-handed."

"Oh, yes. But once you are awake, you will show her who is the head of the household." Though Ammon's voice was soothing, Michael had the feeling that the servant didn't believe his own words.

He sniffed the air. "Is that bacon?"

"Yes," Ammon said, disapproval thick in his voice. "Miss Jane insisted upon it."

Michael gave Jane a lot of latitude, but then again, she was solely responsible for every comfort of his life—including the wonderful meals he ate while out on expedition and even here, in his own home. Before she'd joined his expeditions, the food had been so horrible that he'd worried about starving to death. Once she'd arrived, he'd had to worry more about gaining weight, which more than made up for the innuendos and numerous rude comments his fellow explorers made when they realized Michael had a female assistant. It was an unfortunate fact that even well-educated men could be blind fools.

Michael's stomach grumbled, so he stood and stretched, then allowed Ammon to help him into his robe. Then he crossed to the breakfast tray, heartened by the sight of so many dishes.

"I made coffee." Ammon filled a cup from a small pot as he spoke, the steam curling into the air.

The coffee would be strong, too, for no one made it like Ammon. Michael didn't know how the servant did it, but every cup was hot and rich and held just enough bitterness to engage the tongue and wake up the body.

He lifted the cup and took an experimental sip. "Ah, Ammon. You are a true artist."

Ammon looked pleased.

Suddenly starving, Michael ate. Within moments, he'd finished his bacon, eggs, and kippers, and was spreading marmalade upon a piece of toast. Perhaps it *was* a good thing to leave so early. He would sleep in the coach while Jane made certain they traveled at a decent pace. "I assume we're already packed for our journey?"

"Yes, sir. Miss Jane and I did most of the work last night."

"Good. Put out my clothes, but not the razor. I'm not going to shave." That always irked Jane. *Serves her right for being in my dreams, where she most certainly was not invited.*

He looked at Ammon over the edge of his coffee

cup. "Last night, at the ball, did you notice the man who paid such attention to Miss Jane?"

"Which one?"

Michael set down his cup. "What do you mean, which one?"

Ammon shrugged. "I did not notice any who paid more attention to her than she usually receives."

"When have you seen any men pay attention to Miss Jane?" Michael demanded.

Ammon pursed his lips. "Well, there were the camel traders when we were setting out from old Alexandria. They wished to know how many camels we'd require for her."

"Yes, but that was because they liked how she rode her horse. They went on and on about that, and not because they found her—" Michael waved a hand.

"Attractive?"

"Call it what you will. Personally, I wouldn't give five camels for her."

Ammon lifted his brows.

"Fine, I'd give five camels for her, but only because she's so good at this—" He waved a hand toward his finished breakfast tray.

"She is quite good at organizing, but I assure you that the camel traders did not wish her to organize anything. They were interested in her as a woman. As was the sulfi who held you prisoner. He was most taken with her, too, if I remember correctly."

"Don't remind me of the sulfi. He was as crazed as a Nubian. I had to rescue Jane and risked my own neck to sneak her out of his fortress in the middle of the night."

"She shouldn't have danced for him," Ammon said solemnly.

"I warned her about that, but she was determined to do it. The silly woman thought she could gain the sulfi's favor while I was being held prisoner. What a stupid, harebrained idea *that* was. She's a *horrible* dancer, too. She can't even clap in time. We're fortunate that the sulfi was amused by her display and didn't order us both killed on the spot."

"No, instead he wrote a sonnet to her mouth and offered to purchase her for a casket of jewels."

"He must have been drunk."

"The sulfi does not drink. His religion does not permit it."

"How the hell am I supposed to know how a crazed man thinks?" Michael growled.

"He was a pious man."

"Who wanted to purchase my assistant as if she were a horse!"

Ammon just went quietly to the wardrobe and prepared Michael's clothes.

Michael rubbed his eyes, irritated for no reason he could discern. *That damned dream has set me off this morning.* "I'm in a foul mood this morning. I apologize for my temper."

"Yes, sir." Ammon laid Michael's clothing upon the bed. "If I may ask, why has this topic become of interest to you? You don't normally notice Miss Jane."

"And I don't notice her now, but last night there was a man at the ball who seemed to see her as—" Michael struggled for the word. "Not attractive, of course. But he looked at her as if he were interested in her."

"Ah. And you have never seen her in such a light."

"How could I? She's just Jane." He waved a hand to show how inadequate he knew his phrasing to be, but he could think of no other way to say it.

Ammon apparently agreed, for he inclined his head somberly. "Indeed."

"I suppose I should have paid more attention. Now that you mention the camel traders and the sulfi—"

"And the goldsmith in Syria, the nawab's son in India, and the wealthy trader we met while crossing the Sahara. I'm sure there were others, but those were the only ones who spoke of it aloud."

Michael could only blink. "They were *all* interested in her?"

Ammon nodded.

Bloody hell. "I never knew any of that."

"Because they did not approach you, but her."

"What? They made advances to her?"

"She is not a slave, sir. If she wished to leave you, she had only to say so." Ammon shrugged. "They made offers; she did not accept."

"Ah, offers! Then they were trying to hire her, which I perfectly understand."

"No, sir. Though they offered money, there was no talk of 'hire' as you use it. They wished to own her. For themselves."

Michael tried to wrap his mind around this discovery. "I suppose I should be glad she wasn't wooed away in midexpedition."

"Oh, you'd nothing to fear."

"I should hope not." Loyalty should count for something, after all.

"No, you pay her quite well." Ammon poured some more coffee into Michael's cup, unaware that he'd just sent Michael's lofty thoughts tumbling. "And you are from her home country. That is worth something, I'm sure. She certainly seems less irritated in your company than anyone else's."

Michael grunted and took a sip of his coffee, wondering why he was now in an even grumpier mood. Jane should be thankful he'd hired her all those years ago. Since then, he'd paid her a staggeringly high wage and provided her with excellent working conditions, not to mention including her in the excitement of his expeditions. Furthermore, he never importuned her with salacious offers, which he was fairly certain she would have received from other explorers, many of whom were a rough lot.

Still, it was irksome to realize that one of his employees had been leered at right under his nose and he hadn't been aware of it. But what really grated on his nerves was that she'd never breathed a word about the offers she'd received. Not once. He growled into his coffee cup. *Damn it, I shouldn't discover such things from the servants.*

Downstairs, a clock chimed. "Mr. Hurst!" came a call up the stairs, the voice feminine and undeniably perky.

Michael snapped his cup onto the saucer with enough force to rattle them both, threw down his napkin, and stood so quickly that his chair thunked to the floor. He strode to the door and threw it open. *"I'll be down in a bloody minute!"*

There was a moment of silence followed by *"One minute only,* for if *I* have to be up at this hour, so do *you."*

"By Ra, who is in charge here? *You'll* wait until *I'm* ready!" Michael slammed the door. "That woman is a thorn in my side!"

Ammon, who'd just placed his master's boots beside the bed, wisely didn't answer, and Michael was left to dress in stormy silence.

Within moments he'd finished dressing, slipped his reading spectacles into his pocket, and stomped downstairs.

"Good morning, Hurst!" Jane came forward, looking annoyingly cheerful. She was dressed in her usual gray gown, a brown pelisse clasped about her neck, a bonnet held in one gloved hand. "I was just telling Snape here that we won't be gone long, for we know exactly where we're going to fetch the amulet and—"

"Snape," Michael said to his butler, refusing to acknowledge Jane's cheery ramblings, "send a footman to my room to collect my luggage."

"Yes, sir." The butler bowed and hurried off, dispatching two footmen to Michael's bedchamber.

Jane eyed Michael's face. "You forgot to shave."

He rubbed a hand over his stubbled chin so that it rasped. "No, I didn't forget. I chose not to shave. It's *my* face, after all."

"Hmm." To his disappointment, she merely shrugged and said in an annoyingly happy voice, "It is going to be a *lovely* day to travel."

He didn't answer.

She gestured to the darkness outside the windows. "It's a bit misty and cold this morning, but I'm *certain* it will get better as we trundle along, rocking over the rutted road, jouncing along like a bag of loose bones."

"Sounds delightful."

"I'm sure it will be. I might even sing a bit to alleviate the boredom of the trip."

"Jane?"

She lifted her brows. "Yes?"

"If you so much as hum one word, I shall stuff one of your gloves into your mouth."

"Tsk, tsk." She assumed an exaggerated sad look. "It's like that, is it?"

He looked at her.

She sighed and then plunked her bonnet upon her head, one ribbon tangled at her ear. "Very well. I shall attempt to be quieter. I can't promise, of course, but I can try."

"You'd better."

Her brows rose. "Or?" She held up one of her gloves, dangling it before him.

He could tell from the laughter in her eyes that she hadn't believed his empty words that he would stuff her glove in her mouth, and he wished he could think of a more credible threat that might swipe the irritating smile out of her eyes.

Fortunately, before he could say anything, two footmen brought down several bulging portmanteaus while Snape brought Michael his coat, hat, and gloves. Michael issued some orders for his household, though their patient expressions told him that Jane had already done so.

Irked even more, he turned on his heel and strode to the waiting coach, not waiting to see if his annoying assistant followed or not.

He glanced at the lined-up coaches, a faint sense of satisfaction rising through his gloomy temperament. Jane had done her usual magic. The travel coach was piled with his usual boxes and trunks, while two smaller coaches waited behind, carrying Ammon and other servants, ready to follow at a moment's notice.

"Here we are," Jane said breezily, coming to stand beside him in the cold morning air, every word punctuated with a brisk puff of condensation. "We're off to find the Hurst Amulet! You must be quite excited."

He gave her a basilisk stare.

She patted his arm as if he were a child of two and said in a soothing tone, "I'm certain that once we're under way, your sense of adventure will awaken."

"My sense of adventure will not rise until noon."

"*You* were the one who insisted upon a six-in-the-morning departure time." Her voice was sharper now, far from the fake cheerfulness she'd been exuding in an effort to annoy him.

He narrowed his gaze on her, hoping his sleepy brain would make a sharp retort, but he instead found himself noting how her spectacles framed her mahogany-colored eyes, which were flecked with gold, her thick lashes swooping delicately. *Had her eyes attracted the camel traders? Or had they noticed her mouth, the bottom lip slightly longer than the top and—*

He ground his teeth and turned on his heel. As he climbed into the coach, the coachman said, "Pardon me, sir! Miss Smythe-Haughton didn't say where we was headin' to."

"Oh, yes!" Jane said briskly. "We're to Dover, and then on to—"

"No, we're not," Michael said.

Her gaze flew to his. "But the map said—" She sent a quick glance at the coachman and then said in a low voice, "The map said to look for an isle off the shores of Dover."

"We had it wrong."

"But you said—"

"Get in the coach." Michael turned to the coachman. "Turner, drive the North Road. We're to Scotland."

"Yes, sir," Turner said cheerfully. "Any place in particular?"

"The port town of Oban on the west coast. We're not changing horses unless we find some likely ones, so don't push them."

The coachman bowed. "As you wish, sir."

Michael climbed into his seat inside the coach and tossed the carriage blanket over his lap. The door, however, remained open.

He waited, frowning as the cold seeped in, before he leaned past the footman holding the door to where Jane still stood on the walkway.

She was in the same stance in which he'd left her, hands clasped before her, her eyes wide, as if with surprise. She appeared frozen in place. "Jane, aren't you coming?" he asked impatiently.

She blinked as if waking. "What? Oh. Yes. Of course. I was just—" She shook her head, as if to banish some lingering thought and came forward, though she moved without her usual crispness.

He settled back and watched as she allowed the footman to assist her into the coach. The door closed, and with a lurch they rumbled forward, leaving London under the dark of the cold, chilled morning.

Michael settled once again into his corner and stretched out his legs beneath the warm blanket, noting that Jane sat perfectly still, her gloved hands clasped before her, her expression serious. The coach rumbled along and he realized that he'd never seen her sit immobile for such a length of time.

He let the silence rest as long as he could stand it. Finally, he asked, "What's wrong?"

"Nothing."

"Don't try to cozen me. You're upset. I can tell, so don't deny it."

"I'm not upset, I'm just . . . you surprised me. When did our destination change? The map's markings indicated England, not Scotland."

"True, *if* we'd interpreted the map correctly."

Her lips parted. "We were wrong?"

"Don't look so surprised; *you* were the one who suggested I should have our calculations examined."

"A suggestion *you* promptly said was 'balderdash.'"

He shrugged. "After some thought, I decided it was worth the effort and I sent the map off for analysis by an expert. For the record, we were not wrong. Much."

"No?"

"No. We were purposefully led astray. The original cartographer hid clues about how to read the map within the border of the artifact."

"So there was a guide that we missed."

"Exactly. Then, to further ascertain that no one would break *that* code, he then drew the entire map backward."

"Backward? That's diabolical!"

"I thought so, too," Michael said with satisfaction. "To a certain extent, it also proves the validity of the map."

Her brows shot up, and she said in a thoughtful tone, "No one would go to such trouble with a fake map."

"Exactly. We thought the island where the amulet was located was off the northern shore of England, when in reality it's off the southern shores of Scotland. An island, in fact, that was once—"

"Which island?"

He frowned at the sharp note in her voice. "I'm getting to that. The expert I sent it to—Palmer is his name; you may remember him from when he assisted us when we were attempting to decipher those maps of ancient Alexandria two years ago—said the map is actually of an island in the Hebrides."

She flinched.

Michael found himself staring at her. In all of the years they'd been together, he'd never seen her flinch. Not in the face of flying bullets from a band of thieves trying to waylay their caravan in the desert nor a fierce monsoon that threatened to sweep them away with a blistering wind and sheets of rain. "Jane, what's wrong?"

"Nothing. I was just—" She straightened a bit in her seat, her face assuming a bland expression. "It'll be very cold in the Hebrides at this time of the year."

"It'll be horrid, I've no doubt. Why did you flinch?"

Unfortunately, she'd regained control of herself and gifted him with a cool, disbelieving stare, though her cheeks were faintly stained pink. "I didn't flinch."

"Yes, you did."

"No," she said, her tone sharp. "I didn't."

He narrowed his gaze. Should he call her out? Or would that just make her dig in and refuse to discuss the issue?

If there was one thing he knew about Jane, it was that she didn't suffer prying gladly. It had never been an issue for the two of them, of course, because before now, he'd never bothered to ask her anything of import. But over the years, he'd seen her cut off more than one noisy porter or curious fellow traveler without the slightest remorse. At the time, he'd just thought it was because she felt such questions impertinent, as did he. Now he wondered if it was something more—if perhaps she'd been hiding something all along.

Her steady gaze convinced him to bide his time. He shrugged and leaned back in his seat. "I'm just glad we discovered our error in reading the map before we left town, or we'd have headed in the wrong direction."

She gave a short nod, fidgeting with the edges of her sleeve. "As am I."

She offered nothing more, though her fidgeting increased and she shifted several times in her seat. Finally, she said, "Hurst, are you *certain* about this? Palmer is an excellent cartographer, but I wonder if he had time to thoroughly examine the map."

"I'm positive. What he said makes perfect sense. Here, see for yourself." He reached over to open the seat box. He searched a few seconds and withdrew a small satchel. He kicked the door closed, opened the satchel, and pulled out three matching oblong onyx boxes. "Look at them."

With a flick of his thumb, he opened one box, which unfolded on small hidden hinges until it lay flat. He did the same to the other two boxes. Once they were all flattened into panels, he locked them into place so that they made one large panel. "Here's how we interpreted it, though it was backward all along. We thought this was the northeastern coast of England, but it's not. Instead"—he turned the map around—"it's the southwestern coast of Scotland."

She took the map and held it toward the faint light, staring at it before she turned it around.

Behind her spectacles, her eyes widened.

He leaned back against the squabs. "So now you see. The amulet is located on a small island in the Hebrides in Scotland called—"

"The Isle of Barra," she said in a whisper-soft voice. She stared at the map with an unseeing look.

Michael frowned. "What's the matter?"

She blinked. Once. Twice. Her gaze slowly found him. "Barra," she said again, wonder in her voice.

He examined her pale face. "You know this island."

She stiffened, her fingers visibly tightening on the map before she shook her head. "No." She said it as if in denying it, she could make it so.

So now we'll find out what's what. Michael crossed his arms. "*How* do you know this island?"

She looked down at the map once again, her mind obviously miles away.

Impatient, he leaned forward. "Jane, what do you know of Barra?"

She didn't respond, so he placed his hand upon her knee. "Jane?"

Her jaw tightened mutinously and her gaze locked on his hand where it rested upon her knee. "Remove your hand, if you please."

Michael did as she'd asked, though he had to grit his teeth to keep from snapping at her. "How do you know this isle? And don't pretend you don't, for I won't believe it."

Her lips folded with irritation. "I'm not pretending anything. It's just something I don't wish to talk about. I admit that I'm familiar with the island, and that's all you need to know."

He crossed his arms and quirked a brow.

She gave a frustrated sigh. "I haven't been on Barra for years and years. Most of the information I have is quite old and inconsequential."

"That's for me to decide. I never knew you'd even been to Scotland."

"Well, I have," she said, her voice unusually soft, her gaze suddenly far away. "Aye, but it was a long, long time ago."

Aye? Since when does Jane say "aye"? This was getting more and more intriguing. "How long ago?"

She sent him a look that flashed with caution, and then tapped a finger on the map. "So you think the Hurst Amulet is on Barra?"

She was trying to change the subject. He'd allow it— for a moment. "I'm certain the amulet is there. If I'm reading the map correctly now, then the caves near the southernmost tip hold our final clue."

Her gaze dropped to the map. "The southern caves," she murmured, her gaze unfocusing, as if she saw the very caves before her. "I haven't thought of those caves in so long, but now that you mention them, they would be a perfect place to hide something."

So she knows those caves. Interesting. "What do you know about the caves?"

"They're on the coast and they're treacherous."

"But you've been inside them?"

"Once." Her brow furrowed as her gaze dropped back to the map. She traced a line on the map with the tip of a gloved finger. "There are ancient markings upon a high ledge of the main cave chamber. Odd markings. Ancient, I'd say."

"What do they look like?"

"I don't remember exactly. I was so young when I was last there and—" Her gaze locked with his, her brown eyes gleaming golden with growing interest. "Hurst, do you think that whatever the caves hold will lead us *directly* to the amulet?"

"I'd wager my right arm that the amulet's on that blasted island somewhere, probably very close to those caves."

She clasped her hands together, eagerness brightening her gaze. "Amazing! And to think that I was almost trapped in those caves when I was young."

"How young?"

"Six, maybe seven."

He tried to imagine her as a child of six and was instantly rewarded with the image of a young girl with long brown braids and huge eyes.

She shook her head in wonder. "There have been

rumors for *centuries* that those caverns held treasures, but . . ." She gave an odd laugh. "The Isle of *Barra,* of all places. I simply cannot believe it."

"Why is that so strange?"

Framed by her spectacles, her gaze met his, and for a second, he thought she'd explain; but instead her thick lashes dropped over her eyes and she snapped the map apart, then folded each piece before she packed them back into the satchel and restored it under the seat. "It's a lovely island, but very small. If the amulet is there, we shouldn't have much trouble finding it. We could be there for less than two days if we plan things well."

What are you hiding, my prim little wren? Whatever it is, it's obvious you don't wish me—or anyone else—to know. Well, he'd tried being subtle. Perhaps it was time for some direct questioning. "So you're not going to tell me how you know this island?"

Her brows lifted. "Does that really matter?"

Yes, it did, damn it. He shrugged. "It's a simple question. Why shouldn't you answer it?"

Her lips quirked with humor. "We've known one another for four years and you've never once asked me a single question about my personal life."

"Of course I have."

"Oh? When's my birthday?"

"It's—" He searched his memory, but no answer appeared. He scowled. "You don't know mine, either."

"Your birthday is April second. What about my family? How many brothers and sisters do I have?"

"None. No one could be as bossy as you and have siblings."

She burst out laughing, which made him flash a grin. "Fair enough," she said. "You happen to be right—"

"Ha!"

"—*but* that was luck, not knowledge."

"You don't know those things about me."

"You have two brothers, both older, and three sisters, two older and one younger. Your father is a vicar, and your mother writes lovely long letters about their travels in Italy." She fixed her gaze upon him, triumph in her smile. "Well?"

"You read that in the serial Mary writes under my name. I'm sure she blathers about family business when not making up outrageous tales about crocodiles and arrows."

"Actually, she's rarely mentioned your family. She keeps the serial focused on you and your expeditions, a fact you'd know if you ever bothered to read it."

"I can see that I need to." He rubbed his chin, the stubble rough against his palm. "I suppose you think I should have paid more attention to your personal life."

"No."

He frowned. "But you said—"

"My point is that you *don't* pay attention to those things, and I'm quite happy with that. In fact, I would like it if you'd leave things the way they are—quite satisfactory for us both."

The irritation in her voice made him eye her with sudden caution. She looked a bit put out, and God knew he didn't want to lose his crisp bacon every morning.

But on the other hand, he was afire with curiosity. This entire situation was getting more and more interesting. The hunter in Michael had come roaring to life. His mousy little assistant—mousy in appearance, not in manner—was hiding something. And she was hiding it from *him*.

He was astounded, and more than a little intrigued. Before the events of the last two days, he'd thought he knew this woman well. Better, perhaps, than anyone else. But now he wasn't so certain. Something was going on inside that head of hers, something that had to do with the Isle of Barra. More intriguing yet, the stubborn jut of her jaw told him that it was going to take some finesse to dig the answers from her.

He forced himself to relax against the carriage squabs as he affected an unconcern he was far from feeling. "Jane, don't be silly. I wouldn't have any questions if you'd just state your connection to Barra and leave it at that."

"I wouldn't call it a connection exactly."

"That's for me to decide. I'm not interested in your history for any other reason than that your knowledge of the island could be useful."

She eyed him cautiously. "I suppose that's true."

"You're damn right it's true. Now, tell me what you know about Barra and I'll stop asking questions." *For now.*

She looked down at her hands clasped in her lap, her thick lashes casting shadows over her cheeks. Finally, she looked up at him, her expression reflective. "I don't really know that much. It's been a long time since I've been there."

"I can't imagine things have changed much in the time since you left. You're not that old, you know." He rubbed his chin. "Or are you?"

She chuckled. "No, I'm not. And I can see your point. Nothing much changes in that region of the world. It always seemed frozen in time." She nodded thoughtfully, her eyes the rich brown of brushed velvet. "I suppose some of my recollections might be of help, after all."

Why haven't I noticed her eyes before now? I've seen them hundreds—no, thousands—of times and yet I've never really paid attention to the color.

She frowned. "Why are you staring at me like that?"

Inwardly, he cursed, but then said, "Was I? Sorry. I was thinking. Let's begin with the caves, for you seem to remember them quite clearly. Are they well known to the island's inhabitants?"

"I suppose so. Why?"

"Because if the final clue to the Hurst Amulet was in

those caves, then it is possible that some treasure hunter has already discovered it and spirited it off."

"I don't think so. The caves are very remote and difficult to reach. You can access them only at low tide, and then only for an hour or so at a time."

"So they're underwater most of the time."

"The entryway is, yes, and the bottom of some of the caverns as well."

"That's inconvenient."

"And treacherous. I doubt many people have been in the caves."

"It would only take one, and you did say there've been rumors of a treasure for centuries."

"Yes, but everyone knows how dangerous the caves are, and I'm one of only a few people who've seen the markings on the wall inside the cave."

Her voice had softened, and he detected the faintest hint of a Scottish burr buried among her usually crisp vowels. *Bloody hell, she has an* accent! *Has it always been there and I never noticed? Or is it just audible when she's reminiscing about her home?* "The locals avoid the cave?"

"Oh, yes."

There was a hint of "och" in her "oh," something he was certain she'd never done before.

She continued on, unaware of his locked interest. "When I was young, about ten or so, there were two local lads who entered the cave. They were strapping lads those two, but young, and they dinna—" She stopped. Her surprised gaze found his before she closed her mouth firmly, her lips white.

"So you hear it, too, that touch of a Scottish brogue," he said with satisfaction.

"I don't know what you mean," she returned stiffly, her accent back to its normal clipped tone.

"Unbelievable. All of this time, I thought you were English—but you're a damned Scot."

Her hands clasped tightly together, she said nothing more.

Michael crossed his arms. She didn't *appear* any different. She was sitting in her usual prim and proper fashion, her sensibly clad feet planted firmly on the floor. Everything was the same except her expression, which was guarded. *Hidden.* Whatever she was hiding, he wanted, *needed,* to explore it. "Out with it, Jane. You might as well make a clean breast of it and tell me everything."

"Michael, stop it! Just leave things as they were, comfortable for us both."

Michael crossed his arms and glowered at her. Damn it, he wished this mystery were a simpler one, where all he had to do was crack an ancient text or dig in just the right spot in a vast desert to unearth the treasure he sought. This was far more complex and delicate, and he could tell from her tight expression that he was bungling it badly.

She was right in saying that things would be more comfortable if he'd leave well enough alone, but he couldn't help himself. Something had happened last night when he'd seen that bumpkin eyeing her like an art collector seeing a breathtakingly beautiful painting.

Somehow, over the years, she'd become his. His and no one else's. And he'd be damned if he'd allow anyone to know more about her than he did.

Yet there she sat, stubborn-mouthed and closed to him, her stiff posture challenging him to ask questions she wouldn't answer.

It was infuriating beyond belief. He wasn't used to people telling him no. His irritation bubbled, rising to the surface. She was *his* assistant, damn it. He paid her wages, saw to her safety, and shared her with no one. How *dare* she keep secrets from him?

Caught between a rising tide of anger and the same flush of excitement he always felt when on the verge of a new discovery, Michael reached across the carriage, picked up his plain no-nonsense assistant, and plopped her onto his lap. "There," he said, ignoring her outraged gasp. "*Now* you'll tell me what I want to know."

CHAPTER 4

From the diary of Michael Hurst:

London is good for two things—excellent Scotch and leaving. I miss them both, especially as I often partake of one while doing the other. I find the company stifling, the streets foul smelling and overcrowded, the houses bland and without architectural merit, and the people banal and filled with their own consequence.

No matter how often I leave London, I cannot wait to leave it again. My home is in my explorations. Those always welcome me.

Shocked, Jane's gaze locked with Michael's. Surely he hadn't just plucked her up and plopped her into his lap . . . surely she was imagining this and— But no. Here she was, caught in the circle of his strong arms like the veriest strumpet.

She should be angry and demand to be released that instant, but for some reason, Jane just blinked at him.

She'd worked in some of the most difficult and uncivilized places in the world, and for some of the roughest and least civilized explorers, too. She'd made a name for herself by practicing a tough, unflappable professionalism in the face of all circumstances by never revealing herself as a woman in any way.

Yet here she was, sitting in Michael Hurst's lap and not uttering a single word of protest. The truth was, she didn't know what to say—an unusual circumstance indeed. In her entire life there was only one other time she'd been bereft of speech, and that had involved Hurst, too.

It was the first time she'd met him. She'd heard of him, of course; one couldn't live in Egypt without hearing about the great explorer Michael Hurst. And whenever she could get her hands upon *The Morning Post,* she'd read of his exploits in his serial.

But it was more than that. Hurst was well thought of by other explorers, which was unusual, since they were an unyielding, jealous group. From things her different employers had said over the years, she knew that his work was highly regarded because of his meticulous research and his intuitive way of seeing connections between seemingly unrelated artifacts. But what really drew the admiration of his fellow explorers was the undeniable fact that the expeditions he led always uncovered the most spectacular artifacts. His instincts were exceptional.

It was that flawless reputation that had led Jane to leave her comfortable post with an older, prosy, but secure French explorer and answer the advert that Hurst had posted at an embassy in India. She'd been thrilled when he'd summoned her to an interview.

She'd had no illusions when she'd answered that advert; Hurst was also well known for his sharp-edged temperament. She knew he was an imperious sort, an exacting exploration leader, rude to those he considered inferior, and inordinately demanding. Such was his reputation that, even though he'd offered a superior wage, no one had answered his ad, frightened off by his rudeness. No one, that is, except her.

But what Jane hadn't known about Michael Hurst until the day she stepped into his tent was that this adventurous, driven, gruff, brilliant explorer was also handsome. Blink-twice-and-try-to-breathe-and-still-think-you're-seeing-an-angel handsome.

He was well over six feet tall, with black hair worn a bit too long so that it fell over his brow and emphasized his brilliant blue eyes. Added to that lethal combination was a strong jaw, lionlike grace, and a muscled physique that made every word in her head freeze in place.

Fortunately, Michael's overbearing attitude had quickly melted her frozen-in-place admiration, so she had regained her ability to speak and was quite prepared when he snapped a rude "Sit down!" and then offered her a ridiculously low salary and a list of unacceptable conditions.

But Jane relished bargaining, a strength that had stood her in good stead in her profession. By the time they were done, she'd forced Hurst to double her usual wage, which had left him in a towering rage, but with a new respect in his gaze. She'd found both quite satisfactory.

Thus, their relationship had begun. The respect he'd shown after their first altercation had never wavered in the years they'd worked together. It had offered its own protection, too, as it defined them as employee and employer, boundaries neither of them had crossed—until today.

She put her hands against his chest and tried to rise, no small feat in the rocking carriage, but Michael held her fast. "What is this?" she demanded.

"I'm tired of your evasions."

"My personal life is just that: personal. You don't ask me questions and I don't ask you. That's our arrangement."

His blue eyes narrowed, and he tilted his head to one side.

It was disconcerting to be examined at such close quarters. She was in his lap, her face so close to his that if she leaned forward even the slightest bit, their lips would touch.

The thought created tremors of—amazement? Trepidation? Uncertainty? Whatever it was, it was uncomfortable and to be avoided at all costs. *I know the danger of this,* she told herself. *And I'm no longer a child of eighteen to make such a silly error.* She wiggled, trying to loosen his hold. "Michael, release me this inst—"

"Stop that." His voice was so strained that she instantly froze.

His eyes were closed, his brows lowered, and he bit into his bottom lip as if in pain.

"I'm sorry. Did I hurt you?"

He swallowed hard. "No. But you shouldn't squirm like that."

"Why not— Oh! Your—" Her cheeks heated. "I didn't mean to—"

"I'm sure you didn't."

She was instantly aware of how his voice rumbled in his chest and thus against her arm when he spoke.

He met her gaze now, as bold as ever. "If you don't stay still, I won't be responsible for my reactions."

"You won't be—" She cocked an eyebrow. "Balderdash. You are responsible for your actions, aroused or not."

"I said I wasn't responsible for my *reactions,* not my *actions.* Of course I can control my actions; I'm not a barbarian."

"Then let me up."

"Will you answer my questions?"

"No."

"Then you'll stay right where you are until you do. Just stop wiggling." He settled farther into the corner, pulling her with him, and then tucking her head under his chin, as if it were the most natural thing in the world.

It would be a lie to say she had never wondered what it would be like if he embraced her. How could one not wonder with such a handsome employer? But she'd worked hard over the years to make sure that aimless wondering would never become reality. *I am undoing years of hard work.* "Michael, this is ludicrous."

"You've forgotten who pays the wage."

"My private life isn't covered by my wages."

"Yes, it is."

Her jaw tightened. She didn't wish to tell him anything, blast it, but she supposed that, since they were headed to the Isle of Barra, she'd eventually have to. She sighed her frustration but pulled back to look at him.

"Fine. I was born there. I grew up there. And I lived there until I was sixteen."

Michael blinked. Of all the things he'd thought to hear, that wasn't it. "You were born on the Isle of Barra?"

She nodded. "My mother was English, which is why I don't have as strong an accent as you might expect."

"Until today, you haven't had any accent at all. At least, none that I'd noticed."

Jane flicked him a dismissive glance and said in a perfectly soft brogue, "She dinna ken to a brogue and thought it undistinguished."

"I'd have to agree with her."

Jane's eyes flashed fire as her jaw firmed. He offered bluntly, "I'd never heard of Barra before last night."

"You're not Scottish," she returned promptly, with a strong flicker of pride in her voice. "I've answered your questions, Hurst. *Now* may I return to my seat?"

Michael had pulled Jane into his lap on a wild impulse, but now that she was here, her trim rump pressed to his groin, her wide brown eyes framed by her spectacles, her lush mouth thinned in irritation—suddenly, he could think of no good reason to release her.

Of course, he really should. Decency demanded it.

He sighed and loosened his hold to allow her to stand.

But the second her trim bottom lifted from his lap and she rocked forward to stand, her face came directly even with his.

Their gazes locked, and she froze in place.

If he leaned forward less than an inch, his lips would brush hers. And there was something intensely erotic about the wide fullness of her lips that begged for a kiss. So he did it.

The second their lips met, a shock raced through him, making his scalp tingle, his heart thunder, and his cock rise and harden.

The world stood still, as if uncertain how to handle this new development. Michael's gaze locked with Jane's, neither moving, their lips barely touching.

And then, with the most sensual moan he'd ever heard, Jane closed her eyes, slipped an arm about his neck, and pressed against him.

Desire erupted with a suddenness that would have shocked him if he could think, but he could only feel as roaring passion thundered through him. He grasped her hand, which now rested on his chest, and deepened the kiss, slipping his tongue across her lips.

Jane's eyes flew open and she gasped as if burned, breaking the kiss.

Blinking at him through her spectacles, she pulled away. "Oh, my," she breathed. "That was— I mean, I've kissed someone before— But not like— That was—" She bit her lip. "But it mustn't happen again. We can't confuse things and— No. We can't do this." Her gaze locked on his mouth and a wistful look entered her eyes. "Still . . ."

Michael's mind buzzed from the explosion of sensations. All he knew was that he was damned glad they'd kissed and that she was back in his lap, her bottom pressed to his throbbing cock. *I've never had such a reaction to a mere kiss. And with Jane, who is a perfect innocent—*

She whipped off her spectacles, grabbed his lapels, and kissed him again, only this time it was *her* tongue that slipped across *his* lips.

For a full two seconds, Michael didn't react. He couldn't believe that this was his quiet, efficient, unremarkable assistant. But Jane was in no mood for hesitation; she slid her hands to his shoulders, clutching him closer as she opened her lips beneath his in invitation.

Michael was pulled into the kiss like a fish reeled to shore. His resolve to resist her fled completely and he grasped her to him, his hands greedily exploring the flare of her hips and the delicate curves of her waist. She was just as active, slipping her hands beneath his waistcoat and lower, touching, stroking, driving him mad.

Her passion was as contagious as malaria, and Michael could no more stop her than he could stop himself. He slid his hand over her skirts to the hem, sliding his fingers up her leg to her knee, stopping there, aching to move forward but knowing he dared not.

Not yet.

He deepened the kiss until he was once again the one in control, fanning her desires until she moaned

against his mouth and stirred restlessly in his lap. It felt
so good, so right, so incredibly—

Her teeth bumped into his, and she giggled.

The gesture and her reaction were so innocent
that he closed his eyes and his hand fisted where it had
rested against the enticingly warm skin of her knee. He
couldn't continue this. For all of her enthusiasm, Jane
was as awkward as a colt. *And just as innocent, damn it.*

Michael broke the kiss with a muffled curse. "Jane.
No. We can't." He lifted her off his lap and to the ends
of his knees, giving his aching cock the room it needed
to calm.

She frowned, a wounded look in her brown eyes.
"Michael, please." The name was more moan than word,
and she reached for him again.

"No." His voice croaked like a rusted fence as he
fought the heat that burned through him. Gathering
every ounce of reserve he possessed, he slid his hands
around her waist, lifted her, and then set her on the seat
across from him.

For a moment, they stared at one another. The
coach rumbled on, rocking from side to side. Jane's hair
had come down and hung like rich, chestnut brown silk
about her pale skin. The sheen of her hair added to the
thick sweep of her lashes made her look as exotic as a
harem girl. She looked young and sensual and achingly
beautiful.

Bloody hell, when did that happen? I can't think of her that way. It will complicate everything.

She cleared her throat. "If you don't mind, Hurst, I'd like to try that again." Her voice was faintly husky, a tremor threading through her words. "I—I was just getting a feel for it and—"

"For the love of Ra, I don't *want* you to get 'a feel' for that! Jane, you— I can't— This isn't what should— *Damn it!*" Michael shook his head, trying to clear his numb mind. "I should have never held you."

"But you did hold me," she said in her usual prosaic tone. "And once you'd done that . . ." She tilted her head to one side, regarding him with interest. "I've never been kissed quite like that before."

He wished she'd put her spectacles back on, for it was disconcerting facing that nakedly beautiful gaze. "I'm surprised you've been kissed at all."

"Oh, yes." She looked about the seat for her spectacles. "Many times, in fact."

"Many— Bloody hell! How many?"

Her brows lowered and she held up a hand as she began to count, "Eight, nine, ten—I think that was— No, no. Wait." She bit her lip. "I forgot about those two, so eleven, twelve—" She looked up at the ceiling as if searching for more memories. Finally, she shrugged. "I can't remember them all."

Fury burned through him until he remembered her

awkwardness. "I don't believe you. You've been kissed once, if that."

"How would you know?"

"Because you're inexperienced; I could tell."

Hurt instantly flashed in her eyes, and he fought the urge to apologize, a feeling so unlike him that he growled, "You see? That's the very reason kissing was a bad idea. Now every time I say something, your feelings will be hurt."

She stiffened. "My feelings are not hurt; they're just offended."

"It's the same thing."

"No, it's not. And you can stop glowering at me as if I did something wrong. I'm not the one who initiated that kiss."

He lifted his brows, and she flushed. "Not the first one, anyway," she amended.

"It won't happen again," he returned, unaccountably irritated. The fact that she had reached for him still stirred his blood and made him ache to explore her yet more.

His discomfort made him scowl. "You practically threw yourself into my arms. You should have a care how you comport yourself in the future."

She grabbed up her spectacles and whisked them into place on her pert nose, her back ramrod straight. In that instant, she became the Jane he knew so well. "Don't muddle your facts, Hurst. You kissed me—and quite thoroughly, I might add. I merely responded."

"You threw yourself at me," he repeated stubbornly.

"No, I kissed you back." She sent him a frustrated look. "I vow, is there no man who can talk about physical pleasures without exaggerating?"

He choked. "What do *you* know of men and physical pleasures?"

"Enough to realize that if a man tells you something about them, only half of his story will be true, if that."

The tinge of bitterness in her voice gave him pause. "Someone has lied to you." Perhaps he'd been wrong, and she had been kissed more than once. But whoever had done so had apparently done a remarkably poor job.

Her cheeks turned a deep pink. "It doesn't matter. I kissed you back because I was surprised at how good it felt. That and I was curious. That's all."

"Whatever the circumstances, we'd be stupid to pursue it. It would ruin our arrangement."

"Agreed. However, I must admit that I resent that you believe I'll change the way I react to you because of a simple kiss." She found her pins scattered upon the floor and began to return her hair to order. "I'm not such a ninny that I'd allow such a silly thing to affect me."

"We'll see."

"Yes, we will. And when we do, you'll owe me an apology, which I'll take in two bottles of good Scotch. The same kind your brother-in-law sent to you in Egypt."

"No. That's damned good Scotch."

"Which is why you'll get me *two* bottles."

"By Ra, you're an impertinent, saucy—"

"Careful, Hurst. We just kissed, so according to you, I shall now interpret everything you say in a very negative manner and might burst into tears and run shrieking off to a convent."

She chuckled, smoothing her skirts and looking every bit as proper as she had upon entering the coach. "I never realized until now how little you know about women. Oh, you can discuss Ptolemy III in great detail, but you're a complete novice when it comes to the fair sex."

"You're pushing me, Jane."

"No, I'm pushing you back," she returned, a martial light in her eyes. "There's a difference."

"I wish we hadn't kissed at all," he snapped.

"So do I, but we can't unkiss, so we must deal with it as best as we can. In fact, I'll begin now." She raised up to bang the flat of her hand on the carriage ceiling, bringing her breasts directly in his line of sight.

Michael's mouth went dry, and he found his hands curving as if they were covering those delicate mounds. Why hadn't he done so when she'd been so pliant in his lap—

She returned to her seat as the carriage slowed to a stop. "I'll ride with Ammon while your temper cools. He's alone in the second carriage and I'm sure he'll enjoy a companion."

The coach rocked as the footmen jumped down and Michael frowned, suddenly realizing that he didn't wish her to go. Not until they'd hashed out the nonsense that hung between them. "Jane, don't be ridiculous. We'll just"—he waved a hand—"*make* things go back to the way they were. If you'll just calm down and—"

"If *I* will calm down? *You're* the one who is—"

The coach door opened, and with a flat, unamused look, Jane gathered her pelisse and climbed out. She paused in the doorway and sent him a prim frown of disapproval. "Pray try and get some sleep. It will do wonders for that temper of yours."

With that, she left, and the footman closed the door behind her.

Michael thought about following her and shaking some sense into her, but he didn't trust himself any more than he trusted her. Perhaps she was right and they needed some time apart. "Twenty years might do it," he muttered.

He threw himself into a corner of the coach, rammed his hat onto his head, and yanked the brim over his eyes. He slumped there, arms crossed as he wondered what in hell had just happened. Before yesterday, he'd never imagined Jane as—well, a woman. She was just Jane. But somehow that simple, stable fact had gotten tossed upon its head and he didn't like it one bit.

Perhaps solving the riddle of who Jane Smythe-Haughton really was would rid him of this new, uncomfortable view of his assistant. After all, if she hadn't stoked his damnable curiosity, he would have never had such a heated reaction to a mere kiss. Once his curiosity was sated, his interest in her would be, too.

Pleased to have come up with a sure way to resolve the predicament, Michael tugged the discarded carriage blanket over himself, settled farther into the corner, and fell asleep.

CHAPTER 5

From the diary of Michael Hurst:

Since I've been traveling alone in my coach—which I am enjoying *despite* what certain impertinent assistants may think—I've spent the time summarizing our quest:

- The Hurst Amulet was stolen from the family and then gifted to Queen Elizabeth, recorded among her personal items as late as 1588.

- We know from a letter she wrote that for some reason Elizabeth became fearful of the amulet, and sent it as a gift to a foreign dignitary.

- One hundred years later, an amulet that fits the description of the Hurst Amulet appeared in the inventory of a powerful viceroy of Egypt, who was later assassinated. His goods were dispersed to the winds, but rumors persisted that the viceroy knew he was in danger and he'd sent his treasures to a place of safety, leaving behind a map for his son.

- The map was hidden inside three matching onyx boxes.

- That is the final written record we have of the Hurst Amulet. Until now . . .

They traveled for two weeks, and as the days passed, the roads grew more and more rutted and the vistas more starkly beautiful.

Eventually they turned toward the coast and the sunshine faded, leaving unending gray. It was under just such an inauspicious sky that the three dirty, muddy coaches rolled into Oban, a tiny port town situated upon the western coast of Scotland.

During the trip, whenever they'd come to a stop, Michael made sure to tell anyone who cared to hear that he was enjoying the solitude of his coach. In truth, he'd been bored to death and had passed the time working on tedious translations of various ancient texts that held references to jewels and amulets, hoping for more clues to the one he sought.

Privately, he'd discovered something about himself: traveling alone was not to his taste. Over the last four years, he'd become used to Jane's company. While she wasn't a chatty sort of female who burdened one with a lot of silly comments, she did know how to liven a monotonous journey with interesting conversation, and he found that he missed both her wit and her sharp commentary.

All in all, the journey had been onerous in the extreme. It didn't help that Jane hadn't seemed to miss his company a bit and was her usual sunny self, although he could tell by the way she rubbed her lower back when no one was looking that the roughness of the trip was beginning to pall on her, too.

It was with a sense of relief for all when they finally arrived at the only inn in the small town of Oban. As the carriage pulled to a halt, Michael glanced out the window at the uninspiring building and then returned the scrolls he'd been translating to their protective containers. He'd just finished slipping them into his satchel when the door opened and the footman let down the steps.

Michael tucked the satchel under his arm and descended, looking about him with a frown. "It's damned foggy."

"No, it's not." Jane, just handed down from her coach by a footman, walked briskly toward Michael, her boots clicking on the damp cobblestones. "You're wearing your spectacles and I daresay it's been days since you've cleaned them."

Something in her tone suggested that he was incapable of the task, and he glowered at her. She was wearing her usual gray gown, brown pelisse, and sensible gray bonnet—looking exactly the same as when he'd first met her four years ago. Though she looked the same, since their kiss he couldn't seem to help but notice other things about her. Though her glossy brown hair was sensibly tucked away, a few loose strands curled about her ears. She had a habit of tucking those loose strands away, her slender fingers unconsciously drawing his gaze to her delicate ear, the slender line of her neck, the slope of her shoulder, and the way the material of her modest gown covered her creamy white skin and—

He gritted his teeth and turned away, yanking off his spectacles and tucking them into his pocket. "We need a boat to take us to the island, though the size of this town doesn't make me hopeful that we'll find one easily."

"Nonsense," she said briskly. "Some of the locals do nothing else but ferry people and supplies to the outlying islands. This is a slow time for them, too, so we shouldn't have any trouble arranging for passage."

He sent her a sour glance, noting that her spectacles had fogged to a thick white as she'd spoken. She removed them to rub the glass briskly between her gloved fingers.

"Hot air," he said with satisfaction.

She sent him a twinkling look that made him forget his momentary irritation. "It's better than the icy cold you've been blowing on me since we left London."

"I've been polite."

"Barely. Fortunately, I'm used to your moods." She held up the spectacles, opened her mouth to a perfect O, and puffed warm air upon them.

Michael's gaze locked on her soft lips. They were in the perfect shape to—

He yanked his gaze away. *By Ra, whatever it costs, I've got to stop doing that.* And so he'd been telling himself ever since he'd made his fateful mistake and had kissed her.

He looked glumly at the gray landscape. "It's going to rain."

"It's quite overcast, which is normal this late in the day. I daresay that as the evening breeze rises from the bay, this mist will blow out."

He sent her an annoyed look. "Why are you always so cheery?"

She smiled sweetly. "Because it irks you, and irking you is what I live for."

"Witch."

"Stubborn curmudgeon."

He tried to think of another appellation to toss her way, absently rubbing his cheek where his stubble itched. He'd taken to shaving every five or six days, just long enough to continue and annoy Jane without having to deal with a full beard, which he found bothersome. As he rubbed his cheek, he caught the disapproval in her glance. "I suppose I should shave." He grinned at her hopeful look. "But I'm not going to."

She cast an unfavorable glance at his chin. "It's not a look that suits you." Her breath misted into fog in the chilled air, her cheeks pink as she held up her spectacles and then, apparently finding them still not clean enough, used her gloved fingers to wipe them yet again. "I forgot how damp it is here at this time of the year."

"You look cold through and through. Apparently the foot warmer in your coach didn't have enough coals to melt the cockles of your icy heart."

She merely smiled. "I gave my foot warmer to Ammon. If I'm too warm when I travel, I get ill."

He was pleased to be able to say, "I know."

"I'm sure you do," she said in a dry tone, replacing her spectacles on her nose. "Seeing as how we've traveled together for four years and usually in the same carriage, you could hardly *not* know."

He wisely didn't answer but nodded toward the inn. "I'll send a footman to discover what sort of transport is available. I'd like to leave for Barra within the next day if possible."

"Excellent. I must admit that I'm tired of traveling. It's not as wearing as a camel train through the desert, but it's close. The seats in that coach are not what they should be, and I fear I'll be woefully sore for the next few days."

"My coach's seats are quite comfortable, but then, it's better sprung than the other. A pity you didn't see fit to ride with me instead." He turned to walk toward the inn door.

She fell into step beside him. "I'm sure I was *much* more comfortable in Ammon's coach. But that doesn't alter the fact that this trip has been quite long and the roads atrocious."

"The roads were horrid. I don't care much for Scotland thus far." He opened the inn door and stood to one side. "After you."

She preceded him into the inn, where they were greeted by the innkeeper, a plump woman with iron gray curls and a crooked nose that would have been at home on the face of an Irish boxer. In a deep voice, she informed them that she was a widow and that her name was Mrs. Farquhar.

Jane introduced herself and Michael, and then Mrs. Farquhar escorted them to the inn's only common room. As they went, the innkeeper chattered with such a thick accent that Michael could only understand one of every three words she said. Fortunately, Jane was back in charge of things, and she made some pleasantries that had their hostess grinning as she bowed them into the common room and then toddled off toward the kitchen.

Jane removed her gloves and neatly tucked them into her pelisse pocket before approaching the weak fire that had been laid out.

Michael noticed some firewood in a rack beside the window, so he set his satchel beside the settee and fetched some larger pieces of wood to add to the flames. He dusted his hands as he straightened, the fire already crackling more brightly. "There. That should be warmer. I take it that you ordered refreshments from our hostess? I detected the word 'dram' among her garbled speech."

"Her speech isn't garbled; she merely has an accent."

"I couldn't understand her."

"Only because you weren't trying." Jane removed her pelisse and her bonnet and then hung them upon a peg by the door. When she was done, she straightened her spectacles and sank into the chair closest to the fire. "I vow but though I'm sitting still, I feel as if I'm still inside that wretched carriage. I'd much rather travel by camel."

"They rock just as much."

"Yes, but their gait is much smoother, and they don't toss you about as if you were a loose pebble in a box."

Michael shrugged out of his overcoat and tossed it over the back of the settee, then dropped into the chair opposite hers. "The carriage smells better than a camel."

She curled her nose. "I'd forgotten about that." The fire crackled cozily and Jane leaned toward the warmth, holding out her hands to the flames, her spectacles reflecting the fire. "Coach or camel, I'm glad we're finally near our destination."

He grunted. "This cold and relentless travel makes me long for the warmth and comfort of the sulfi's palace."

She chuckled. "I never thought I'd hear you say that about our prison, velvet lined as it was."

"I almost grew fond of that place; my brothers took so long to procure my release. It took them *months*."

"If I'd had another week or so, I'd have won our way free. The sulfi was beginning to show signs of reason."

Michael had to stare. "You have gone completely mad. He was not beginning to show signs of reason. You were too busy flirting with him to notice, which made for a very difficult situation when the time did come to leave."

She sniffed. "I was *not* flirting."

"You danced in front of him wearing the most revealing, low-cut—"

"Nonsense. I performed a perfectly acceptable regional dance while wearing perfectly proper clothing for that culture, which you would know if you'd get your head out of a book once in a while."

"Acceptable? Proper? You wiggled your hips like a . . . a . . . a . . . I can't even say it. And I won't even begin on your choice of clothing."

"The sulfi's wives helped me select those."

"I couldn't believe you were willing to expose yourself like that. The whole thing was quite undignified, and your dance—I don't wish to be cruel, but you lack a noticeable amount of grace. I've seen bears dance better."

He'd thought to irritate her, but instead she chuckled. "It was quite fun. Besides, you must admit that he treated us better after that. We were moved to better quarters and given more servants, better food, and even access to his library."

"He always treated you well. *I* was the one held captive."

"Yes, in a silk-lined suite of rooms, with nine personal servants to see to your every whim."

He rubbed his chin, scratching at the itchy stubble. "The rooms were quite nice, but I couldn't even go outside without guards escorting me with muskets."

"Please note that you were given nine servants *after* I performed that dance." She shot him a laughing look, her brown eyes sparkling. "Admit I was good."

"I will admit no such thing." He'd been beyond shocked when Jane had offered to perform the dance usually done by one of the sulfi's many wives. She'd been quite horrible at it, too, and the sulfi had been reduced to chuckles, but still, there was no disguising the man's interest in Jane after that. Michael had been outraged and furious, though there had been precious little he could do about it.

Jane smiled serenely, ignoring his glower. "It was all part of my master plan to make him forget that we were his prisoners and see us as guests instead. In his country, dancing doesn't have scandalous intentions the way our culture might see it. It's merely a way to show appreciation for—"

"Balderdash. The only thing that dance expressed was that you needed a good talking to. And don't tell me that it didn't complicate things. When my brother arrived to rescue us, the sulfi refused to give you up, and I then had to rescue *you*, which was a pain in the ass."

She waved an airy hand. "Don't pretend you didn't enjoy storming the castle. You loved every minute. Your face was positively aglow as you ran through the courtyard firing your pistol in the air." She sent him a look of approval, which surprised him. "I never met a man who liked storming a castle better."

"It's in my blood. The Hursts are a dangerous mixture of royal Norman stock and brutal Scottish blood."

"You sound invincible."

He showed his teeth in a smile. "You'd do well to remember that."

"Humph. Be that as it may, I didn't need your help— dramatic as it was—to win my freedom from the sulfi; I'd already found a way to escape and was just biding my time."

He gave her a flat stare. "Normally, you're a sane woman. But I think being shut up for those long months disturbed your brain in some way. I—"

Footsteps in the hallway announced the arrival of the landlady with a tray bearing glasses, a bottle of amber liquid, a plate of bread and cheese, and two bowls of fragrantly steaming stew.

Jane rose and went to the table where Mrs. Farquhar was spreading out the fare. The two conversed for a few moments in low tones and then the landlady left. Jane took her seat before a bowl of stew. "You should eat while it's hot."

The wondrous scent of the stew made his stomach growl, so he reluctantly rose from his chair and went to join her at the table.

Jane picked up her spoon and then said, "Mrs. Farquhar believes her nephew has access to a boat large enough to carry us to Barra. She's going outside now to talk to the coachman and give him her nephew's name."

"Good." He hungrily dug into the stew. The delicious flavor spread through his mouth and instantly eased his ill temper. The savory broth was rich with carrots and onions and large bits of meat and a mixture of spices that made the stew the best he'd ever had.

Across the table, Jane peeped at him from beneath her lashes, noting with satisfaction the look of bliss on his face. Though they'd eaten almost every meal together since their disagreement, he'd been distant and chilly. She'd replied in kind, although it had weighed down her spirits far more than it should have.

It was odd how one missed something only when it was gone. Until now, she hadn't realized how much she counted upon their leisurely conversations while traveling or over the dinner table. But she had missed them dreadfully this last week.

It was unfortunate that Michael was right; their kiss had indeed changed things. Not from her end, of course, but from his. After the kiss, he'd been so different, so distant. He was an intense man who did things his own way, with a passion and fervor that was unmatched. It was the trait that made him so successful. It was also the trait that demanded that their relationship stay professional and nothing else.

She watched as Michael picked up the bread and tore a crusty piece from the loaf, which he immediately held out to her. She smiled as she took it, the scent a pleasing complement to the stew.

That was one of the things she'd always liked about him; though he could be notoriously rude in the things he said, he possessed an old-style courtesy, which she attributed to being raised by a very forceful mother as well as being among a large number of siblings.

She tasted the stew and was pleased that it was as good as Michael's expression had indicated. As she ate she watched him surreptitiously, noting how his dark hair was falling over his brow and into his eyes. He was due for a trim soon and a shave as well. She wished he'd allow her free rein with her shears, for she'd like to see him far more neatly shorn.

Not that it really made any difference: long hair or short hair, stubble chinned or not, Michael Hurst was a devastatingly attractive man. He lifted a spoonful of stew to his lips, unaware of her attention. What made him so much *more* than other men? Was it his coloring— the brilliant blue eyes and black hair? Or the way his mouth was so masculine and sensual? Or the way his—

His gaze locked with hers.

Her face burned at being caught staring and she hurried to say, "We should look at the map here, before we go to the island."

He placed his spoon in his empty bowl. "Why?"

"I'm not sure what sort of accommodations we'll find once we're on the island. There used to be an inn on the southern end, but I'm not sure it's still open after all of these years. We might be forced to make do with our tents."

"That's unfortunate." He cocked a brow at her. "I assume you brought our tents?"

"Of course. So while we have the chance, we should make use of this fine table and the excellent lamplight."

He looked about the small room, which was now quite cozy, thanks to the crackling fire. "I hope that inn is still open."

"So do I, but it's been a long time since I was there, so . . ." She shrugged.

He poured some whiskey into a glass, the liquid swirling in glowing gold as his dark blue gaze locked on hers once more. "How long has it been since you were on Barra?"

"Fourteen years."

"So you were—" He frowned. "How old are you now?"

She placed her spoon into her bowl and pushed it away. "That's no question to ask a lady."

"You aren't a lady." He took a drink of the Scotch and grinned.

"And you are no gentleman," she retorted. "No gentleman I know would ever ask a woman such a rude question."

"I never said I was a gentleman." He appeared quite pleased about it, too, his blue eyes mischievous in the lamplight.

"And I never said that I was a lady, so we're at an impasse. Again." She hid a grin when she noted his smile fading. "Hurst, pray pour me some of that wonderful Scotch. In return I'll fetch the map."

"How do you know the Scotch is wonderful?"

"The same way I knew the stew would be good: I saw your face when you tasted it. You have a very expressive face and it reveals your every thought."

"Balderdash. Go get that damned map and let's see what we can make of this adventure."

She arose and brought back the satchel. She opened it and pulled out the three onyx boxes, then dropped the satchel on the bench tucked under the table. In a very short time, she'd removed the onyx boxes from their velvet sheaths and had them unfolded and locked in place.

Jane placed the assembled map on the table between them, took the seat beside his, and pulled the lamp closer. "I can't believe I didn't realize this was the Isle of Barra. It's so clear now."

"You should give yourself credit for realizing it was a portion of this country at all. At one time, I was certain it was part of Constantinople."

"It took me a while to realize it, but this"—she touched a faint word etched below the map—"is an ancient term for *island*. And then this symbol"—she traced an odd etching beside what they'd assumed was a river—"has been used in ancient texts to indicate what we now call the British Isles."

"Both are still correct, even with the new interpretation of the map."

"Yes, but I was on the wrong side of the country. Whoever put the words upside down to hide the true orientation of the map was very clever." She made a wry face. "I was so certain that the amulet was hidden in some rocky outcropping in the bay near Dover. I'd have bet gold on it."

"You were supposed to think that. Our mapmaker was very skilled in hiding his intent, which only confirms to me that he was hiding something very valuable."

"The Hurst Amulet."

"It must be."

She noted how Michael's brow lowered as he looked at the map. Since the first day she'd met him, he'd made no secret that finding the lost family heirloom was of immense importance to him. And he'd worked tirelessly to track the long-lost amulet, too.

He stirred restlessly. "It didn't help our cause that the map doesn't show the entire island, but only a portion of it, so that it was even easier to be led astray."

"True," she said. "Otherwise we could have simply looked for a coastline that matches."

He nodded his agreement and then traced his fingers over the etched surface of the map. "Someone tried very, very hard to be as obscure as possible, and they succeeded."

She sighed. "Still, I grew up on Barra and I should have recognized it. It's a very small island and I've ridden over every inch, time and again. I know every cove, every curve of the shoreline, every glassy loch and grass-covered hillock, and yet—" She shook her head.

Michael's gaze lifted from the map to rest upon her face. "You miss it?"

"I miss being that young." As she pulled the lamp closer so that the golden pool of light spilled over the etched metal, she tried not to notice how it reflected across Michael's face and made his blue eyes glow. "I thought anything was possible if you only wanted it enough, which was stupid. As an adult, I now know that just wanting something won't make it so. You must also have opportunity and luck on your side. A few casks of gold aren't amiss, either."

He rubbed his chin, his gaze still locked on her. "Interesting. In all of the time we've worked together, I don't think I've ever heard you utter such a pessimistic sentiment."

"It's not pessimistic to admit a universal truth." She took an absent sip of her whiskey and allowed the

warmth to spread through her. "But back to the map . . .
I recognize some aspects of the island, now that I know
the map for what it is. For example, the shoreline is a
bit different." She touched a small bay in the southern
part of the isle. "This is Castle Bay, and it's much deeper
now than depicted here; no doubt it has been eroded by
storms and whatnot over the centuries. There's a town
now, too."

"Where?"

"Here." She touched the edge of the bay. "The
town's name is Castlebay."

"And the name of the bay is Castle Bay?"

"It is."

"That's original."

She chuckled. "So it is."

Humor warmed his blue gaze. "What else has
changed?"

She pointed at a squiggled line. "That's not a river as
we'd thought, but the western shore of the island."

"So this represents the sea." Michael touched upon
a row of upside-down *v*'s, his fingertips tracing the
raised portion of the etching. "Not mountains as we'd
thought." He couldn't help but feel a certain appreciation for the long-gone cartographer who so cleverly hid
his meanings while still offering up a trove of clues. "We
need to compare the old map to a new one. I bought
one before we left London."

Her glance was warm with approval. "Well done, Hurst."

He found the satchel beside their bench and pulled out a small tube. He removed a number of maps, paging through them. Finally he found the one he wanted. He handed it to Jane, who spread it on the table beside the map made by the boxes and bent over it, her brown hair set to a golden gleam by the lamplight.

He decided that he liked that particular shade of hair color; it was rich and shimmered with red and gold lights. Oddly enough, his fingers itched to touch her silken hair. *Which is ridiculous,* he told himself, focusing on returning the other maps to the tube.

Her brow suddenly lowered. "Hurst, this map is dated 1812, and yet it is missing some very significant features."

"You said it had been a while since you'd been to Barra."

"Yes, but an entire castle?"

"There's a castle?"

She sent him an impatient look. "Why else would they call it Castle Bay?"

"Ah, yes. This is Scotland, too. You can't swing a dead cat in this country without hitting a fortification of some kind."

"That's because of the warriorlike nature of earlier times."

"And by 'warriorlike nature' you're talking about the Scots themselves."

Her eyes sparkled. "I'm talking about *most* earlier societies. They were *all* more given to violence."

"Some, I'll grant you, but your people have been a contentious lot since the beginning. Far more than most."

"I prefer to think of the Scots as strong-minded."

"I daresay you do, seeing as how you're one yourself. However, I've read hundreds of histories about ancient societies, and with the exception of the Spartans, I believe the Scots are *the* most contentious society to ever walk the earth."

Her gaze narrowed behind her spectacles. "Are you done?"

He grinned and pulled out his own spectacles. "For the moment." He slid his spectacles in place and then leaned forward, his shoulder touching hers. "So the new map isn't accurate?"

"Apparently not. Kisimul Castle is represented on the ancient map, just not the current one. See?"

He glanced to where her finger touched beside a crudely represented castle etched in the metal map and then to the blank space on the newer version. He shrugged. "Perhaps the newer cartographer didn't mark dwellings."

"So I'd think, but they've drawn several dwellings— two, in fact, neither of which I know." She placed her finger on the northern side of the isle and murmured, as if to herself, "This one is drawn especially large, as if it were a manse of some sort. Who would build a house here, one large enough to be placed upon the map? It could only be— But no. That would be a waste when . . ." She frowned and fell silent.

"What would be a waste?"

"Nothing." Her gaze lifted to his, though her expression gave away none of her thoughts. "I was just thinking aloud." She ran her finger over a line that appeared on both the maps. "This is the main road. It circles the entire island and hasn't changed at all, so navigating will be simple."

He'd leaned forward when she'd traced the road and now her scent tickled his nose: light lavender and something else . . . a hint of rose, perhaps? He had to fight the urge to bend down and run his cheek along the delicate line of her neck and soak in the scent. She'd just thawed after their last physical encounter; he wasn't about to allow her to retreat again. *Just one kiss, and she and I were uncomfortable for almost two weeks. I will not allow that to happen again.*

He returned his attention to the maps. "The caves are marked on the southwestern shore, but . . . what's this?" He pointed to another symbol on the ancient map, this one an upside-down triangle. "What's here? It's too obviously placed not to be of some importance."

"That's a glen." Her expression softened a moment. "A very beautiful glen at that. When I was a child, I used to ride my horse through there. There's a loch, a ruin, and some delightful fishing, if you like that sort of thing."

He lifted his brows. "Did you fish?"

"I still do, when I have the chance. I am very good at it, too."

"Of that, I have no doubt." He leaned back in his chair. "If we reach the isle this evening, as we hope, then in the morning we'll search that glen."

"And the caves?"

"We'll ride by them and get an idea of the lay of the land. You said they're available only at low tide, so it will take more planning to investigate them."

"That makes sense." She pursed her lips, the soft bottom one glistening with moisture.

The innocent gesture instantly made Michael's body react. He was so drawn to her, so *interested*. He couldn't seem to stop watching her, wanting by turns to touch her, taste her, feel her—

He scowled. *Stop it. I must control these urges. They'll only make things miserable for the two of us.* He forced himself to smile and say lightly, "The caves must hold the final clue to the—"

"Pardon me, sir." Ammon stood in the doorway. At his side, her eyes wide, her mouth open, was Mrs. Farquhar.

Jane stood and crossed to the landlady. "Ah! I see you've met Ammon."

The landlady nodded mutely, her gaze still glued to the tall servant, her fingers moving across her cheek, as if she were tracing the path of the servant's scars on her own skin.

Jane smiled up at Ammon. "Did you perchance find a boat to hire?"

Ammon inclined his head, ignoring how the landlady's gaze followed his every move. "Mrs. Farquhar's nephew possesses one that is well suited for our task. I hired it and trust it will be sufficiently large to carry us all, as well as the trunks. He will return for the horses."

Jane turned to the landlady. "Thank you so much for recommending your nephew's boat."

The landlady nodded, her gaze still glued to Ammon, her mouth still hanging open.

Ammon sighed, though he never gave her so much as a glance. "Mr. Hurst, if it pleases you, we're to leave in three hours with the tide. The pier's not far from here, so we've no need to hurry. We're to sail down the Sound of Mull and then to Castle Bay on the Isle of Barra."

"Who will care for the horses during their crossing?" Jane asked.

"Turner and two footmen will stay with them and make sure they are well cared for. The other footmen will come with us."

"Well done, Ammon," Jane said. "I believe we'll wait until it's closer to the time to leave before we come to the pier. A few hours of rest will do us all some good. I hope everyone has eaten?"

"Yes, miss. We've all had stew. It was well made." He inclined his head toward Mrs. Farquhar, who started as if someone had goosed her.

"Och, did ye? I'm pleased ye enjoyed— That is, 'tis an old recipe and I— Not that yer people dinna have guid recipes, too, fer I'm sure they do, not that I've ever had any food from yer land, but my family is known fer makin' the best stew providin' we have a bit o' mutton to—"

"Thank you, Mrs. Farquhar," Jane said in a soothing tone, patting the landlady's arm, as that lady seemed well on her way to getting lost trying to find the right words.

Ammon bowed. "Miss Jane, I shall return for Mr. Hurst and yourself in an hour and a half." As if relieved to be away from them all, he spun on his heel and left.

Mrs. Farquhar let out her breath as the inn door closed behind him. "Gor', ye dinna tell me ye was travelin' with a heathen. I aboot jumped from me skin when I saw him in the yard."

"That's because we *aren't* traveling with a heathen," Michael said, his gaze hooded.

Mrs. Farquhar was impervious to the sharp note in his voice. "La, tha' giant scared me witless, he did!"

"Which wouldn't take mu—" Michael started to say.

"Of course!" Jane quickly spoke across him. "Mrs. Farquhar, there used to be an inn on Barra. You wouldn't happen to know if it's still in existence?"

If there was anything more powerful than Michael Hurst when he decided to be charming, Jane didn't know what it was. And Mrs. Farquhar was no match for that blindingly handsome grin or the way his blue eyes sparkled with mischief.

Mrs. Farquhar blushed a lovely shade of pink and immediately embarked on a disjointed outpouring of information. "Och, now, I do know a bit, as me cousin Rory Johnston lives there now and he comes through when he brings his kelp t' sell. 'Tis a lovely isle, lush and green, with lovely lochs and white sands upon the beaches. It's a wet land, though, and some say it rains more than it shines."

"That can be depressing."

"Aye, the people are oft given to fits o' the sullens fer thet."

"I can imagine."

"Aye, but ye'd best take care whilst there, fer me cousin says there be dark magicks upon the isle, too— powerful forces at work. Barra is filled with mysteries the likes o' which have ne'er been seen." The landlady's voice lowered. "'Tis inhabited by fairies, witches, selkies, and ghosties as yell in the night."

"Ghosties, eh?" Michael asked, amusement in his voice.

Mrs. Farquhar nodded, but looked disappointed. "Well . . . only one ghostie, though me cousin says she's a wild one, she is."

Michael smirked. "I suppose this ghostie was once a beautiful woman who died a horrible death."

"She was barely a woman, but aye, she was a beauty. She's the lost daughter of the MacNeil clan who died fourteen years ago when Kisimul Castle burned to the ground—"

"*No.*" The word was torn from Jane's lips. Through the haze that spread through her shocked mind, she heard the words echo and she shut her eyes. *Not Kisimul. Please, not my home.*

CHAPTER 6

From the diary of Michael Hurst:

I've been an explorer and an adventurer for well over two decades. In the last fifteen years I've seen it all—amazing treasures revealed, lost tombs uncovered, ancient cities discovered, and centuries-old mysteries answered. Yet none of this has been as bone-shocking as what I discovered today: the plain brown wren that I hired four long years ago to be my assistant is actually a Scottish princess . . . and a dead one at that.

*M*ichael paused in lifting his whiskey glass to his lips. Jane stood stock-still, her hands fisted at her sides, her face white, her lips parted in shock, her eyes squeezed closed, as if to ward off a horrible sight.

He put down his glass. "Jane?"

She opened her eyes but didn't move, her gaze locked on the landlady.

Mrs. Farquhar looked concerned. "Lassie, are ye well? Ye're so white ye look like a ghostie ye'self—"

"The castle," Jane managed to gasp out, her voice raspy and harsh. "It *burned*?"

"Aye," Mrs. Farquhar said, looking confused. "'Twas a horrible accident, to be sure, fer it killed poor Lady MacNeil the verrah night o' her—"

"But the castle—I don't understand. It's been there for centuries."

"Och, lass, so 'twas, and a more beauteous castle ne'er stood. I can see it now, rising proud in the middle o' Castle Bay, pennant flyin' in the wind." Mrs. Farquhar tsked. "'Twas a horrible loss."

"It . . . it burned to the ground?"

"Nay, no' all the way, fer the outer walls were of stone. Still, the fire was so fierce tha' the main beams, which were thicker than my body, turned to ash. Once they were gone, there was naught to hold up the outer walls; one wall crumbled before the fire had cooled, whilst another is leanin'. 'Tis dangerous to even walk near it, fer one day 'twill all crash down, one wall upon t'other."

Jane swallowed, a hand pressed to her temple. "What caused the fire?"

"Tha' is something we'd all like t' know, miss," the landlady said ominously. "Ye'll have t' ask the new laird aboot tha'."

Jane's eyes widened. "The new laird? Wait . . . you think the *laird* set the castle afire?"

"Who else stood to gain so much?" Mrs. Farquhar looked over her shoulder and then leaned in to say in a dark voice, "We all know 'twas no' an accident, and many ha' no' been quiet aboot it, neither, fer it put an end to any talk o' marriage, it did, and left him wi' all o' his cousin's fortune, too."

Jane slapped a hand over her eyes. "Oh, no!"

"Aye, we were all just as shocked as ye are now," Mrs. Farquhar said, tsking loudly. "Puir, puir bairn, t' die so. She was a bonny lassie, she was, lively as the mornin' and with a smile like a ray of sunshine. She had her father's disposition, she did, always laughin'. I saw her once't, ridin' through the glen on Barra." Mrs. Farquhar sighed. "'Twas a tragic death."

Jane dropped her hand from her eyes and Michael perceived the intense note in her voice as she leaned forward, "Mrs. Farquhar, I'm sure this fire—whatever caused it—must have seemed convenient for the new laird, but I *know* him, and he would *never* do such a thing."

The innkeeper's face grew dark with suspicion. "Ye know him, miss?"

"Not well, of course—I haven't been on the island for years and years—but . . . I can't imagine him doing such a thing."

"Then imagine a bit harder, miss, fer 'tis as plain as the nose upon yer face wha' the new laird wished. He got it, too—freedom to wed someone other than his own cousin, whom he dinna like, and he got away from the watchful eye of his da as well."

"Pardon me," Michael said, unable to hold his tongue a moment more. "The new laird was engaged to wed Lady MacNeil, then?"

"Aye. He was her cousin and they were nearly raised together, the two o' them."

"So you think he *killed* her to get out of the marriage?"

"Ye dinna know his father. He's a dire man, he is. Full of dark plots and evil ways. He was determined to wed his son to the miss and thus make his son the laird."

"So the new laird didn't wish to marry."

"He opposed it as much as the lass, tho' 'twas a brilliant match fer him."

"Thus far, he sounds like an honorable man," Michael said.

"Except for killin' the lassie—who was like a sister to him!—just t' get out o' his promise t' wed her!" Mrs. Farquhar huffed. "'Tis well known tha' he had his eye upon another well before the weddin'. No' two weeks had passed after the puir lassie had died tha' he was upon the doorstep o' another woman, beggin' fer her hand."

Jane gasped. "Two *weeks*?"

"*If* that!" Mrs. Farquhar nodded vigorously, apparently glad to have elicited some proper indignation.

"That *fool*! What a blockheaded, chuckle-nubbed— *Oh!*" Jane's jaw was tight with anger, and she actually began to pace the floor. "No wonder people think— And after I went to so much trouble to— By Ra, I'll *kill* that man the next time I see him. *Kill* him until he begs for mercy!" Her lips thinned, and Michael had the impression that she was trying hard not to say much, much more.

Mrs. Farquhar nodded in sympathy. "We all felt th' same way, miss. And now ye see how 'tis tha' we all know the truth o' it, though the new laird's ne'er spoken his cousin's name in well over fourteen years."

"I do, indeed," Jane said grimly. "It looks damning, I admit it. Still, say what you will about Jaimie MacNeil, he is not capable of injuring another. Why, he's as mild mannered as a mouse. Perhaps more so."

"Ye're right aboot tha'. The new laird's a weak maw worm of a man, and we all know it. Tha' is why he got his father, David MacNeil, who's as evil as the day is long, to do his dirty work fer him."

"But you said Jaimie had the MacNeil lass murdered because his father was demanding they wed. So how could Jaimie include his father in his plans?"

Mrs. Farquhar pursed her lips. "I dinna know, fer no one has ever asked me tha' particular question, but . . ." She frowned, her brows knit. After a moment, she brightened. "Perhaps the laird won his da o'er to his way o' thinkin' *before* the murder, sayin' they'd *share* the winnin's."

"No, no, no. If Jaimie wasn't afraid of his father, then there was nothing stopping him from just setting the MacNeil lass aside and marrying whomever he wished."

"He wouldn't be the laird, though. The lass had to die, fer th' title rested in her hands."

"Yes, but she could have ceded the title to him directly and then just"—she waved a hand—"left."

Michael's brows rose. *Is that what you did, my mysterious Scottish princess?*

Mrs. Farquhar frowned. "Can ye do tha', miss, just cede o'er a title? I've ne'er heard o' such a thing in all me life."

Jane's eyes widened. She looked at Michael.

He shrugged. "Neither have I."

Jane pressed a hand to her cheek. For a moment, it didn't look as if she could speak. But then she let out a long breath and said in a panic-filled voice, "Oh, dear. Oh, dear, oh, dear, oh, dear."

Michael added, "So all we really know is that there's a new laird, a burned-down castle, and a missing young lady who is now a ghostie."

"Aye!" Mrs. Farquhar beamed that Michael had followed her story so closely, though she managed to look melancholy when she added, "So there ye have it: the puir lassie is dead in her ashy grave, the castle burnt to the ground, and then, wi'in a fortnight the new laird engages with a new bride, whom he brings home the day he finishes building her a manor house fit fer the court o' Edinburgh . . ." The innkeeper shook her head, her iron curls swaying. "Wha' more proof o' murder do ye need?"

Jane's shoulders sank, as if she were suddenly carrying a heavy weight on them. "What a bloody, foolish mess. When I get to Barra, I'll—" She folded her lips, as if she didn't trust herself to say another word.

Michael sipped his whiskey, watching every expression on Jane's face. *You'll do what, Jane? Fix things more to your liking?*

"'Tis a sad, sad story," Mrs. Farquhar said. "The laird can claim his innocence all he wishes, but we all know wha' is wha' and who's to blame fer the lass's death, *especially* after the new laird married tha' *woman.*"

"Elspeth MacQuarrie," Jane said almost tiredly.

The landlady looked suspicious. "Ye know her?"

"I've never met her, no."

"She's a demon, she is, wi' all her fancy English ways, though she's as much a Scot as I am. She wouldna' allow the laird to rebuild the castle and instead forced him to build her a huge house on the best piece o' property on the northern end o' the isle."

"Ah, yes," Michael said. "We saw that house marked on a map and wondered about it."

"Eoligary House, 'tis called. 'Tis a monstrosity tha' sneers down upon the crofters' huts tha' dot the land aboot it. In a way, 'tis a guid thing tha' the auld castle burned, fer no one would be happy seein' the likes o' *her* at the long table in the Great Hall, sittin' beside the laird in a seat as belonged to Lady J—"

"Please!" Jane threw up a hand. "Mrs. Farquhar, I-I'm sure you're right, but there's no need to— We don't need to hear every scrap of gossip—"

"Actually," Michael said, coming to stand near Jane so that he could better see both her and the landlady, "we *do* need to hear every scrap of gossip about the Isle of Barra. Local rumors often lead to intriguing finds."

"No," Jane said stubbornly, her eyes snapping fire at him from behind her spectacles. "We *don't* need to hear more."

"Oh, yes," he replied. "We *do*. Though you may chase poor Mrs. Farquhar out of the room, nothing— and I mean *nothing*—will keep me from following her to the kitchen and hearing the rest of this fascinating tale."

Jane glowered before she stomped to the table and

snatched up her glass of whiskey, turning her shoulder in his direction.

Michael bowed to the landlady, who'd been watching the exchange with a wide, interested gaze. "Mrs. Farquhar, pray continue with your tale about the lost daughter of the MacNeils. Her father was the laird, correct?"

"Aye, t' the rest o' the clan, she was a princess."

"A *princess*? How interesting."

"Oh, *please*," Jane said, huffing her outrage between words. "I would hardly call a laird's daughter a princess. There's no crown, no royal standing, no—"

"*I* say she was a princess," Mrs. Farquhar said, her fists resting on her hips. "I dinna know who ye are, miss, but no Sassenach can tell me aboot me own history."

Jane opened her mouth, then closed it, then whirled on her heel and faced the window, where she crossed her arms, her back as stiff as a board.

Michael smiled at the landlady. "Forgive my assistant. She's a factual sort and not given to legends."

"Why, 'tis no legend, but fact!"

"Indeed, it is," Michael said soothingly. "Mrs. Farquhar, what was poor Lady MacNeil's Christian name?"

"Och, 'twas Jennet. Jennet MacNeil, she were."

Jane had to fight the urge to close her eyes. It had been so long since she'd heard that name. Years.

"Jennet." Michael's deep voice wrapped about the word and caressed it. "Jane, did you hear that? The poor ghost's name is Jennet. That's a Scottish version of your own name, isn't it?"

Jane sent him a cold look. "I heard. I'm only a few paces away."

"I thought you might be. Mrs. Farquhar, tell me more of the mysterious princess of Barra, the tragically dead Jennet MacNeil."

"Puir Lady MacNeil was barely sixteen when she died, she were. She was raised by her father, the old laird, after her mither died. Though an English woman, her mither adopted our ways and raised her daughter t' understand what was due her name. I fear it took a firm hand, fer the lass was high-spirited."

"High-spirited," Michael repeated. "Jane, did you hear—"

"I heard," she snapped. She snatched up her glass of Scotch and took a hefty drink, scowling all the while.

Eyeing Jane uneasily, Mrs. Farquhar continued, "When the laird's wife died of the ague, Lady Jennet was no' but twelve and 'twas just her and the laird from then on. The laird loved his daughter more than life itself and he dinna have the firm hand as his wife had."

"Ah, so Lady Jennet was spoiled, was she?"

Jane, in the middle of taking a sip of whiskey, choked.

Michael said in a solicitous voice, "Careful, Miss Smythe-Haughton. Scottish whiskey is stronger than our usual fare." He turned back to the landlady and raised his brows.

She obligingly plunged back into her story. "Aye, once't her mither died, Lady Jennet ran wild, she did, fer her da could no' find it in his heart to say to her nay. Still, they loved one another verrah much and they were happy as clams there upon Barra 'til the day the laird's horse was startled by a rabbit. The horse bucked and the laird fell and struck his head upon a rock. He died instantly."

Michael slid a glance at Jane, but she'd turned her face away from him and was holding her glass of whiskey as if her life depended upon it, her fingers white where she gripped the glass. Perhaps that explained her extreme independence. First she was indulged by a father who was missing his beloved wife, and then she was left to roam an island kingdom on her own, when her father was ripped from her life as well.

Some people would use such a tragedy as an excuse to become weaker, but not a woman like Jane. No, she'd see the hardship as a challenge tossed in her teeth by life itself. She'd rise to the challenge, too, and she'd beat it.

Mrs. Farquhar sighed. "We were shocked at his death, fer the laird was a master horseman and a brawny man, too. The lass was left alone, the sole inheritor of the castle, the isle, and all the gold in the treasury."

"She was wealthy, then?"

"'Twas rumored tha' she was worth her own weight in gold."

"Just *rumored*," Jane said.

"There had to be gold in the castle's treasury," Mrs. Farquhar said in a pragmatic voice. "Why else would ye have a treasury?"

"I daresay there were many large wardrobes in that castle, too," Jane returned sharply, "but that doesn't mean they were full of silks and satins. More than likely, they held moth-eaten blankets and burlap sacks for covering the windows in the cold."

Mrs. Farquhar sniffed. "If the lass was no' wealthy, then why did all of those suitors come?"

"Suitors?" Michael asked, startled by this new twist.

"Aye! Before the laird's body was cold, hordes of suitors descended upon the isle like starving locusts. The lass was followed and harassed and couldna even mourn in peace."

"A bunch of mustering maggots is what they were," Jane said, frowning.

"So they were." Mrs. Farquhar tilted her head to one side. "Lass, how do ye know o' this?"

"Yes," Michael said. "How do you know?"

Jane sniffed and turned away.

Mrs. Farquhar sent her a curious glance, but continued. "We all feared one o' the suitors might steal the puir, unprotected lass away, but then 'twas revealed that the laird had left his daughter in the care o' a guardian, his cousin, David MacNeil, a man the lass thought of as her own uncle.

"I'll ne'er understand wha' the laird was thinkin' to

leave Lord David in charge o' the precious bairn." Mrs. Farquhar's brows knit in disapproval. "The man is a mean one, he is. He arrived wi' his son, a lad aboot the same age of Lady Jennet. The lad was no stranger, as the old laird had had a kindness fer his nephew, and so little Jaimie had stayed at Kisimul almost every summer fer years."

"At least Lady Jennet had a friend."

"So ye'd think. But the lad was under his father's thumb and had no backbone at all." Mrs. Farquhar shook her head sadly. "It was a confusin' time fer us all, especially the lass. Lord David sent the suitors packing. We were relieved at first, fer the lass was no longer importuned day and night."

"But then?" Michael asked.

"But then we discovered why Lord David had saved the lassie; he wished t' marry his own son t' Lady Jennet."

"Out of the frying pan and into the fire."

"Aye, but she would ha' none o' him."

"Somehow, that doesn't surprise me."

"'Twas a fiery courtship, and och, the yellin' and screamin' tha' went on—" Mrs. Farquhar shuddered at the memory.

"Again, I'm not surprised."

Jane sent him a withering glare, which he met with a wink and a grin. Her lips reluctantly quirked into a smile before she turned away again and hunched her shoulders in his direction.

He was glad to see that her sense of humor was returning. To see her so pale and upset had shaken him deeply—far more than he cared to admit.

He turned his gaze back to the landlady. "So the Scottish princess refused to wed, did she?"

"Aye, though no one blamed the lass for refusin' Jaimie MacNeil, who is a lack-witted muttonhead. Unfortunately, her outspoken ways maddened her uncle, who thought her too wild. They had horrible rows, yellin' at one another. Finally, he would take no more and locked her away in her bedchamber, sayin' she'd stay there until she agreed to wed her cousin."

Michael stroked his chin, watching Jane from the corner of his eye. "It's a pity this uncle wasn't fond of Egyptian dancing."

Mrs. Farquhar blinked.

Michael added in a polite tone, "Had Lady Jennet's uncle been a fan of Egyptian dancing, I'm almost *certain* she could have escaped."

Jane sent him a withering glare. "You're incorrigible."

Mrs. Farquhar looked from one to the other and scratched her head. "Wha' has dancin' to do wi' escaping?"

"Exactly," Michael said in a soothing tone. "I was merely making an obscure reference to an imaginary incident that Miss Smythe-Haughton is fond of recalling. What happened after Lady Jennet was locked away?"

"Och, the puir lass! She was left in her room, but she was spirited, she was, and she refused to bend. And so her uncle—och, I canna say it wi'out gettin' angry, but he said he'd enou' and ordered the lass locked in the dungeon."

Michael's humor disappeared. Until now, he'd been willing to tease Jane about it. But this—to lock a young girl, and Jane, at that—in a dungeon? His jaw tightened until he could barely speak. "That blackguard!"

"Aye, and the puir, puir, *puir* lassie was no' given food nor water."

Jane gave a superior sniff. "I daresay a 'puir lassie' who'd been raised in such a castle as Kisimul might know a way out of a dungeon that she had played in from the time she was a wee bairn."

Michael found himself grinning from ear to ear. *I should have known she wouldn't stay locked away.* "So Lady Jennet was very resourceful."

"*Very*," Jane said. "She might also have been aware that it wasn't in her best interest to let her uncle realize that she had access to such an escape."

"So she was canny, too."

Jane took a sip of Scotch. "I would also conjecture that she wasn't starving, either. She had friends among the people of Barra, who are renowned for their generosity."

Michael had to resist the urge to crow. *What a magnificent woman, even at sixteen. Has nothing ever cowed her?*

Mrs. Farquhar brightened. "I ne'er thought o' that, miss, but ye might be right. I'm sure the people of Barra did what they could. She was much loved." Her face fell. "But there was no one assistin' her when the castle burned. Her bones were found among the ashes and she was buried on the isle. What a sad ending fer such an angel. Puir little thing."

"Little, was she?" Michael held up his hand until it was a few inches taller than Jane. "About this tall?"

"Och, no! Far smaller than that."

He lowered his hand until it was even with the top of Jane's head. "Maybe this tall, then?"

"Aye. Somewhere aboot there."

"And slender, I'd assume."

"Aye."

"And her coloring?" He looked inquiringly at Mrs. Farquhar.

"I dinna know aboot her eyes, though her hair was the color of peat."

"Brown, eh? Then I'd assume that her eyes were brown, too."

"Mayhap. She had a piquant face, quite like a pixie. And the voice o' an angel. Well, before she was a screamin' ghostie, tha' is."

"I vow, but your description is so vivid that I can almost see her . . ." Michael let his voice drift off.

Jane cast her brown eyes heavenward, as if praying for patience.

Michael flashed her a satisfied smile before he turned back to the landlady. "I daresay your ghostie is far more active in the mornings when she's trying to interrupt an honest man's sleep—or so my experience with Scottish harridans has been."

Jane gave an exasperated sigh.

"Och, no," Mrs. Farquhar said, "ye only hear her when storms are nigh."

"Oddly enough, I can almost hear her now. Mrs. Farquhar, that's a *fascinating* story. Thank you for taking the time to tell it." He took the innkeeper's rough hand between his own and bowed over it. "I hope we didn't keep you from anything too important."

Mrs. Farquhar turned three shades of red. "Och, now, I canna say— I mean, I've never meant to be so— Of course, 'twas a pleasure to tell ye—"

Jane thunked her glass upon the table, a fixed smile on her face. "Mrs. Farquhar, would you mind packing a bit of food for us to take to the isle in case we can't find lodging at the inn right away?" Jane dug into her pocket and pulled out several coins. "I'll pay for it now, *if* you can promise that it'll be ready soon."

The landlady brightened and quickly pocketed the coins. "Of course! I'll see to it now. I'll take these empty dishes, too." She gathered the dishes, bustling happily. She was almost humming when she finally left.

The second she was out of earshot, Michael turned to Jane and crossed his arms over his chest. "So, Jennet MacNeil, what do you have to say for yourself?"

"My name is not Jennet."

"It is, too."

Her brown eyes locked with his. "It *was*. *Now* my name is Jane."

"Jennet, don't be ridiculous. I'll—"

She spun on her heel and swept to the pegs by the door, where she removed her pelisse and bonnet. She slapped the bonnet upon her head, the ribbons dangling untied, and yanked on the pelisse, leaving it unbuttoned. "I will never answer to that name."

"But it's your real—"

"Hurst, do you or do you *not* wish me to go with you to Barra? For if you don't, then call me by that name just one more time." Her voice was crystal cold and crackled at the edges as if covered in ice.

By Ra, she's serious. Michael reflected that if there was one thing having three sisters had taught him, it was to know when he'd gone too far. "Fine. Have it your way. But don't think we're done speaking about this."

"I don't *think* anything." She buttoned her pelisse, her movements jerky. "I *know* we're done speaking about this."

"Jane, you can't ignore—"

"Yes, I can. And if you know what's good for you, you will, too. My history is *my* business and no one else's." She turned toward the doorway.

"Where are you going?"

"To check on the arrangements for our passage to

Barra," she said as she marched to the door. "Be at the docks within the hour."

"Jane, wait. You can't stay outside in that weather for an entire hour."

"Ha!" Jane whipped out the door, her booted heels rapping smartly on the hallway floor. A second later, the front door slammed.

Michael was instantly aware that the room felt suddenly colder and far more empty without Jane. "Touchy, are we?" he said to the silent air.

Sighing, he picked up his glass of Scotch and ambled to the front window, where he watched Jane march across the cobblestones to the street beyond, her head bent against the wind, one hand slapped upon her head to hold her bonnet in place, the untied ribbons dancing behind her. "Amazing how things can change with just a few short sentences."

He'd never in a million years expected to discover that the prim and ever proper Miss Jane Smythe-Haughton was anything other than what she appeared. *And now look at her,* he told himself. *She's a bloody Scottish princess. A dead one, true, but still a princess.*

He leaned against the window frame as she turned down the cobblestone street toward the pier. Jane didn't move with the graceful sweep his sisters employed, especially Caitlyn, who seemed to float when she walked. Jane's walk was firm, quick, and efficient. Yet the purposeful tread didn't stop the very feminine sway of her hips.

He'd always thought that voluptuous women were the most delectable, and none of the women whose favors he'd enjoyed in the past had been smallish in frame. But seeing Jane marching off, her trim behind outlined as the wind tugged her billowing skirts this way and that, he realized he was beginning to develop an appreciation for small, delicate women.

He finished his Scotch and set the glass down, still watching Jane's retreating figure. *What other secrets are you hiding, my little wren?*

The answers lay on the Isle of Barra. Once there, he would pursue the truth with the same determination he'd used to unlock the many secrets of the pharaohs. *You, Miss Jennet MacNeil, have no hope of keeping your secrets. By the time we leave your precious isle, I'll possess two things—the Hurst Amulet, and the truth about you.*

CHAPTER 7

A letter from Michael Hurst written to his sister Mary from an inn in Oban while waiting to set sail for Barra:

If you're in the process of writing one of your overly thorough letters to our cantankerous grandmother, pray tell her that I've just been given a glimpse of a Highlander's pride and that it has astonished me in both its depth and its stubbornness. Furthermore, I am maddened at their refusal to bend knee to anything resembling common sense.

That will make her very happy.

I now have a new appreciation for her spouse, our long-dead grandfather. Any man who would knowingly court a Scotswoman has given up on all reason, and has decided that prickles would make a more interesting bed than down. Such foolishness deserves every cut he gets.

*T*he sea winds were brutal. Jane tugged her voluminous cape closer and held it tightly about her neck, but no amount of wool could keep out the vicious breath of the Hebrides. A bonnet would have blown off in this weather, so her hair flew wildly, the pins long gone as the silky strands tangled about her cheeks, then were tossed away, only to return, clinging to her cold skin.

Though it was bone-bitingly cold, she refused to go below deck, and stayed where the fresh scent of the wild sea could wash over her.

I'm going home. She'd thought the words over and yet they wouldn't sink in. She simply couldn't believe she was upon a ship cutting swiftly through the rowdy Sea of the Hebrides, the dark green ridge that was the Isle of Barra growing on the gloomy horizon.

She shivered as a particularly strong gust swept over the deck, whipping the bottom of her cape and skirts. She hoped Michael was prepared for the icy weather that awaited them, for it would be a shock.

She frowned. *The last thing I should worry about is whether Hurst is cold. He's been positively insufferable. I can only be thankful that he's had the good sense not to call me by that name again, for I might have been moved to violence.*

It was a small thing to be thankful for, but for the last two days, that was all she'd had. Though they'd planned on sailing straight to Barra from Oban, the weather had stopped them at the mouth of the Sound of Mull, and they'd been forced to seek port for a day in the small town of Tobermory. The stop had not been a welcome one; the crew was unhappy, for they made no money as they waited. Plus, she'd been tense since her argument with Michael at the inn, which had been made worse by the realization that he was now watching her with eyes bright with curiosity.

She'd sighed with relief when the skies had proven less threatening this morning and they could set sail once again.

Of course, "less threatening" did not mean the passage was smooth, for the Sea of the Hebrides was never peaceful. As she looked out at the whitecapped sea, the ship hit a wave and rocked high upon its crest. Jane grabbed the wooden railing, icy air frothing her skirt and chilling her wool-clad legs.

And with the wind came her fears. *Surely no one from Barra will recognize me. That would undo all that I tried to accomplish . . . if it hasn't already been ruined.* "Jaimie, you fool," she muttered. "What did your father talk you into this time? You promised to hold firm. You *promised.*"

She scowled at the green sliver of land growing before her. *Perhaps it's a good thing I've come home, at least for a few days. It will give me a chance to measure how things stand. Given enough time, perhaps I can even right what's been wronged.*

Her inclination to institute order was soothed by this thought, and she watched as they closed the gap between the sea and the mouth of Castle Bay, swinging starboard as they approached. Her hand tightened about the railing and she took a deep breath to slow the hammering of her heart. *Perhaps it's fortunate that everyone believes I'm dead, for they won't be searching for any similarities between the long-dead Jennet MacNeil and the English assistant to a famed explorer searching for an ancient relic.*

She'd changed a lot over the years, too, which would help. She was no longer a gangly youth, and her hair was lighter because of her exposure to the sun, the dark brown shot through with gold. Her skin was darker, too, from being in hotter climes. *I should be safe enough, providing I don't let that Scottish burr slip into my words. It's difficult, though, when I hear others speak with it. Somehow, it curls upon my tongue like a cube of sugar and melts into my words—*

"It's too cold to be on deck." Michael's voice cut through the wind. "Come down below before you catch an inflammation of the lungs."

She turned as he walked toward her, his cape swirling about his black boots, his dark hair tossed by the wind. His blue eyes seemed bluer today, probably because they were the only touch of color on him.

She clutched the railing tighter, her fingers growing numb inside her gloves. "I'm not coming in. I get sick in the hold, as you well know."

"Seasickness won't kill you; an inflammation might."

"Cold weather never affects me. I grew up here . . . remember?"

"Oh, I remember. I'm still astonished by that fact." A hint of admonition deepened his voice.

"Hurst, we've traveled together for four years now. It's your own fault for not asking me where I came from."

"What would you have said if I *had* asked?"

"I might have told you."

"Balderdash. You would have prevaricated, and you know it."

She shrugged.

"Ho, don't even pretend. You've done nothing but hide yourself since the day we met. You're worse than the damned Sphinx."

"I've been in plain sight. *You* just never bothered to look." She had him there; she could tell by the way his jaw tightened.

He came to stand beside her, walking effortlessly on the pitching deck. "And to think that all of this time, I've been traveling with a dead Scottish princess."

"Jennet MacNeil was no princess."

"Our landlady in Oban seemed to think you were. Are. Hm. You're a conundrum of tenses."

"I'm in the present and I intend on staying here. You'd be much more satisfied if you did the same."

He grunted, as if he didn't deign to give her an answer, though she suspected that he was really too busy trying to think of some way to trick her into revealing more than she wished. She leaned against the railing and watched a seagull swooping in the wind. "It's unfortunate that Jennet has turned into a legend over the years."

"I find it amusing. It's one thing to be a dead princess and quite another to reach ghost status, all while still alive."

"I'm not the least amused."

"Odd, for I detect some humor in your usually somber gaze, my evasive little princess." He shot her an unabashed grin that crinkled his blue eyes and set her heart tripping even harder.

Jane opened her mouth to make a retort, but at that moment, the boat lurched and she lost her hold on the railing and staggered backward.

Her heel found a coiled length of rope and tipped her even farther backward, where she teetered for a horrible moment, arms flailing, the deck icy beneath her unsteady feet.

Michael stepped forward, slipped an arm about her waist, and tucked her against him, his natural balance and firm footing holding them both upright as the boat settled back into place.

The wind gusted against them, swirling his cape about her. Jane knew she should step away, but she was so toasty warm in the circle of his arms.

But it was more than warmth that held her there. It was the strength of his powerful arms, and the width of his broad chest. It was the masculine scent of his clothing, a mixture of leather and boot blacking and the damp wool of his cloak. It was also the way that her body melted against his, as if she'd been waiting for this very moment all her life—which was ridiculous. Her dreams of her future had always been about travel and adventure and her own independence. Nothing else.

Still, some quiet, unheard-'til-now part of her clung tightly to Michael's broad chest, savoring the hard feel of him beneath her hands.

The ship rolled beneath their feet. Water sprayed across the railing and misted them. The wind whistled in the rigging high above their heads. And yet neither moved.

Jane was powerfully aware of the way his hands remained firmly clasped upon her back, pressing her cheek to his chest. *Does he enjoy this, too?* The thought startled her. It was one thing to privately lust after him, something she'd done since they'd first met. It was another matter altogether to think that he might be lusting for her.

They could *not* step past the boundaries they'd established. She'd already witnessed the changes caused by just one kiss. Had he been a less complex man—or if she didn't love her position as his assistant so much—perhaps things could have been different. But things *weren't* different.

Her entire world was pinned upon two things—her precious independence, and her ability to support herself in this crazed, unfriendly world. Both depended upon her keeping herself, and her feelings, untangled from those she worked with—and for.

She wasn't about to give up her plum position as assistant to the most successful explorer in the known world. Few men would pay her as well, and even fewer would be as acceptable as an employer.

More importantly, Michael wasn't a man to trifle with a woman. When he was interested in something, he pursued it with an intense fascination that defied description. But as soon as he had it—whether it was an ancient Egyptian vase or a woman—his interest waned and he was on to the next mystery.

With great reluctance, she stepped away, freeing herself from his embrace.

He let her go easily, his warm hands slipping from her shoulders seemingly without regret. "Back on balance, are you?" His deep voice rumbled over her.

"Oh, yes." She managed a brisk smile as she grabbed the railing again and hauled herself against it, determined to look in charge of the moment, though her throat was tight. "That coil of rope took me by surprise.

I'm sorry that I fell and then, um—" Her cheeks heated as she struggled to find the word. Finally, she settled on a lame, "Clung. Yes, that's what I did: I clung."

His lips twitched and he stepped across the coil of rope to stand beside her at the rail. She admired the way he maintained his balance. That was one of the things that had drawn her to him—the ease with which he traveled. No matter how they went—ship, camel, or foot—he adapted to it seemingly without effort. After working for a fussy Frenchman who'd demanded the best of everything while constantly complaining of being too hot or too tired or too something, Hurst had been a delightful change.

He leaned against the railing beside her now, blocking some of the wind, and she was instantly glad he was there, which was at odds with her other feelings.

She was wary about his interest in a way she'd never been before. His insatiable curiosity made him the explorer he was, and being the focus of that never-ending curiosity was very unpleasant.

He looked out at the approaching bay. "Even in this gray weather, it's a lovely island. How long have people lived here?"

Glad he was no longer looking at her, Jane said, "Barra has passed through many hands over the centuries. She was once inhabited by the Norse, and many of her names are still from that language. When I was a child, a farmer found Norse utensils and a breastplate deep in the dirt in the glen. He brought them to my father, who displayed them in the Great Hall."

"Interesting. So there was a settlement here at one time."

"Yes. There's also an ancient Nordic grave on the isle that once had a magnificent headstone. I never got to see it, because it was stolen when I was young. My father said it was carved on one side with a Celtic cross, while the other bore some odd runes."

"I'd like to see that."

"So would I. I've always thought—" Her gaze flickered past him and her attention was caught. "We're almost there. We'll be rounding the sound into Castle Bay in a moment and you'll see Kisimul Castle—or what's left of her." It was impossible to keep the bitterness from her voice. Kisimul Castle was as much a part of Barra as the rocky shores.

They were making the final turn into Castle Bay. She almost didn't want to look, but even as she had the thought, the promontory that protected the bay on one side slid into view and a memory struck her.

She'd been about seven, and had been riding with Lindsee MacKirk, her best and only friend. There were only a few children upon the isle, and even fewer who weren't working with their parents in the fields or at a trade. Lindsee was the daughter of a well-off widower, and she and Jane had been riding along the promontory on their ponies when Jane's father—speaking with some fishermen on the shore—had seen them. He'd instantly grinned and lifted his arm in greeting, the wind ruffling his sleeve.

It was an odd snippet of memory, for it had no importance, yet she could see her father as clearly as if she were still that seven-year-old astride her fat pony. He'd looked so young, but of course Mama had been alive then, too. He'd aged quickly after Mama had died. So had Jane.

A swell of emotion threatened and she brushed aside the troubling memories. There was no benefit in reliving the past, good or bad. As Father used to say, 'twas better to live today than lament a yesterday already gone.

Still, she couldn't help but wonder about the pieces of her past that might still be present on Barra. Where was Lindsee? As a girl, she'd been as determined to leave Barra as Jane. As Lindsee grew older and lovelier, she'd drawn the attention of suitors from the surrounding isles. Jane had no doubt that Lindsee was now married and living somewhere nearby, probably in a castle much larger than Kisimul.

Which is how it should be. Leave the past in the past and all will be well. Jane pulled her cloak closer to her, her booted feet beginning to ache from the cold.

"Kisimul," Michael said in a musing tone. "That's an usual name."

"Some call it Caisteal Chiosmuil, which means 'castle of the rock of the small bay.' Others say the original name is from *cios mul,* which is Gaelic for 'the place where taxes are paid.'"

"Did the MacNeils build it?"

"Aye. We settled in Barra in the eleventh century. Parts of the castle originate from within a hundred years of that time."

"They must have been a very hotheaded family to think they'd need a fortress."

"You have no idea. Some claim the MacNeils are descendents of Niall of the Nine Hostages."

"Ah, the high king of Ireland. Interesting."

She shot him a surprised glance. "How do you know of Niall?"

"My grandmother is as much a Scot as you, and she spent more time than she should have filling the ears of her eager grandchildren with tales of old."

"She sounds lovely."

"She's cantankerous and outspoken and rude."

Jane grinned. "Like I said, she sounds lovely."

"She is certainly a brave woman," he said, watching Jane from the corner of his eye. "*She* has no issue with claiming her family in public."

"It's not my family I don't wish to claim. It's my name."

He faced her now, his blue eyes locked on her face. "Why is that, Jane?"

She frowned. "We came to Barra to find the Hurst Amulet, not to dig about in my past."

"Why don't we do both? It could be fun."

She tugged her cloak tighter. "I hope we find that blasted amulet quickly."

"Already in a hurry to leave your beloved home?" He tsked. "We haven't even arrived."

Her hair blew across her face and she brushed it back. "I'm in a hurry to get back to warmer weather so I can thaw. Years of working in Egypt have thinned my blood."

He reached down and wrapped his large hands about the fluttering edges of her cloak. With an easy tug, he tightened it about her. "I'm glad I'm not the only one to hate this biting cold. Once we land, we'll—" His gaze lifted over her head to focus on something close by. "Ah! Your castle."

Jane's eyes widened behind her spectacles and she spun around.

Michael looked over her head. The blackened ruin stood forlornly in the middle of the small bay. At first glance, the castle appeared to be sitting in the middle of the water on the barest sliver of rock, but as the ship sailed closer, he could see that there was a decent-size beachhead to the east where a small skiff could tie up. Around it was a ring of rocks set at even intervals. Pilings to tie off larger ships, perhaps? "The MacNeils had ships?"

"They were pirates, some of them. They used to have a large galley that they sailed up and down the sea, taking what they could from foreign vessels. They were widely feared."

So she was the descendant of pirates, too? "Next you'll be telling me you're a direct descendant of King Arthur."

She offered no comment, her hair obscuring her expression from view.

He turned back to the castle. The walls that were still standing were three stories or higher. Two towers sat at opposite corners, one quite large, while the smaller one seemed more ancient in its design.

It wasn't until the ship began to sail directly past the castle that the real damage could be seen. The entire western wall had collapsed, and a pile of rubble and great stones filled what must have been a courtyard. Another wall was leaning dangerously, supported only by the thick walls of the tower. Michael eyed the shapes and placements of the parapet stones. *Hmm. Mid-fourteenth century, perhaps older. The shape of the smaller tower could mean—*

The faintest sound came from Jane. He turned to look at her, her hair streaming behind her so that he could now see every line of her face. Her gaze was locked on the castle as a single tear ran down her face, her lips quivering.

Michael felt like every sort of fool. Here he was, evaluating the site as he would any other ruin he'd been sent to examine. But to Jane, this wasn't just a castle; it was her childhood home.

He looked back at the blackened ruin and wondered how he'd feel if this had been Wythburn Vicarage, where he and his brothers and sisters had grown up. His throat tightened. *There is something special about the place one grows up. And no matter how much Jane may wish to forget it, this was her home.*

Bloody hell, what should he say now? He was horrible about this sort of thing, and for once he actually wished for Mary's advice. After a moment, he managed to say gruffly, "I'm sorry."

Jane had already pulled a handkerchief from her pocket. She quickly wiped her tears and then hurriedly tucked it away. "That's quite all right." She fixed a firm smile upon her lips. "She was a formidable castle, wasn't she?"

"She's larger than I expected."

"Aye, 'tis just as well that I saw her burned and broken firsthand and got it over with."

Her brogue was more marked, though he didn't think she realized it. He nodded toward the castle. "The great tower is impressive."

"My father always thought the Watch Tower, which is opposite the Great Tower, was the older of the two, though he was never certain."

"I agree with him. The shape of the upper windows look as if they're from an earlier period."

"I'm fairly certain that the oldest portion of the castle is the chapel, which is—was—inside the wall."

"Perhaps we can take a look at it later. More may be standing than you think."

She nodded, a faraway look on her face. "There were several structures inside the castle walls of varying ages. According to the castle records, the last structure was built by Marion of the Heads. That one, which is—I'm sorry, *was*—quite airy and had its own fireplace, was called the Marion Addition." A faraway look settled in Jane's eyes. "Marion was a fierce one, she was. They said she ordered two sons from her husband's prior marriage beheaded so that her own child would become the chieftain."

"A real harpy, eh?"

"Mayhap. Then again, it could just be an old wives' tale—you've already seen how the Scots love their stories. Her son did end up being the chieftain, but perhaps it was his time. His brother built another castle on the other side of the isle. A smaller one, meant only for observation in times of conflict."

"There are *two* castles on this small island? Bloody hell, we *are* in Scotland."

She laughed, a gentle peal that made him feel as proud as if he'd discovered an ancient tomb on his own. Her eyes twinkled as she said, "Yes, you're definitely in Scotland. The other castle is more a tower and is called Dun Mhic Leoid, or MacLeod's Tower. There are some interesting stories about that tower, all bloody and bold."

"Your people are the most contentious, argumentative, complicated—" He shook his head. "It's a wonder any of you survived your own families."

She laughed again, and he grinned back at her, feeling like he'd won some sort of a prize.

She placed her hand over his, and though it was gloved, he was still aware of the chill of her fingertips. "Thank you," she said softly.

His throat tightened in an odd way and he was relieved when she turned back to look at the castle as they left it behind them. She removed her hand and pointed toward a small dock that protruded out in the far end of the bay. "That's where we're going. It's the only dock on the island now that Kisimul is no more." She looked at the castle as the small ship rounded it. "She was a fine castle."

"I can see that. What other buildings are inside the walled ring other than the chapel and Marion's Addition?"

"There's the Great Hall, which is a black house."

"Ah. No fireplace, just a fire pit in the center of the room."

"Which left the walls black with soot. When I was a child, I used to draw on those walls with a stick. My mother would get very angry, for my clothes would be smudged and I'd need yet another bath."

He couldn't imagine it. The Jane he knew was always neat. Well, except for right now, with the wind whipping her hair about her pink-cheeked face. She looked younger and . . . less staid, perhaps? *There's something about Scotland that agrees with her.*

Unaware of his regard, she continued. "Beside the Great Hall, there's the Tanist's House—"

"Tanist's?"

"That's another name for 'heir.'"

"Ah. So he'd be close by, but not too close. Seeing how Marion treated her stepsons, perhaps a little distance is not amiss when attempting to live with one's Scottish relatives."

She nodded, the wind whipping long strands of her hair over her shoulders. "There's also a gokman's house—that's for the guards—a kitchen house, and—oh, under the Watch Tower is the dungeon."

"No castle is complete without a dungeon. Especially when you have cantankerous family members."

"You laugh, but it's said that Black Roack MacNeil threw his own parents into that very dungeon. They made a written complaint to the Crown about it, too."

"I begin to understand why no country was able to subjugate this nation." He looked back at the great castle. "As impressive as Kisimul is, the center of the bay is a poor place to build a fortification. If you were encircled by attackers in boats, you'd easily be starved or left without water."

"And therein is the magic that is Kisimul Castle," she said. "It has its own freshwater well."

His gaze locked back on her. "In the middle of this saltwater bay?"

Her smile could only be described as smug. "Oh, yes. The well's under shelter, too, safely tucked under the eaves of Marion's Addition. So when there was an attack, the people inside the castle were safe and had access to both water and food."

"Food from the storerooms?"

"And fish, too. There are ways to net fish without going outside the walls."

"Amazing. Now that I know its secrets, I can't imagine a better-situated fortification."

"Sadly, its only weakness was from within its own walls," Jane said. "Betrayed by her own laird." She shook her head as if the thought were too bitter to hold, and then turned her back on the fading castle and faced the land.

Hearing the sadness creep back into her voice, Michael was glad when the captain of their ship yelled for the small crew to prepare to moor at the small dock at the head of the bay. A small grouping of stone houses and huts marked the town of Castlebay.

Soon they were standing on the sandy shores of Barra while the crew unloaded their belongings on a rather decrepit-looking dock that had made Jane's mouth thin with displeasure. Ammon oversaw the unloading of their trunks, ignoring the stares of the crew, while Jane approached a youth who'd arrived at the dock in a cart pulled by a plow horse. From the snippets Michael overheard, she was attempting to hire the cart to take them and their luggage two miles down the shore to the inn.

Michael listened as Jane haggled the man's already reasonable price even lower, her accent growing with the exchange though she'd regained her usual clipped manner of ordering people about. Satisfaction warmed him. Perhaps here, on this windswept isle, he'd discover the answers to the two greatest mysteries of his life: the location of the elusive Hurst Amulet, and the true history of the long-dead princess of Barra.

If he didn't, it wouldn't be for lack of trying.

CHAPTER 8

From the diary of Michael Hurst:

The skies over Barra seem to have the normal cloud cover one can expect from Scotland—gray and dismal, plump with rain, and with the promise of more ill winds than a soul can bear.

It's so moist here that I would not be surprised to discover that mushrooms can thrive in midair. Even damper in spirit are the inhabitants. I've received nothing but suspicious looks and sullen stares since I crossed the border. What have I done but visit their wretched country and spread good English coin? Does that deserve such foul looks? I'll never understand how Jane—sensible, commonsense, pragmatic, perfectly calm though sometimes annoyingly happy Jane—sprang from this wind-buffeted, dour-faced isle.

*M*ichael leaned against the window frame and watched the rain beat upon the cobblestones. They'd arrived yesterday slightly after noon, navigating their way on a road that had been neglected until it was nearly impassable. It had begun to rain the second they'd carried the last trunk into the small farmhouse referred to as an "inn," and it had rained ever since.

He'd gone to sleep with the thrum of a steady rain, and awakened to it. He eyed the muddy road that curved beyond the courtyard and wended a small distance along a bluff before the sea. The sea itself seemed beaten down by the rain, for it was as gray as the clouds above it, the only color the verdant green of the rolling hills. He scowled and turned from the window. Rain or no, he'd be damned if he'd sit in this tiny "inn" for an entire day.

Especially not this inn. His bedchamber was appallingly small, the floors creaky, the bed narrow and far too short. The mattress was lumpy, too, and damp. But worst of all were the thin walls. He'd hardly slept, able to hear every step Jane took, every murmur she made, every turn she made in her creaky bed. There was only one comfortable part of his room and that was the pillow—which he'd belatedly realized must have been placed there by Jane. His pillow must have been stored in her trunk, too, for her lavender scent filled his senses every time he tried to sleep.

He'd been awake when Jane had risen at dawn from her creaky bed after finding her spectacles on the table nearby—he'd heard the scrape of the metal rims as she'd pulled them close. When she'd thrown open her shutters to peer outside, he'd been unable to keep himself from imagining what she looked like—her long dark hair mussed as she stretched and yawned, then padded barefoot from the window to the washstand before dressing.

If he closed his eyes now, he could see her slender figure as she—

Blast it, I've slept in the same tent with that woman with nothing more between us than a curtain. Why am I so aware of her now?

Whatever had caused it, he'd better stay in his room until his blood cooled—though, at this rate, he might be here until Michaelmas. Scowling, he reached for his shirt, which was hanging on a peg by the bed.

He finished dressing and went downstairs, having to duck along the narrow passage. "Bloody hell, was this house made for children?" he grumbled as he turned the corner into the common room.

Jane was already there, looking neat and unflappable as ever. Beside her stood their landlady, a woman named Mrs. Macpherson, who was as tall and thin as her husband was round and short. She glared at Michael to let him know she'd heard his comment before she thunked a steaming pan of food on the plank table before the fireplace.

Jane frowned at him. "Hurst, Mrs. Macpherson brought us breakfast. Her husband is seeing to the horses in the barn, as Turner's ship landed this morning and arranged to have them brought here."

Her tone clearly let him know what she thought of his lack of manners.

The last thing he felt like doing was apologize, but he could tell that Jane would settle for nothing less. Grinding his teeth, he inclined his head toward their landlady. "I'm sorry I'm a bit ill-tempered this morning. I haven't had my coffee yet." He glanced at Jane.

"Ammon's making your coffee now and will bring it as soon as it's ready."

Mrs. Macpherson folded her thin arms across her chest, her jaw a thin line of disapproval. "That servant of yers aboot scared me nigh t' death this mornin'. He came creepin' into the kitchen and—"

"Creeping?" Michael asked, lifting his brows. "He's well over six feet tall."

Mrs. Macpherson flushed an ugly red and said in a defensive tone, "He walks wi'oot a sound, he does. Like a ghostie."

"There seem to be a lot of ghosties on this island." Michael walked to the table to look into the steaming skillet. "Whatever's in that skillet smells delicious. It's making my stomach growl and—" His head thwacked into a low-hanging beam. "*Ow!* Bloody mo—"

"Mrs. Macpherson," Jane said immediately, even as she winced. "I'll ask Ammon to make more noise when he walks."

Mrs. Macpherson gave a sharp nod. "Thank ye, miss."

Michael had clapped a hand over his head and was now glaring about the room as if trying to decide which piece of furniture he should throw first, so Jane said in a soothing voice, "Hurst, just sit down. If you stagger about, you'll hit your head again, and this time it could hurt one of the beams. This is an old house and was not built to take such abuse."

He growled but sat on the bench at the table. He tried to put his legs under the table, but it was too low. "Blast it, this house is *tiny*." He locked an icy stare upon the table, as if to freeze it into growing longer legs.

Jane had to press a hand to her mouth to cover a giggle. He was right—everything in the house was built for a family of much smaller stature. While it all fit her perfectly, Michael's towering height didn't fit in any part of the room. Unfortunately, no one had ever built a real inn on Barra. Instead, over sixty years ago the enterprising Macphersons, after building a new house on the bluff behind the farmhouse, had converted their old home into the island's only inn.

Jane was just glad it was available. She turned to

the housekeeper and smiled. "Thank you for bringing breakfast, Mrs. Macpherson. It smells wonderful."

"Aye, there's eggs and bacon, and some bannock and a nice pot of tea."

"Where's Ammon with that damned coffee?" Michael slid the skillet closer and peered inside.

Jane and Mrs. Macpherson shared a look. "Men," Jane said under her breath.

"Lord love 'em," Mrs. Macpherson agreed. "I've often said tha' men who canna—" The innkeeper tipped her head to one side, her gaze suddenly locked on Jane. "Excuse me, miss, but now that I see ye in the light, ye look a mite familiar. Are ye related to the MacN—"

"*No.*" The word burst from Jane's lips before she realized she meant to say it.

Mrs. Macpherson's brows shot up. "I'm sorry, miss. I dinna mean to insult ye."

"Oh, no, no! I'm not insulted at all. I'm just—I'm not related to anyone who lives in"—Jane waved a hand—"Scotland."

"Not one?"

"No. Not one." Jane realized that Michael was now watching her with interest. *Blast it, just go back to staring at your breakfast and let me handle this.* She smiled at the innkeeper and said in her best voice for negotiating with difficult people, "My name is Miss Jane Smythe-Haughton. I recently returned from Egypt. Mr. Hurst here is a brilliant explorer, and I am his assistant."

"Egypt, eh? That's far away, is it no'?"

"Very. We've discovered many important historical finds. I lived in Egypt and the surrounding countries for the last fourteen years. Before that I lived with my parents, who are from—" Her mind, up until now flicking along at a brilliant rate, chose that moment to freeze. And it didn't freeze a tiny bit; it froze into an icy, unthinking block.

Later, she'd wonder if her inability to finish the sentence came from an odd sense of guilt at denying her own father on the very soil he'd once presided over, or if it was something subtler; but whatever it was, she couldn't find a single word to finish her sentence.

Mrs. Macpherson glanced uncertainly at Jane, and then at Michael, and then back at Jane, suspicion growing. "Yes, miss? Your parents are from?"

From where he sat at the table, Michael's deep voice rumbled, "Miss Smythe-Haughton's parents are from Cheapstowe, I believe. Isn't that right, Jane? They lived there from the time Jane was born until she was a small child."

Cheapstowe? Jane was only vaguely aware of that particular area of London.

"Oh?" Mrs. Macpherson said. It was a polite "Oh?" one that implied that the listener had heard quite enough, but apparently Michael wasn't finished.

"Oh, yes," he said, his voice rich with satisfaction. "They had to leave once Jane's father was thrown into gaol for—what was it, Jane? Forgery? Thievery? I can never remember."

Why, you—

"After Mr. Smythe-Haughton was sent to gaol, Jane's poor mother, Mrs. Smythe-Haughton, was forced to make her way by becoming a s—"

Jane managed to make a strangled noise, her voice still locked tightly in her chest.

Michael's brows rose and he said in a polite tone that was as unlike him as it was maddening, "Yes? Did you say something?"

The humor in his blue eyes finally loosened the invisible bonds that held her voice. "Thank you, but I'm *certain* Mrs. Macpherson has heard more than she wished to know. She doesn't need to hear my entire family history, *unsavory* as it apparently is."

He leaned back in his chair, though it creaked noisily. "I was just trying to help."

She didn't deign to reply, but firmly thanked a gawking Mrs. Macpherson for the lovely breakfast and assured her that their accommodations were lovely, all the while herding her to the door. Soon Mrs. Macpherson was bundled back into her cloak, the hood up to protect her hair from the rain as she scurried out the back door to the small kitchen located across the garden behind the inn.

That done, Jane joined Michael in the common room. Since he couldn't fit at the table, he'd filled two plates with the contents of the skillet and had carried them to the small table by the window. He'd pulled two seats up and now slid one of the plates toward the empty chair. "I thought we'd eat here."

She gathered the napkins he'd left behind, then sat in the chair and scooted closer to the table. "Ammon should be here shortly with the coffee."

"He'd bloody well be."

She placed her napkin in her lap and placed his in front of his plate.

"Thank you." He dropped the napkin into his lap. "You're lucky I saved you any; I'm starving."

She picked up her fork. "It's more than the daughter of a forger should expect."

His eyes sparkled. "You didn't like that, eh? Did it make you miss being the daughter of the laird?"

"It didn't make me anything except surprised—although I owe you for saying something. I don't know why I couldn't think of an answer to her question, but I couldn't."

"I'm surprised a person with your experience in telling elaborate fables should have difficulty in thinking up such a simple tale, but I suppose it's a different issue when you have to think quickly rather than spend time thoroughly developing your story."

"I'm sure that's it," she replied blithely, cutting her bacon into small bits. "I'm also sure that my skills will grow over time. I just need to practice, practice, practice. Did I ever tell you about the dragon I owned when I was a child?"

"No, and you're not going to. Our landlady thought she recognized you." He lifted an eyebrow. "Did you really think you could return here and no one would know you?"

She was putting marmalade on her toast, but she paused long enough to grimace. "I had hoped so."

"If our landlady saw the resemblance, then others will, too. You need to have your story ready or you'll be discovered."

She nodded, feeling oddly chastised. Perhaps it had been naïve of her to hope to escape notice, but it had been so many years and she'd experienced so much in life as Miss Jane Smythe-Haughton that she felt like a different person from that girl of so long ago. A girl who really *had* died, as far as she was concerned.

She realized that Michael was regarding her from beneath his lashes, his expression inscrutable.

She hid a sigh. His dark hair was too long again, falling over his brow. His dark skin gleamed golden in the wan lamplight, and his eyes were thickly lashed and the darkest of blue.

An odd heaviness sat in the pit of Jane's stomach. She knew him so well, and yet there were times, like right now, when she felt that they were miles and miles apart.

She pushed the marmalade pot toward him. "Perhaps I was foolish to think no one would recognize me, but you really didn't give me time to think it through. I didn't know we were coming to Barra until we were under way, and I couldn't say no. Plus, the amulet is here, and we've been looking for it for so long. I couldn't turn my back on the opportunity."

"I can't fault you for that. I'm rather excited about it, too." He glanced at the rain-washed windows. "If it will just stop raining."

"It's getting lighter. Hopefully, it will be down to a mist by this afternoon."

"And if it's not?"

"Then we don cloaks and go anyway. It's the rainy season now, so it could rain for days. We can't let it slow us down."

"Lovely. This almost makes me miss the heat of Egypt."

Jane had to grin. "As wet as this is, *nothing* will make me miss the heat of Egypt."

Ammon entered from the back door carrying a pot of coffee on a tray.

"Thank Ra," Michael muttered.

"Watch your head!" Jane called to the servant.

She needn't have worried, for Ammon's dark gaze was already fixed on the closest beam. He set down the tray, then removed his dripping cloak and hung it on a peg by the fireplace. Then he reclaimed the tray and came to the table, ducking another beam on the way.

Michael leaned forward as coffee was poured into his cup, the fragrance lifting his spirits. "Ammon, you are a saint."

The servant chuckled, his teeth flashing white in the dim light. "I knew you'd need your coffee, sir. I daresay you did not get much sleep in that small bed."

"I noticed that you escaped to the barn. Was it comfortable?"

"Yes, sir. I made a bed of hay and slept well indeed."

"No leaks?"

"A few. No more than expected."

"Very good. Take care you dress warmly. This cold, damp air can be difficult if you're not used to it. How are the horses? Were they affected by the crossing?"

"No, sir. Ramses is restive, though, and will need to be ridden."

"Have him and—" He looked at Jane.

"I'll ride Alexandria. We'll leave within the hour."

The servant bowed. "I'll tell Turner to saddle the horses. Will there be anything more, sir?"

"Not now. Thank you for the coffee."

Ammon inclined his head again and then returned to the fireplace, ducking beneath the low beams as he collected his cloak and left.

Michael took a grateful drink of his coffee. "I dislike this climate. The rains in Egypt were heavy but rare.

The dampness here permeates even the air indoors and leaves one just as wet as if one had jumped into a pond."

"The rains are persistent," Jane agreed. She wiped her fingers on her napkin and then rose and walked toward the windows. "We can at least visit the site of the cave today, even if it's too late in the day to enter."

"We can ride to the glen, too." Michael refilled his cup and rose to join her. The gray light washed out her features and stole the warmth of her brown gaze. Yet it also showed the delicate line of her cheek and brow, highlighting her serene nature.

"I'll be glad for a long ride, though these roads are not in good repair. We'll have to be cautious." Jane's brow creased. "I noticed the state of the roads yesterday. And the dock, too. Both are in disrepair." She shook her head. "That should never be."

"Oh? Is this the daughter of the laird speaking now?"

She shot him a frown. "Tax money is collected from the good people of Barra for just such repairs. Or it used to be. But I've been away a long time and who knows how things stand now?" She managed a smile. "I should leave well enough alone."

"Ah, but can you?" he mused aloud. Through the window, he caught sight of Mr. Macpherson as he led a horse pulling a cart through the courtyard. The man stared openly at Michael and Jane, suspicion clear in his expression. Michael had had a lively conversation with the man the day before about boarding the horses.

Macpherson's idea of boarding them was to charge an exorbitant amount for hay.

Perhaps that's why this rain irritates me; it reminds me of these damn Scots. They eye me with caution, offer no help nor information without some sort of bribery, and leave one dissatisfied with whatever small answer they deign to deliver. "Secretive, prideful people," he muttered. "And so damn suspicious."

Like the rain, he could feel their gazes filtering across him like a thousand wet cobwebs, tickling his face and nose and lashes and mocking an honest man's attempt at staying dry. "Give me a good English rain any day of the week," he said, looking at the endless gray sky.

"Oh, yes," Jane said in a brisk tone. "Because English rain is ever so much drier." She twinkled at him. "I'm going to change into something more suitable for exploring. You should do the same." She walked toward the staircase. "And watch the beams, or you'll spend the rest of the day with a headache."

"Thank you for that word of wisdom," Michael called after her.

"You're welcome." Her voice drifted down the stairwell. "That's what I'm here for."

CHAPTER 9

From the diary of Michael Hurst:

Today I visited the cliff above the cave that harbors the final clue to the Hurst Amulet. I also met an intriguing inhabitant of Barra, a woman who just might hold the truth about the recalcitrant Miss Smythe-Haughton.

Though I've yet to see the sun shine on this grassy rock, the world seems a little brighter now.

The rain had slowed to a hazy drizzle by the time Jane and Michael left the inn. Jane had changed into a sensible gray riding habit that would offer some protection from the weather. By the time she reached the courtyard, Michael was astride Ramses, and they appeared menacing when silhouetted against the gray sea.

Once she was mounted, Jane turned her horse and led the way down the muddy road, the misty coolness doing her spirits good. They had to keep the horses to one side, single file, on the part of the road that was less slick. It was tedious riding, but at least they were out of that too-small house. Jane led the way to an old bridle path where she turned inland, Ramses clopping behind.

As they rode, Barra rose to greet Jane. The hillocks were more pronounced inland, the ground lush and green.

Michael said in a musing tone, "There are very few trees."

"They were cut down to make boats and furniture," she answered over her shoulder. "Except for a copse on the southern end of the island, there are no forests left. That's one of the problems with many of the islands:

there's a never-ending need for building materials. They have to either ship or float it over from the mainland."

"At least it hasn't diminished the beauty of the land."

A flicker of pride made her smile. Barra did indeed possess a fairylike beauty, something she had tried hard to forget. The green land was broken by silvery gray stones that dotted the fields, the southern slopes filled with pale purple heather.

"Where are we now?" Michael asked from behind her.

"We're northwest of Castlebay, near Loch Tangasdale." Jane urged Alexandria to a trot down the path. Though she enjoyed the freshness of the air, she was glad for the hood on her cloak, as it kept most of the water droplets from her spectacles.

As they rounded a bend in the trail, a tall standing stone surrounded by heather came into view. Jane pulled Alexandria to one side and turned to Michael as he halted Ramses beside her. Water beaded like pearls across his broad shoulders and in his black hair.

She gestured toward the path. "Would you like to see MacLeod's Tower? It's not far from here."

"How old is it?"

"Fifteenth century, but it stands on an ancient dun that holds evidence of an earlier settlement."

Interest warmed his blue gaze. "By all means, then."

With a flush of reciprocal excitement, she turned Alexandria down a path that passed beside the standing stone and led between two hillocks. They followed the path as it narrowed, turned sharply, and then opened onto a glen that widened to encompass a beautiful lake. She paused to soak in the sight, her heart beating painfully at a sudden rush of memories. As a child, she'd loved this lake. She'd swum in it almost daily and sailed upon it in a small boat she'd kept hidden on the far side.

Michael pulled up beside her, and they looked across the loch to a small island where a crumbling three-story tower of moss-covered stones stood watch over the glassy water. "It's a picturesque place, though I can't imagine needing a fortification in that particular location."

"Oh, there's a reason it's placed where it is, but you'll have to visit the tower to understand. I sometimes wondered if an older edifice was there before this."

"It's possible. We've discovered that most fortresses are built upon the sites of older ones."

"There's an old Viking grave here, too."

From beneath his hood, Michael's eyes brightened with interest. "I'd like to see that."

"The headstone is missing, but I know where the grave is."

He glanced at the dripping sky. "Another trip, then? Perhaps tomorrow, if it's not raining as much."

"Perhaps." She pointed to a shallow section of the loch. "I used to keep a boat hidden in that cove when I was a child. I would bring bread and cheese and row to the island, and spend the day pretending to be a princess in a castle."

"By yourself?"

"Oh, no. My friend Lindsee made a much better princess than I did, for try as I might, I could not make it to MacLeod's Tower without a messy gown."

"I can't imagine," he said politely.

She sent him a laughing look. "My father and I fished here, too. I caught quite a few brown trout in this loch."

"It's certainly an idyllic place," Michael admitted grudgingly. Barra's beauty was unsurpassed. *Try as I may, I just can't match Jane's pragmatic, no-nonsense view of life to this fairy-tale island.*

A distant rumble from the gray clouds overhead made the horses prance nervously, and Jane frowned. "If you wish to see the cave entrance, we should go now. It looks as if a storm is brewing to the west."

Michael nodded, and they rode out of the glen the same way they'd entered. As they rounded the bend leading to the main road, they pulled up their horses at the sight of a lone mare standing in the center of the road. It wore a fancy English saddle, a broken rein trailing on the ground.

"Oh, dear." Jane stood in her stirrups and looked down the road, but the shrubbed hillocks gave her very little view. "Someone must have been tossed."

"The mare's eyes look a bit wild, so it was probably recent."

Jane had to agree. The animal blew nervously and jumped a bit, turning, as if considering a gallop in the opposite direction.

Michael was off his horse instantly. He handed his reins to Jane and carefully approached the lone horse. The mare skittered back, but Michael was already close enough to grab the longer of the broken reins. "Easy, girl," he murmured.

Jane watched as he calmed the horse, speaking in a low, even voice and patting its lathered neck. "You've always been good with animals. Well, except camels."

He sent her a grin. "Blasted spitting creatures of hell that they are."

She chuckled. "That mare is a beautiful creature. Someone must have paid dearly for her." Jane's smile began to fade. "I wonder who— Oh, there they are." She pointed up the lane. "There."

A woman in a brown riding habit came limping down the lane, leaves sticking to her skirts. "I'll go and see how badly she's injured," Jane said.

Michael took Ramses' reins. "I'll calm the mare and then bring her on."

Jane spurred her horse forward, noting that the woman's fashionable habit, tall hat and veil could have easily fit in Hyde Park. It was odd to see such high fashion on Barra.

As Jane reached her, the woman looked up, the brim of her hat shading her eyes, the fashionable veil obscuring her face.

Jane pulled her horse to a stop and slipped off. As she did so, the woman pushed aside the veil.

Jane's mouth fell open. *"Lindsee?"*

The woman blinked at her. She was still beautiful, with dark gold hair and rich, brown eyes. Recognition flickered, then flared and she gasped. *"Jennet?"*

Jane nodded and was instantly enveloped in a swift, laughing hug. "Jennet, I can't believe— How did you come— When did you— I've wondered—"

Jane glanced over her shoulder and was relieved to see Michael examining the mare's hooves, apparently making certain it hadn't thrown a shoe. "Lindsee, I'll explain all, though I haven't time right now."

"Och, you haven't changed a bit!" Lindsee's gaze shimmered with excitement. "I've thought of you so often over the years, wondering where you were or—" Her eyes widened. "Wait. Does Jaimie know you're here?"

"No." Jane sent another covert glance at Michael and grimaced to find him now watching them. He was too far away to hear, thank heavens. "Here, let me brush the leaves off your habit."

"Oh, never mind those. Jennet, it's so good to see you!"

"And you. I never thought you'd still be on Barra. The night I left, you said—"

"Yes, yes, I said I'd be gone within a fortnight, but things didn't happen as I'd wished and so—" Lindsee frowned. "Does your uncle David know you're here?"

"No. No one knows. Is David still on the isle?"

Lindsee tucked a curl behind her ear. "I hear that he visits frequently."

"Oh, no. Jaimie has the spine of a piece of fresh bread and will never withstand his father, even though I told him time and again that there's naught to fear of David other than a lot of hot and unkind words."

"Aye, I know you thought you left your cousin in a good position, but he's—" Lindsee shook her head. "Jennet, 'twas a grand plan, but things haven't progressed as you'd hoped."

"I know. I saw Kisimul." Jane couldn't keep the choke of tears from her voice.

"I'm sorry," Lindsee whispered. "It was horrible. Everyone thought you were dead, and other than David and Jaimie, I was the only one who knew differently. Though it was hard, I didn't tell a soul. I knew you'd want me to keep quiet."

"I don't know why they felt they had to kill off Jennet in such a spectacular fashion, but I'll find out soon enough. My cousin is due a visit. And perhaps David, too." Jane frowned. "What's happened to Barra? The roads are nigh impassable, and I noticed that the dock at Castlebay needs repair. Where's the tax money going?"

"I suppose it's all going to Eoligary House, for 'tis a grand one. Jaimie built it for that sour-faced wife of his."

Jane ground her teeth. "By Ra, Jaimie will answer for this."

"Jennet, what can you do about it? They had you declared dead."

"Jennet MacNeil may be dead, but Jane Smythe-Haughton is alive and well, and capable of handling anything Jaimie and his father toss my way."

"So you mean to stay and right things?" Lindsee looked concerned. "Oh, Jennet, are you certain—"

"Hold. I can't stay, but I *can* at least deal with my cousin and uncle before I leave. If I'd known that Jaimie would ignore his duties as laird, I'd have never left."

Lindsee looked doubtful. "I'm sure you'll try to fix things, but if you didn't come back to stay, then why did you return?"

"I work for an Egyptologist and we've information that a famed amulet is hidden somewhere on this isle."

Lindsee's brown eyes brightened. "Is it valuable?"

"It's worth more than money, as 'tis a family heirloom." Jane hesitated but, encouraged by Lindsee's eager expression, added, "They say it holds an ancient magic, though I don't know that I believe it. I've seen many things thought to be magic over the years, and none of them turned out to be so."

Lindsee tugged her cloak higher against the rustling wind. "Still, if the amulet is ancient, as you say, it must be worth something."

"I hope so. Once Hurst and I find it, we'll go on to our next expedition."

"*Next* expedition?"

"We've been on many and plan on several more. I've been to Egypt, India, Greece—"

"Oh, Jennet, you've been having such adventures!"

"Too many of late. We arrived at Castlebay yesterday. We're staying at the Macphersons' and—" While she'd been talking, Jane had peeped around Alexandria and caught a glimpse of Michael walking toward them, the horses trailing behind. Jane whirled back. "Here comes my employer. Mr. Hurst is a prying sort of man and would no doubt ask you hundreds of questions if he knew you were my childhood friend. You must promise not to get drawn into conversation with him; he's a wily one and determined to find out about my past."

Lindsee didn't look convinced. "Jennet, I—"

"*Jane.* Please, this is important."

Lindsee's gaze narrowed suspiciously. She stood on her tiptoes and peeked over Alexandria's shoulder. "Your employer is a handsome man. Wouldn't it be easier if you just told him the truth?"

"You don't know Michael Hurst. If he were a different kind of man, I could just tell him a bit of what's occurred and say I wished to explain no more, and he'd accept that, but Hurst has never settled for half of the truth about anything. Discovering secrets is what he does, and I'm not about to be some sort of artifact he's dug up just to get a closer look at before he boxes it up and ships it off to some museum!" Jane could hear the clop of the horses getting agonizingly close. She grasped one of Lindsee's gloved hands and said in a low voice, "Just trust me on this. I'll come and see you and explain all."

"You must. I only hope you will—"

"Good afternoon." Michael's deep voice jolted Jane and made her realize that she still held Lindsee's hand.

Jane patted the back of it. "I'm so glad you weren't injured, Miss— Ah, I'm sorry. What is your name?"

"It's Lady MacDonald," Lindsee said with a shy reserve. She held her hand out to Michael. "And you are?"

Michael took her hand, his eyes widening as he caught sight of her lovely face. "I'm Michael Hurst. It's a pleasure."

Lady MacDonald? Jane wished she'd had more time to talk to her childhood friend. There was obviously much yet to be discussed. "Lady MacDonald, I hope you didn't hurt yourself when you fell."

"Oh, no," Lindsee said. "I only hit my—" She patted her rump and then glanced at Michael and blushed. "I mean, I'm fine. Just a small bruise, if that."

"Even a small bruise can be painful." Michael handed his horse to Jane. "Allow me to fix your reins so that you can get home safely. One was broken during your fall."

"Thank you, Mr. Hurst."

"It's nothing." He pulled out a pocketknife and cut a length from the unbroken rein and began to weave it together with the broken one. "Tell me, Lady Mac-Donald, are you a longtime inhabitant of this charming island?"

Lindsee sent an imploring glance at Jane, who hurried to say, "Lady MacDonald is new to the island and only visits now and then."

"That's right," Lindsee said, obviously relieved.

"Ah. That's a pity," Michael said. "I was hoping to find someone who knew the history of Barra."

Jane added, "I was telling Lin—Lady MacDonald about how we came to the island to look for an old family relic of yours."

"So she did," Lindsee said in her soft brogue. "I hope you find it."

"We will." Michael tugged the woven spot to check its strength. "We will find all of Barra's secrets or we won't leave." He handed the patched reins to Lindsee. As he pressed them into her gloved hands, his eyes gleamed and he smiled. "There, that will at least get you home."

Jane's heart stuttered, a totally unfamiliar feeling entering her heart. Lindsee had always been a beauty. When they were younger, Lindsee had possessed all that Jane had wished for—a rounded figure and creamy skin, laughing brown eyes, and thick, dark gold hair that shone with a gloss that Jane's messy mane could never replicate.

Lindsee was a bit rounder now, her face softened, her eyes larger in her heart-shaped face, and she was every bit as beautiful or perhaps more so. It wasn't fair, Jane decided.

Her gaze slid to Michael, whose gaze flickered appreciatively over Lindsee, lingering on her more obvious curves. "I'm glad you took no real injury in your fall," he said with a faint smile. "Or if you did, it's not where one can easily see it."

Jane blinked. *By Ra, he is* flirting *with her! Surely not.*

Jane cleared her throat. "Lady MacDonald, I hope you don't have far to ride?"

Lindsee laughed, her smile making her look even prettier. "Och, no. I live at Dunganon House, on the eastern shore. You know the shore ro—" She caught herself and said in a more demure voice, "It's not far. You just take this path to the shore road and go north. 'Tis upon a bluff there."

"That's not far, then," Jane said, trying not to lose her smile. "I hope you— Oh! Did you hear the thunder! Michael, we should be on our way or we'll be caught in the rain."

"I didn't hear any thunder," Michael said, his gaze still locked on Lindsee, as if fascinated. "Lady Mac-Donald, I hope Lord MacDonald isn't too worried about you."

Instantly, Lindsee's expression turned sad. "Och, no. I'm a widow."

"I'm very sorry," Michael said.

"Thank you. Lord MacDonald passed two years ago when his fishing boat sank. He was very fond of fishing, he was, and would go out in the worst seas. I warned him, but . . ." She shook her head, the picture of lovely widowhood.

Michael murmured his sympathy and then asked how such a young and lovely widow stayed busy on such a small island, which sent Lindsee into a thorough and exhaustive description of each and every amusement there was to be had on Barra.

Soon they were talking as if Jane didn't exist. She watched them uneasily, realizing that Michael was only charming when he wanted something, and she worried that she knew exactly what he wanted—and it had nothing to do with Lindsee.

Still, Jane couldn't help feeling a bit of envy. Lindsee was one of those naturally beautiful women who were so used to their own beauty that they didn't expect it to garner notice. They did, however, enjoy the attention that beauty brought them. Right now Lindsee was laughing at something Michael had said. She was toying with a curl that reached down over one of her shoulders, the gesture provocative in some way that Jane couldn't define, though she recognized it well enough.

Blast it, why can't I be more flirtatious like that?

Michael chuckled, the deep sound raking along Jane's nerves as Lindsee tilted her head to one side and smiled. Jane was certain that if she attempted to look that way, she wouldn't look either adorable or lovely, but like a moonstruck cow. She was equally certain that Michael wouldn't smile as he was now smiling at Lindsee, but would scowl and tell her to stop being a chucklehead. Worse, Jane didn't think she'd blame him. She simply wasn't that type of female.

Lindsee seemed to realize that she'd left Jane out of the conversation, for she gave a startled blink when her gaze met Jane's. "Och, I should get home now," she said quickly, and then said to Michael, "It was nice of you to help. I don't know what I would have done if you hadn't caught Merry for me."

"Oh, Michael is very good at leading horses," Jane returned dryly. "I've often told him that if exploring grows old and banal, he could easily become a groomsman."

Michael bowed over Lindsee's hand. "Lady MacDonald, may I visit you soon?"

"That would be lovely. Please bring Miss—" Lindsee frowned.

"Her name is such a long one," Michael said, patting Lindsee's hand instead of releasing it. "Just call her Jane. I'm sure that would be easier for all of us."

Jane cut him a hard look. *What does he mean by that?*

But nothing in Michael's expression betrayed his thoughts. Instead, he said easily, "I daresay you find it lonely here on this island. I'm surprised you haven't re-moved to Edinburgh."

"Oh, no," Lindsee said. "I traveled to Edinburgh once but found it far too noisy to my liking. I didn't sleep a wink for all of the creaking carts and yells and dogs barking and other noises."

Ha! Michael will stomp that utterance into dust. He has no pa-tience with people who complain about bearing with changes whilst traveling. He always scoffs and says, "What fools expect sameness when traveling and—"

"Too true," Michael said. "I would imagine even Oban would seem noisy after living upon this lovely, peaceful island."

Jane stared at him.

He caught her look and lifted his brows, his dark blue eyes glinting. "Your mouth is open."

Jane snapped her mouth closed, her irritation ready to boil over.

Michael continued. "As I'm sure Jane has men-tioned, I'm on a quest for a lost family amulet. It might be helpful if you could spend a few hours showing me about the island, as I'm sure you know it well and—"

"Us," Jane said quickly. "Shows *us* about the island."

"Oh, no," Michael said. "Just me." He smiled at Lindsee. "I would love an escort."

"Pardon me," Jane said firmly. "But *I* can escort you around Barra. I can take notes of our discoveries, and mark the maps where we—"

"How diligent of you," Michael replied. "But you haven't been here in years. If Lady MacDonald has the time, I'd prefer to go with her."

Jane knew what would happen next—Lindsee would blush and agree in that breathless way of talking that always drove men mad with lust. Jane couldn't blame her, of course. What woman in her right mind could resist Michael when he was at his most charming, as he was now? It showed in the faintly amused smile on his lips, and in the twinkle in his dark blue gaze.

Lindsee sent Jane a look meant to reassure her before setting a time with Michael to explore the island the next day. Then Michael slipped his hands around her waist and lifted her into the saddle.

As she settled into place, her gaze flew over Michael's shoulder to where Jane stood miserably watching. Unaware of her friend's turmoil, Lindsee winked.

She looked so much like the old Lindsee that Jane felt all of a foot tall for having such uncharitable thoughts. She managed a quick smile and a nod. It wasn't Lindsee's fault she was so beautiful or that she couldn't see through Michael's stratagems.

Still, it was a relief to see Lindsee ride off down the path, the dappled sunlight reflecting off her golden hair.

"Interesting," Michael said.

Jane turned to find him watching her, not Lindsee's retreating figure, one brow lifted, as if he were asking a question.

"What?" she asked.

"I was about to ask you that same question." He led his horse to where Jane stood beside her own mount and offered his laced hands to assist her in climbing back into the saddle.

She tossed her skirts over her arm, placed the tip of her boot in his hands, and was immediately tossed into the saddle. *Of course, Lindsee was placed in her saddle like a glass doll.*

Michael made no move to climb back into his saddle but remained by her knee, looking up at her. "Ever since we arrived on this island, you seem different from the Jane Smythe-Haughton who ran my expeditions so efficiently."

"How so?"

He eyed her with a thoroughly considering gaze. "I haven't quite figured it out. But I shall."

Jane fought the urge to smooth her hair and arrange her skirts in a more decorous manner. Her cheeks heated, which was simple foolishness on her part. All he was doing was looking at her. Why should such a thing discombobulate her so?

Above them, a deep rumble of thunder rolled across the gray sky. "Ah," Michael said, "real thunder, unlike what you said you heard earlier. I'm many things, my dear, but deaf is not one of them."

Jane was uncomfortably aware of the breadth of Michael's chest near her leg, of the masculine line of his firm lips, and the way his dark hair fell over his fore-head. She'd looked at Michael Hurst a million times before, but for some reason, he'd never appeared so *dear*.

Yet that was what he was . . . he was dear to her. It suddenly dawned on her that her life for the last four years hadn't been taken up with adventuring so much as it had been spent taking care of Michael. *That* was what she'd enjoyed doing. *That* was what had made their adventures so challenging and fun.

Taking care of Michael like a wife might if she were traveling—

Stop that! she told herself, almost breathless with the direction her thoughts had taken. She'd never *ever* allowed herself to think such things about Michael, and she wasn't about to begin now.

She firmly collected her galloping thoughts and forced them to settle back into safer realms, where she was the personal assistant of the dashing, exciting, intelligent, and painfully handsome Michael Hurst, and nothing more.

More thunder rumbled, following by a streak of lightning. She gathered the reins. "We had better return to the inn. We can visit the cave another time."

He glanced at the sky. "I suppose you're right, damn it. But, before we go, I want to know why meeting Lady MacDonald upset you so. You've done nothing but scowl since." He watched her expression the way a hawk watched a rabbit.

"Upset me? Nonsense. She seems like a nice enough person."

"Yes. Did you know her from before?"

Blast it, was there nothing *she could keep from him?* "It's possible, though it's been many years since I lived here and—"

"Oh, you know her," he said softly. "I'm certain of it."

A blazing bolt of lightning flashed, followed by a crack of thunder so close that the ground rumbled. The horses whinnied and tried to bolt, but Jane kept firm control of the reins while Michael moved to Ramses' head.

As soon as the horse was calmed, Michael climbed into the saddle with an easy movement. "Have your own way, my prickly Scottish princess. For now."

He gestured for her to precede him down the path, and she did so, wondering how she was going to keep him from his promised ride with Lindsee.

Chapter 10

From the diary of Michael Hurst:

I never thought to be intrigued by an icy, god-forsaken pile of rocks, but Barra promises to reveal many secrets. How can such a small isle hide so many? When I look at a map of the island, it hangs from the Hebrides like the wicked tail of a dragon, ready to wreak havoc upon the weak and unsuspecting. Fortunately, I am neither.

*A*lone in the common room, Michael set down his empty coffee cup and leaned back in his chair, wincing as it protested. It was very peaceful, as immediately after breakfast Jane had disappeared outside, saying she needed to speak to the groom about the horses.

The back door opened and he could hear Jane entering, humming a tune of some sort. "The horses will be ready in an hour," she said.

"An hour? I wished to leave immediately."

"Yes, but Ramses has a loose shoe, and it must be repaired immediately. Fortunately, Mr. Macpherson has all of the necessary tools and it can be done here."

"So we're stuck here, waiting in this miserable weather." Michael glared at the solid gray sky that hung over the inn yard. "Curses to you, blasted rain."

"If that helps, let me know." Jane came to the window, and he realized she was carrying a vase full of flowers. She'd taken off her cloak, and the bottom hem of her gown was drenched, her hair damp so that it fought the neat chignon she'd pinned it in.

The dewy freshness of the flowers was mirrored in her face.

"Where did you get those?" he asked.

"From the garden in the back. Mrs. Macpherson has a remarkably green thumb. Though it's already late in the season, she still has a lovely assortment of flowers and herbs. She has thyme and basil and mint, roses and—"

"Don't tell me the name of every flower and herb in the blasted garden. I'm bored, but not that bored."

Her lips quirked. "I'm glad to hear it."

"I was, however, bored enough to make friends with our recalcitrant landlady. According to Mrs. Macpherson's gouty left knee—which, I'm told, is never wrong—we're in for one more day of this relentless rain."

"Only one? I'm astonished."

"And I'm relieved. There's no reason why we can't at least give the caves a good preliminary scouting today. If we're to visit them, it would make sense to get a feel for the excursion beforehand."

"And then we'll know what equipment we'll need."

"Exactly."

"That can be done, although I fear we're in a spring tide."

"But it's October."

She'd been arranging the flowers in the vase, but at this, she shook her head. "Spring tide doesn't refer to the time of year, but to the height." At his curious look, she said, "There are spring and neap tides. Spring tides come with the full moon and are high, while neap tides come with the waning moon and are low."

"Ah. And we have a full moon now."

"Almost. Which means the cave won't be out from underwater for very long. When we visit it, we'll have to slip in and out as quickly as we can."

"We'll just have to make it work."

"Very well. I'll gather rope, candles, and the other supplies we'll need and have them packed on the horses in the morning."

"Good. I'll—" A horse rode into the courtyard, and Michael stood to see who it was. "Ah, there's Ammon. I wondered when he'd return."

Jane set the vase of flowers in the center of the table before she joined Michael at the window. "I didn't realize you'd sent him out."

Michael looked down, though all he could see of her was the top of her head, her hair darkened from the rain. "Oh, yes," he said, moving so he could see her face. "I sent Ammon with an invitation for the charming Lady MacDonald."

Jane's brows snapped low, and she sent him a dark look. "You're wasting your time if you think to find out something about my past from her."

He shrugged. "Then you've nothing to fear from my visiting the delightful Lady MacDonald."

"I didn't say I was afraid," Jane returned stiffly.

She hadn't said it, but oh, she was; he could feel it in the air about her. "I daresay I'll be gone awhile, for I intend on having a long talk with Lady MacDonald. We'll probably speak on a number of topics. The weather. How she came to be on this forsaken isle. Her favorite color. The sort of books she enjoys. Memories of childhood friends . . ." He grinned at Jane.

She didn't so much as blink. "You're not going to give this up, are you?"

"No."

Ammon, having tied his horse to a large ring on the outside of the farmhouse, now entered, water dripping from his cape.

Michael stepped forward. "Did you get an answer?"

Ammon withdrew a small folded note from the voluminous folds of his cloak. "With Lady MacDonald's compliments."

Michael pulled out his spectacles and read the note. "Excellent!" He took off his spectacles and tucked them back into his pocket. "I am to visit her this very afternoon."

Jane sniffed. "Go. Talk to Lady MacDonald. You won't learn a thing."

"One never knows where one might find a clue. Ammon, she asks for no reply, so I've merely to arrive at her home at two. Was it difficult to find?"

"No, sir. It is the only house on that stretch of road. It's a fine edifice, too."

"Lady MacDonald doesn't strike me as the sort of woman to live in anything less. Thank you, Ammon. Oh, and Miss Smythe-Haughton and I will be going for a short ride this morning ourselves, just as soon as Turner has fixed Ramses' loose shoe. Please ask Mrs. Macpherson to have a luncheon waiting at noon when we return."

Ammon bowed and left.

Michael was aware of Jane glaring at him. He faced her now, his brows raised politely. "If you don't say something, you'll explode."

"Had I known you weren't coming to Barra to search for the amulet, but to engage in senseless flirting, I wouldn't have bothered to accompany you."

"I wouldn't call it *senseless* flirting."

Her gaze narrowed. "You're just going riding with her to ask about my past?"

"Jane, please. You're not the focus of every conversation I have. In fact, I doubt you will even come up. Of course, if you do . . . naturally, I will listen to whatever Lady MacDonald has to say." He headed for the stairs. "We should change our clothing if we're to go mucking about the cave site today. I'll meet you back here in ten minutes."

He climbed the stairs, noting that the day seemed much brighter. Oddly, discovering the truth about Miss Jane Smythe-Haughton was almost as exciting as finding the Hurst Amulet. Almost.

Humming, he found his riding clothes and began to change.

*   *   *

A half hour later, Michael pulled the horse to a halt and looked around at the thick underbrush. "How do we reach the cave entrance from here? You said it was at sea level, and we're far above that."

"There's a path." Jane slid off her horse. She'd worn a sturdy gray gown instead of her riding habit, in order to have much more freedom of movement. "The path is cut into the cliff face and it starts there." She pointed to where the earth seemed to disappear from sight over the distant vista of the ocean. "It's rather steep in places."

Michael swung down from his mount, tied the horse to a shrub, and then walked to the sheer cliff edge. Below, the surf pounded furiously against sharp rocks. "Where exactly are we?"

"At the southernmost point of the island. This"— she gestured to the cliff edge, which curved in a crescent above the tumultuous sea—"is Devil's Height."

"Ah. Named by whom?"

"Sailors. There are many ship hulls on the bottom of this cove. The tide is strong here and the reefs treacherous. Once a ship gets caught, it's done for."

"I can only imagine." A fat drop of rain plopped on his sleeve, and he glanced up at the gray sky. "The rains won't hold off for long."

"Which is why we must hurry," Jane said. "We should at least go a short way on the path to make certain it's still there. It's been years since I was here, you know. It could have crumbled into the ocean in that time."

"That's hardly reassuring." He joined her at the head of the path.

Jane tucked her gloves into her pocket and tramped ahead, Michael following.

She'd been in a much better mood by the time they'd started their ride, and he could only surmise it was because she'd sent poor Ammon off with another note for the suddenly popular Lady MacDonald, warning her not to divulge any secrets.

If Michael hadn't expected such a stratagem, he might have been upset, but he trusted in two things to make his afternoon adventure worthwhile—first, the tendency of women (other than Jane) to artlessly blurt out every thought in their heads, even when they knew better; and second, his own charm in getting the lovely Lady MacDonald to reminisce about her history. He would wager a golden ankh that those memories would invariably hold some reference to Jennet MacNeil.

He looked at the barely visible track they were following. "You're a bit free with the term 'path.'"

She threw him a quick glance, amusement twinkling in her brown eyes. "What's wrong, Hurst? Worried?"

"Do I look scared, Smythe?"

"No, you look as you always do—smug and arrogant."

"And you look as you always do—impertinent and fresh."

She chuckled, her booted feet moving swiftly along the cliff head, her skirts rustling in the grass. "Oh, look, it's low tide now. What time is it?"

He pulled out his pocket watch. "Twenty-one after ten."

"Then that's the time we need to be at the bottom of the cliff tomorrow."

He followed her into the brush, where the path became more obvious. It wended along the cliff face for a short distance, overlooking magnificent views of surf and jagged rocks. Michael enjoyed both views—those offered by the cliff, and the sight of Jane's trim derriere as she marched in front of him.

She was completely feminine and yet unaware of it. He found that rather entrancing. He was considering saying something to her on the topic, when the path suddenly turned and seemed to plunge off the cliff.

Jane halted, lifting on her toes to peer over the cliff.

Michael grasped her arm and yanked her back.

She landed firmly against him, her chest against his.

He held her there, aware of how small she was compared to his height. "Are you trying to kill yourself?"

She blinked up at him, surprise in her piquant face. "Of course not. I was just looking down at the path."

"The path is gone. It must have fallen into the sea."

"No, it's still there." At his blank look, she sighed and walked out of his arms, back toward the place where the path disappeared. She pointed down at it.

"It's steep right here, but once you're on the path, it's not as bad."

He came to peer over the edge, his stomach tightening at the sight of a narrow path—more like a goat's trail—that hugged the cliff face. "That's bloody steep."

"It's more of a climb in places. I used to go down it backward, using the sea grass as an anchor."

"This path is dangerous. Maybe we should—" But it was too late. While he'd been talking, she'd tucked her spectacles away, dropped to her knees, and then disappeared from sight.

"Damn it to hell! You can't climb down that— And without your spectacles, too. How will you see where—" But he spoke to blank air. "Damn it," he muttered, hurrying after her. "Is *nothing* ever easy with you?" Michael reached the edge and looked over, an icy ocean-scented wind buffeting him, as if to warn him away.

Jane had already climbed down the few feet that were so steep and was making her way along the narrow shelf cut into the cliff face.

"Hold there, you fool!" he called, eyeing the sheer drop. "By the hand of Ra, you could fall—" He frowned as he realized that she was once again out of sight.

He gritted his teeth, dropped to his knees, and crawled down to the small ledge. Once there, he stood and hurried after her. Three steep steps turned sharply to the left as the path followed a natural ledge along the face of the cliff. One side was sheer rock, on the other a sheer drop into a cove where the icy ocean beat against deadly sharp rocks. "Damn it, Jane," he muttered under his breath, turning his gaze to the narrow path where he could just see her again.

She was carefully edging down the path, her hands flat on the surface of the rock, her body facing it.

At least she was trying to descend safely. Or as safely as she could while following cliff ledges to a sea cave. Muttering under his breath, he did the same and slowly caught up to her. As soon as he was within hearing, he announced, "This is ludicrous."

She looked amused. "What part of 'dangerous cave' didn't you understand?"

"None of it, apparently. You took this path as a child?"

"Several times."

"Your father should have been shot."

"He didn't know." Her brow was knit as she concentrated on each spot where she placed her feet.

"Always a rebel, eh?"

She flashed a sudden smile that made their tenuous positions seem rather commonplace. "Don't pretend to be surprised."

"I'm only surprised that you'd so openly admit it, especially when so much about you is a secret." They continued on for a few moments in silence, the surf crashing below. "Surely there have been accidents?"

"Many."

"I was afraid you'd say that." He edged toward her, noting how she made her way so surely down the narrow path. She was a resourceful woman, and he could learn a lot from watching her. Fortunately, it was a pleasure to do so, one that increased each day.

"Who made this atrocious path?"

She paused and glanced back at him, and he realized that her spectacles had been hiding her long lashes.

"I was just wondering that myself." She edged around a small corner. "It has always been here. But I could never ask my father about it, since I was forbidden to use it."

"It appears to be hewn by pickax."

"So it does. I've often wondered if—" A rock loosened under her booted foot and she stumbled, the rock bouncing down the cliff face, the sound soon lost in the roar of the surf below.

Michael's heart gave a sick thud as Jane teetered on the edge of the path, too far for him to reach, fear on her expressive face. "The grass!" he snapped.

Her frantic gaze found the small outcropping of long grass at the same second and she desperately grasped at it. Though some broke off in her hand, the thick tuft held, and she was able to regain her balance.

Breathing loudly, she pressed herself against the cliff wall.

A million admonitions burned on Michael's lips as

his heart thundered in his ears. "You . . . you . . ." was all he could manage.

Jane turned a white face his way, a plucky smile immediately coming to her lips when she caught sight of his expression. "You look exactly the way you did when you were in that tomb near the southern valley in Egypt and found those snakes."

"Just be bloody careful," he ground out, unable to see the humor in anything at the moment. "Or do you want me to have an apoplexy right here on this cliff face?"

Her lips twitched. "Not here, of course, but . . ."

"Then go! Let's see this cave opening and decide what preparations should be made, and then get to safety."

They made their way in silence for a goodly distance, the path ledge slowly descending the face of the cliff. Michael forced himself not to relive the sheer terror he'd felt watching Jane teetering on the path, though it was difficult. For some unknown reason, he'd lost his usual calm sense and was beset with reactions about her.

Michael's hands grew cold holding on to the rocks, his neck exposed without a scarf, and the warmth from his coat stolen by the wind. The air grew chillier and damper as they made their way closer to the pounding surf.

A fat raindrop plopped on Michael's cheek, and he glanced up at the darkening sky overhead. Thunder rumbled deeply, a faint wind stirring bits of dirt and causing small rocks to tumble down the cliff.

Michael listened over the sounds of wind and surf. "I can't tell if the rocks are hitting rock or the water."

"It doesn't matter. If you slip, it's such a long fall . . ."

He kept his focus on Jane after that, noting that as she descended, she paused every now and then to see if he was keeping up. A few times, she noticeably slowed in her progress after seeing where he was.

He frowned. "You're going slower because of me."

She chuckled. "Your feet are larger than mine. I thought you might need more time to decide on the best place to set them."

He'd been doing just that. "Thank you." Another fat plop of rain was followed by several more. On impulse, he glanced back over at the ocean and let out a long string of Egyptian curses at the gray sheet of rain racing toward them.

Her gaze followed his. "That's a deluge." Her voice was sharp with worry. "We must get back to the horses before that rain gets here." She was already coming his way. "Blast it, I really wanted to reach the cave mouth. It's so close."

"We'll make it tomorrow, if Mrs. Macpherson's knee is to be believed." He turned and headed back toward the safe edge of the clearing above, climbing as quickly as he dared.

A few more drops pelted them, the amount steadily

increasing, a faint roar announcing the closeness of the wall of rain. "Hurry," Jane said, her voice low and urgent.

He did so, wishing she were ahead of him now. If she had been, she'd already be safe on the ledge above them.

All he could do was concentrate on putting one foot in front of the other as quickly as he could, but it was too late. The rain slammed into them, and within the space of a few moments, Michael's head, shoulders, and back were wet through.

Not only were the rocks now slick, but he also couldn't see a thing. Sputtering, he reached out and grasped Jane's wrist and continued making his way up the path, his foot slipping here and there as water washed over the rock path.

Jane welcomed the warmth of Michael's grasp, though she wished he'd use his hand to balance himself. Her foot hit a rock. Wet with rain, the dust that coated it had now turned into a slick slime that sent her boot shooting out from under her.

For a heartrendering moment, she balanced precariously. Michael yanked her forward so that she could grasp the face of the cliff once again, her hands tangling in the sea grass.

"Thank you," she gasped, the rain pouring down as if from an overturned bucket. "It's so heavy—" She choked and looked down, struggling to breathe.

Michael squinted against the heavy wash of rain at

the cliff edge overhead long enough to see the problem. "The cliff is channeling the rain over the edge like a waterfall, and we're taking the worst of it."

Jane sputtered against the water as her hair, weighted by the rain, fell about her face, sticking to her cheeks and neck. But worse than that slight inconvenience was the way the rain weighted down her skirt and filled her boots, until it felt as if she were trying to wade through mud. "We . . . must . . . hurry."

He took in her predicament at a glance, his eyes dark with concern. "Damn it," he muttered. He increased his pace. "Stay close."

She continued on, doing as he'd said and staying only a step or two behind him. Two more times she slipped, her heavy skirts tugging her off balance, and both times he yanked her back. Meanwhile, he grimly held on to the cliff face as safety came ever closer.

Was the path this dangerous when I was a child? I never thought so, though I know Father did. Looking at it through adult eyes, I wouldn't wish a child of mine on it, either.

"Almost there," Michael said, his deep voice soothing and calm.

He was always soothing and calm under adverse situations. She, meanwhile, was battling the desire to yell unkind things at the rain.

Finally Michael reached the steep drop that marked the beginning of the path, the rain easing now that they were no longer directly under the edge of the cliff.

"Stand still." He released her wrist and then reached up and hauled himself over the final turn in the cliff path.

She edged closer, wondering how she'd pull herself and her wet skirts over the rise. She was so tired and her arms ached and—

Strong hands reached down from above to grasp her and lift her clear. As she was pulled over the edge of the cliff face, she saw the strain in Michael's face as he carried her, wet skirts and all, away from the pathway and into the safety of the copse.

Just as they reached the horses, Michael slipped on the wet grass, and with a gasp, they both went tumbling backward.

CHAPTER II

From the diary of Michael Hurst.

So there I was, flat on my back, Jane sprawled across me, both of us completely soaked, rain pelting down as if it had a vendetta against us . . . I had every reason to jump to my feet and—dragging Jane—find shelter, which is what a sane man would have done.

But instead I just stayed there. On the ground. Holding her. And damned well not willing to let her go.

Somewhere between Oban and this cliff side, I've gone stark, raving mad.

*J*ane expected Michael to release her once they'd come to rest, but instead his arms enveloped her and he held her in place. She grasped his lapels and buried her face in his wet shoulder as her heartbeat returned to normal.

Though the rain was shivery cold, Michael radiated warmth. She pressed her forehead to his coat and felt his chin lower to the top of her head as she lay upon him, the rain beating down.

It was heavenly, and she realized how afraid she'd been moments before. Now, nestled against him, her heart slowed with each breath as she soaked in Michael's heat.

She rubbed her cheek against the wool of his coat, her body shivering from both the cold and something else. Something Michael. She shifted, seeking . . . she didn't know what, only that she was restive and wanted, needed, to be even closer to him.

He used his wet sleeve to wipe some of the water from his eyes, his hat long gone, his hair wiped back from his face. "That was exhilarating."

She nodded as the rain pelted the back of her head and ran down her neck. "We should find some shelter."

"Why?" His blue eyes crinkled as he flashed an unexpected smile. "So we can stay dry? There's not a scrap of dry clothing on either of us."

She chuckled. "True."

"So what's the hurry?"

His deep voice rumbled in his chest and through her own. She shivered at the pleasurable feeling.

His smile disappeared. "You're cold."

"Not a bit." She shrugged. "I'm just suffering from a belated reaction to our misadventure."

His gaze narrowed on her and a reluctant smile touched his hard mouth. "It's going to be a miserable ride home."

"Not as miserable as if one of us had fallen over the edge." Just saying it aloud made her stomach ache as if she'd been stabbed with a pickax.

"I'm glad we don't have far to reach the horses." Michael sighed. "After climbing that cliff face, it seems that here, close to the earth, is the safest place to be."

Jane laughed and rolled to one side and rose, pushing her wet hair from her face. The rain pelted them relentlessly as Michael rose as well, and then, as if mocking their escape, the rain grew harder, roaring as it poured.

"Oh, no," Jane muttered, following Michael as he plunged into the thicket, the rain splashing onto his sopping-wet coat.

They reached the horses just as a huge split of lightning dashed across the sky, dazzling in its brightness. Both horses began to prance.

Michael grabbed both sets of reins. "Get on!" he yelled over the sound of the rain.

She reached for the saddle but Michael was faster, swooping her up and depositing her and her wet skirts upon her horse. She was secretly glad; it would have been difficult to maneuver with yards and yards of soaked material hanging from her waist like so many bags of wet sand.

Soon they were on their way back to the inn, the thunder escorting them. Michael watched Jane as she rode ahead of him. Small and neat, she rode as if born to the saddle. Now he knew why: during her entire childhood, she had been riding across the deeply sloped, rough hillocks of her island kingdom.

The path widened as they grew closer to the inn. Jane's wet hair hung down her back in long brown strands. Michael urged Ramses forward until they were abreast. With her hair slicked back from her face, her profile was as pure as an alabaster statue's. *Has she always had such a perfect nose? Even the—*

Her horse stumbled on the wet, uneven path, and he reached impulsively toward her reins. She shot him a hard look, and he retracted his hand immediately.

"I am fine. The trail is a bit slick, is all."

For some reason, it irritated him that she never seemed to need his help with anything. *Ever.* "You were daydreaming and not minding your horse."

She stiffened. "I was not daydreaming."

"You've done nothing but daydream since we came to this island." He flashed her a smile, knowing it would irk her. "It's time to wake up, Sleeping Beauty."

To his surprise, she met his sally with a sudden grin. "I've never been called Sleeping Beauty before. Or princess. I could get used to that."

That's because most men are damned fools and see only what they expect to see. The thought came unbidden, tinged with regret, for he'd been guilty of the exact same thing.

They turned onto the main road and it was only a short ride until they arrived back at the inn. They rode the horses directly into the barn, where Turner met them. He took the horses, calling for the footmen to come and rub them down.

Dripping wet, Michael and Jane made their way to the inn. Mrs. Macpherson didn't look at all happy to see them, tsking loudly as they both dripped steadily in front of the fireplace. "I warned ye aboot the rain," she said to Michael.

"So you did. I'm glad to know it'll be better tomorrow."

She nodded toward the stairs. "Ye both need to change into some dry clothes. If ye'll peel off the wet ones and put them outside of yer rooms, I'll spread them afore the fire in the kitchen and let them dry." She took their cloaks and coats. "I'll take these to the kitchen and spread them out and then come back to get the clothes."

"Thank you," Michael said to her retreating back. He turned to Jane. "I hope there's a fire in my bed-chamber, though I somehow doubt it."

Jane hiked her skirts and began to wade toward the stairs, the wet cloth dragging about her.

"You look like a duck."

"I feel like one, too. My skirts are as heavy as two brick-loaded portmanteaus."

"Take them off."

Jane sent him a startled glance. "I can't undress here."

"Why not?"

"Someone could come in and there I'd be in a wet chemise. It's not—"

Michael scooped her into his arms and carried her up the stairs.

"Just what do you think you are doing?"

"Quieting your ridiculous complaints." He strode up the stairs as if they were flat ground, not even winded at the exertion, leaving Jane speechless.

As he neared the top, he looked down at her. "I'll carry you to your room but you're on your own after that. I must get ready for my visit with Lady Mac-Donald."

Jane had to clamp her mouth closed over a very unladylike retort. It would have been easy to pretend that Michael's efforts meant more than the impulse of the moment. A weaker woman might have slipped her arms around his neck. A more needy woman might even have pressed herself to his strong shoulders and enjoyed the feel of his strength as he carried her. But Jane was neither weak nor needy, so instead she made a fist and punched the lout in the shoulder.

He gave a muffled "Oof." "What was that for?"

"I know why you're going to see Lady MacDonald, and I don't like it."

"What I do with my free time is my own business. And need I remind you who is the boss here? I don't require your permission to visit anyone."

"Jackanapes."

He favored her with a brief smile. "Weakling."

She crossed her arms and stared straight ahead. "Barbarian."

"Froofy female."

"Overmuscled Viking spawn."

"Weak-kneed bluestocking."

Aha! She gave him a superior smile. "I *like* being called a bluestocking."

"Good," he said, kicking open the bedchamber door and stalking across the floor. "Then I'll call you that every chance I get." He paused by the bed, his eyes suddenly alight. "You know what happens now?"

Something in the way he spoke made her suddenly breathless as she imagined the possibilities. Would he place her on the bed and then join her? Hold her in his arms and kiss her senseless? She shivered at the thought as she asked in a breathless voice, "What happens now?"

"This." And with that, he threw her onto the bed with such vigor that she bounced twice before coming to a lopsided rest.

"Oh! You . . . you . . . you . . ."

He laughed and turned on his heel. "You should call for a bath to warm you up. I'd take one, too, but I don't wish to be late for my visit with Lady MacDonald."

Jane propped herself up and scooted to the edge of the bed, her clinging clothes making even that simple action difficult. "I don't know if you've noticed, but it's still raining. *Hard.*"

He stopped by the foot of the bed and sent her a glinting smile. "Oh, I'd noticed. That's why I'm not changing my clothes."

"But you're wet through!"

"And I'll be even wetter when I arrive at Lady Mac-Donald's. She'll invite me in once she notices and take pity on me, while secretly being pleased that I went through a storm to reach her. I'll get much more information from her then."

Jane was astonished at how correct he was. That was exactly the sort of quixotic gesture that would appeal to

Lindsee. "You are becoming quite manipulative, Hurst. I don't like that about you."

"Was it manipulative when you told the sulfi who was holding me prisoner that you enjoyed the Phrygian dominant scale in Egyptian music, when I know for a fact that you find it discordant? Or when you told those traders in India that you love coconut milk, when you think it tastes like—"

"I see your point, but in those particular circumstances I was attempting to form a bond in order to garner useful information."

"Which is exactly what I plan to do. Lady MacDonald can help me solve a mystery."

Jane scowled at him and stood. "You, sir, are annoyingly stubborn."

"As are you. Although . . . if it bothers you that much, I might be willing to stop my questioning of Lady Mac-Donald."

That was hopeful. "You should leave her alone."

Michael leaned against the tall bed post, his smile glinting. "And so I might . . . *if* a certain someone—you, for instance—would offer me an incentive."

That wasn't what she'd hoped to hear. She crossed her arms over her chest. "It's come to bribery, has it?"

He chuckled and bent to cup her chin, turning her face to his, his voice deep and intimate. "Tell me, Jane. What would you offer me *not* to visit Lady MacDonald?"

His hand was so warm against her skin that it sent a shiver through her. Jane looked into his eyes and wanted nothing more than to throw her arms about his neck and press herself to him and forget everything—her past on Barra, the poor state of things here, her suspicion that her uncle was stealing from the island's funds, and most of all, how complicated things would be if she were discovered.

All of that piled one onto the other and tried to weigh her down, but the warmth in Michael's eyes offered something else . . . something more . . .

"Jane?" His voice whispered her name, rich and silky.

Her skin tingled and her heart beat against her throat as an overwhelming yearning to lean toward him swept over her. Surely it wouldn't hurt to give him a kiss. Just one. Or perhaps two, if that's what it took. Besides, she yearned for it so.

She stood on her tiptoes, closed her eyes, and offered her lips to him.

Nothing happened.

After a moment, she opened her eyes to find Michael regarding her with a knowing look.

He dropped his hand from her chin. "Just as I suspected: you're desperate to keep me from seeing Lady MacDonald, which makes me all the more determined to see her." He winked at Jane and walked to the doorway. "I'll see you when I return."

"Oh! You-you-you *dog*! To tease me so is just— *Oh!*" She wished she had something to throw. "Somewhere along the way, you've become a complete scoundrel, Michael Hurst. A complete and total scoundrel."

He chuckled again. "I know. Don't wait up for me; I may be a while. I have a lot of questions to ask Lady MacDonald. A *lot*."

With a wink, he left, closing the door behind him.

Jane listened to his footsteps as he went down the steps and to the front door, which he closed with an exuberant slam.

Jane grabbed her pillow and flung it at the door, where it landed with an unsatisfying thud. Then, sighing her frustration, she threw herself back on the bed and stared at the ceiling. "Blast you, Hurst! I hope you catch your death of the ague."

CHAPTER 12

From the diary of Michael Hurst:

If it doesn't stop raining soon, I shall be forced to kill someone.

*Y*ou do not need me to go with you?" Ammon peered through the growing darkness at the manor house that rose before them.

"No. Just wait here with the horses. I shouldn't be long."

"Yes, miss." He eyed the house. "It's a very large edifice."

"Too large," she muttered. Eoligary House was large by any standards, but it was especially large given the fact that it had been placed on a bluff so that it towered over the entire end of the island. The house was three stories tall and of rich red brick covered with thick green vines. The front portico boasted no fewer than eight large columns, and a side terrace looked out over the sea. *How can Jaimie afford this?* she wondered. She knew the land's income well, and there was no way he'd be able to pay for the upkeep of such a house. *Just the coal to heat this house would take half of Barra's income.*

She noted that light burned in only two rooms, one on the lower level and one on the middle. Hopefully one was a sitting room where the family was gathered, and the other a study or library where she might find Jaimie alone.

She turned to Ammon. "Don't be surprised if you hear loud noises. Some people might think I'm a ghost and raise an alarm before I can explain otherwise."

"A ghost, miss?"

"A spirit."

"Ah," Ammon said, though his tone let her know he didn't.

"Just stay here and hold the horses. I'll be back soon." She started to leave and then had another thought. "Oh. And just so you aren't surprised, I might not use the front door."

"Pardon, miss?"

"I don't want everyone in the house to know I'm here; just one person, so I may slip in a side door. Or a window. I don't know yet."

"So you are skulking." There was no mistaking the disapproval in the servant's tone.

"No, no. I'm not skulking. I'm just being discreet."

"It looks like skulking."

"Well, it's not," she said sharply.

"Very well, miss." Ammon seemed far less certain now, his dark eyes flickering from her to the house and then back. "Perhaps I should bring the horses closer, in case you have need of some assistance. Then, I could hear you more clearly if you called out."

"No, no. That won't be necessary."

"But, miss, if you enter through a window, someone might mistake you for a thief and shoot you."

Jane chuckled, thinking of Jaimie being moved to violence. She just couldn't fathom it. "I'm in no danger, Ammon. I promise."

"You know this person you visit, then?"

"He's a relative. A cousin."

Ammon's brows rose.

Jane sighed. "I know that sounds odd, but the owner of this house and I used to be very close and I'd like to visit with him without having to include others, which is what I'd have to do if I walked up to the front door and rang the bell. Jaimie and I need to talk alone."

Ammon's concerned expression relaxed a little. "Very good, miss. I will await you here, then."

She nodded and, glad to see that the sun had finally sunk below the horizon, started to slip toward the house, pausing behind various shrubberies and trees as she went.

She realized she was tired, though that shouldn't have been a surprise. She'd arisen early, had been caught in the excitement of the cliff face climb, and then had gotten thoroughly drenched. After a tepid bath, she'd spent a fretful few hours waiting on Michael to return from Lindsee's.

Those hours had been difficult because she couldn't stop imagining that meeting. Lindsee was a beautiful woman and Michael—when he wished—could be devastatingly charming.

The thought had driven Jane to distraction. Not that she was jealous, for she wasn't. She was just—

She frowned. She didn't know what she'd been, but it wasn't a feeling she wished to feel ever again. When Michael hadn't come home by twilight, she'd realized that she needed something to do rather than fret, and so she'd had Ammon saddle two horses and she'd come to visit Jaimie.

And now here she was, skulking about like a thief in the night.

Well, it couldn't be helped. Jane reached the house and crawled through the low hedge, ignoring how it tugged and picked at her gown. She reached the house and peeked in the window of a darkened room. She couldn't see the furnishings or their colors, but with persistence, she eventually made out a huge marble fireplace and a harp off to one corner. "So Elspeth took up the harp, did she?" Jane murmured.

She tried the window, but it was locked. Moving on silent feet, she went to the next window and tried it. After four more tries, she finally found an unlocked window. She slowly swung it open, peered into the dark room, and then slipped inside, her foot entangling in the long velvet curtain. "Blast it," she muttered, hopping on one foot as she twisted first to one side and then the other. She finally regained her balance, but in the process, she fell against a small table filled with knickknacks, all of which went tumbling, bouncing, and breaking.

It wasn't the sort of entrance she'd wanted to make, and she could only be glad that no one was inside the study at the moment. Heart pounding, Jane replaced the fallen objects, listening for footsteps outside the door. None came and she breathed a sigh of relief as she shook out her skirts, grimacing at the grass stains from where she'd crawled through the hedge. "Not very ladylike," she told herself. She closed the window and looked about the room.

She'd walked no more than three steps when she froze in place, her jaw dropping. Except for two items— the walls were plaster instead of stone, and the number of palm fronds growing from pots in every corner—the room looked like a duplicate of the study at Kisimul Castle. Every piece of furniture was grouped here as it had been in Kisimul, the two wing-backed chairs flanking the fireplace, the settee with a matching chair by the windows, even the large mahogany desk. Someone had saved the furnishings from Kisimul.

The chairs had been recovered in an expensive damask, but she knew each piece of furniture as well as the back of her hand, and no amount of red-and-gold-striped material could disguise it.

She ran a hand along the desk, which had been her father's favorite place to sit in the evenings, tracing her fingers along a dent she'd made when, as a child, she'd knocked the mace from the hands of a suit of armor and it had landed on the smooth wood and scarred it. She next touched the chair behind the desk and then noted the books. "By Ra," she breathed. "They saved the books, too."

Tears sprang to her eyes and she was painfully grateful. It was all so familiar and so dear. When she'd heard that Kisimul had burned down, she'd assumed that all of it had gone up in flames, including this, the family furnishings, the mementos of her father's life, the family records he'd so carefully recorded, every tradesman's receipt and—

She blinked, looking slowly around the room. *There is only one way all of this could have been salvaged, and that's if Jaimie and his father removed the furniture before—* She pressed a hand to her chest and slowly sank into her father's chair. *Surely not. Not even my uncle David is capable of such an act.* Her gaze found the banner that hung over the doorway. Embroidered over three centuries ago, it carried the Mac-Neil heraldry and displayed the family crest. It had once hung high over the hearth of the Great Hall. It would have been almost impossible to remove in a fire.

They knew the castle was going to burn down. They knew because they're the ones who set the fire. But why? Why did they burn Kisimul?

Her stomach clenched at the thought. Her home, the place she loved more than anywhere else on earth, set afire like a pile of rubbish. *What benefit could they have possibly garnered from—*

A sound outside the door made her freeze in place. The large brass doorknob began to turn, and she scrambled away from the desk and dove behind a large marble table just as the door opened.

She peered out through the fronds of the large palm, watching as Jaimie MacNeil entered the study and closed the door behind him. He went to the desk and lit one of the lanterns that sat upon it, the light sweeping across him and casting eerie shadows on the walls.

It had been fourteen years since she'd last seen him, and the years had been kind to him. Where before he'd been a painfully thin youth with large ears and a thin and warbly voice, he'd since filled out and now carried himself with the grace of one used to physical exertion. His dark hair was fashionably cut and fell over his brow, emphasizing his brown eyes. His hair, though, was streaked with silver, which was surprising, given that he was younger than her by two years.

He sat down at the desk, pulled out a sheath of papers, and selected a pen from his inkwell. He looked somberly at the papers, raked a hand through his graying hair, and then began to add up columns of numbers.

She noted that the papers were marred with large ink blots, as if someone had struggled to collect the information, whatever it was. And indeed, Jaimie looked equally serious, a worn expression marring his face.

Jane smoothed her gown and then stood. "Hello, Jaimie."

He gasped and dropped the pen upon his desk, a splash of ink spattering across the page. His eyes were wide, his mouth opening and closing before he suddenly jumped back, almost tipping his chair over in the process. "Y-y-you can't b-b-be!" he said in such a loud voice that she winced.

"Whssst, Jaimie! Do you want to awake the entire household?"

He shook his head no, though he didn't seem able to look away from her, his face completely white. "Jennet? Is that . . . is that really you?"

"Of course it is, fool!"

He sagged. "You scared me to death! I thought you were a ghostie."

"Do I *look* like a ghostie?"

He looked her up and then down. "No."

She rolled her eyes at the uncertainty in his voice. "I told you I'd come back one day."

"Yes, when we were both ninety."

"Ninety?" She bit her lip. "Oh, yes. I did say that, didn't I? Well, I'm a bit early, then."

"You're here. I just can't—" Jaimie wiped his brow, his hands shaking. "Good God. Where have you been? Where are you staying?"

"I'm staying at the Macphersons' inn right now."

"Ah. I'd heard there were strangers staying there— someone even said one of them looked like a MacNeil— but I never thought it would be *you*." He shook his head. "I can't believe it."

"Well, believe it, for I'm here, standing before you."

"I know. It's just—I'm surprised."

"I'm glad to know that the Macphersons think I look like a MacNeil, but not Jennet MacNeil."

"Aye, that's something, although I don't know how no one's recognized you yet. Jennet, I—" He shook his head. "I can't believe you're here."

"I look a good bit different now."

"You've more color to you and your hair is a mite lighter, but other than that—lass, you look exactly the same. Who have you met since you arrived?"

She read the truth in his gaze and had to swallow a wince. *Good God, I was truly deluding myself, wasn't I?* "I've only seen the Macphersons, Lindsee, and some people on the docks in Castlebay."

"'Tis a matter of time, then." He hesitated. "Are you planning to stay? Jennet, you . . . you didn't return to take Barra, did you?"

"Of course not."

He looked relieved.

Too relieved, in fact, so she added, "Unless, of course, I find that you've been mucking things up." She crossed her arms. "What have you been doing since I left, Jaimie MacNeil?"

He flushed, awkwardly moving the papers on the desk, as if to arrange them in some order he wasn't sure would work. "I've been doing as you asked."

"Balderdash." She walked to the desk where he

stood and ran her hand along the glossy surface. "How is it that Kisimul burned until she fell in upon herself, and yet all of my father's valuable furniture made it safely here, to your lovely new study?"

His gaze flickered, roving here and there, but never meeting hers. "There was a ship nearby, so we loaded what we could and—"

"Pah! Don't lie to me, you miserable fool!"

He shifted from foot to foot, looking far too much like the boy she'd left behind.

"And where did this fire begin?" Anger snapped through her veins like a living thing.

"I-it started in the kitchen house and then spread to the Addition. I-I don't know what began it; probably a hot coal that rolled out of the fire and—"

She slapped her hand upon the desk, and he jumped. "You bloody fool, this desk was in the top of the Watch Tower! Had the fire begun in the kitchen, no one could have gotten into the Watch Tower, for the doors are beside one another!"

Sweat beaded Jaimie's brow, and he gaped at her. "Jennet, don't— Please, you have to believe, it wasn't my idea to burn Kisimul, but Father said—"

"Damn you to hell, Jaimie MacNeil!" She was yelling and no longer cared. "I knew you burned the castle on purpose! I can't believe you'd— Kisimul was— And now she's *gone*!" Her voice caught on the last word and tears blurred her eyes. She ripped off her spectacles and began wiping them with her sleeve, her lips quivering. "She stood on Castle Bay for centuries, and with one thoughtless act, you wiped her away as if she were nothing but—"

"No, no! That's not how it was! I was desperate! You—you were gone and you'd taken so little that it looked as if I'd— Good God, I was afraid to sleep, for people were so angry and saying—" He opened and closed his mouth as if he'd run out of words.

The sheer panic in his voice gave her anger pause. "You thought they'd come for you? Who?"

"The people of Barra. They loved you. Jennet, your plan sounded so wonderful—we both thought it would work—but as soon as you'd left, people began to ask after you, and when I told them you'd left on your own will, they looked at me as if— It was horrible. The servants were muttering and someone threw a rock into my bedchamber window and shattered the glass and someone else left a bloody rabbit's head outside my door—" He shuddered. "Thank God Father came back before I was murdered. He'd heard how people thought I'd killed you in your sleep and tossed you into the bay—"

"Bah! No one who knew you would ever think you capable of murder."

"But no one really knew me."

"You grew up on this isle! You stayed with us every summer for years—"

"And because of that, when you left, people saw me as an usurper, a snake hidden in the bosom of the family!"

"No one said that to you."

"Oh, but they did. Mrs. MacJamison."

"The housekeeper?"

"Aye. She passed last year, but she never spoke to me again after you left. She was certain I'd harmed you. And she was only one of many." He spread his hands wide. "Jennet, I'm not saying 'tis your fault, for God knows I agreed to that mad plan. But I'm not you. The people of Barra don't love me the way they love you. I'm not as talkative and people don't react the same way. I tend to keep to myself. Father said my shyness made me look even more guilty."

She blinked at him, thoughts slowly settling into line. By Ra, her plan—her lovely, perfect plan—had been a disaster. "But . . . I left documents saying you were the new heir, that I relinquished all rights to Barra."

"Documents that you wrote and signed yourself, without a single witness . . . except me." He shook his head, looking like a confused bear. "No one believed me. After a few weeks facing everyone's suspicions, I began to doubt myself."

She closed her eyes and sank into the chair opposite the desk, her knees as weak as butter. "Which would make it all look even more damning."

He shuddered. "They kept looking at me, hating me. I feared someone would kill me in retaliation." He rubbed his forehead. "It was horrible. There was nothing I could say to fix things."

She sighed, suddenly so tired that she could barely keep upright. "I never once thought that people would assume I'd been *murdered*. I told everyone I wished to leave. Kept maps upon the walls of my bedchambers. I was constantly announcing my intention to leave. It never occurred to me, not once, in all of those weeks of planning, that they'd assume something different." She rested her elbows on her knees and dropped her head into her hands. "Ah, the follies of youth! I was so naïve."

"Both of us were. I thought it the greatest plan I'd ever heard. We both got what we wanted. You got your freedom and I got Elspeth."

She sighed and leaned back in her chair. "It seemed so simple."

"Yes, it did. But I was hated, Jennet. *Hated.* I still am, to some extent, as there are those that still doubt. Not everyone, mind you, but enough." A flicker of a smile touched his worn face. "When you left, they at first thought I'd locked you in the castle. Then the rumors began that I was attempting to starve you to death."

"Pssht. Even your father couldn't keep me confined to the dungeons of my own castle."

"I'm sorry for that. He wished us to marry, and you were so adamant."

"Och, I used to play in that dungeon; it held no fear for me." She grinned. "I'd been escaping from it since

I was three when you and Lindsee would lock me in it when we were playing Roman soldiers."

"She didn't play that game for long." He wrinkled his nose. "She's a prissy woman, is Lindsee. I'm still shocked she agreed to explore the cave with us."

"She would go only once."

"Aye. As I said—prissy. She grew worse after she married MacDonald."

"She was a good friend to us. Isn't she still?"

He hesitated and then shrugged. "I see her often enough." He smiled sadly. "Ah, times, they've changed, haven't they?"

"Unfortunately, yes." They were quiet a bit as they each thought of their past. Jane finally bestirred herself. "How did David finally calm the suspicions that you'd murdered me in my bed?"

"He staged a grand return banquet for you and hired a servant girl from the mainland to come wrapped in a cloak. She pretended to faint as she got off the ship, and he carried her to your bedchamber and then declared that she—or rather, you—had smallpox. That kept everyone away."

"David is a very intelligent man."

"He went to great lengths to convince everyone it was you and that he and I were both devastated at your illness. He even brought a specialist from Oban to visit you. The servant girl played your part until we staged the fire. It wasn't until the people of Barra saw the bones in the ruins that they believed you dead." He gave her a wry smile. "You're a hard woman to kill, Jennet MacNeil, even in imagination. You ride like a Gypsy, swim like a fish, shoot a pistol like a highwayman, sail a boat like a pirate—you were almost a legend in the minds of the people of Barra. It would take something spectacular to bring such a woman to the earth, so . . . it was Kisimul or nothing."

"I should be flattered, I suppose." She cocked a brow. "Where did you get the bones?"

"Father shot a deer." Jaimie shrugged. "We put the bones in the fire."

"And the servant girl?"

"She left with a pocket full of gold, determined to make her way in America. We've not seen her since."

"What a mess I left behind. I had no idea. Still . . . Jaimie, I don't mean to complain, for I can tell you were in a difficult spot, but couldn't you have burned something other than Kisimul?"

"What? A crofter's hut? Something you'd have easily escaped? Somewhere the laird's daughter would have never been? The people here see Kisimul as you. We had no choice. And burning the castle worked. We had a grand memorial ceremony and people came from all of the islands when we placed the bones in your tomb."

A laugh bubbled to her lips. "I have a *tomb*?"

"Of course. A lovely one overlooking Barra Sound."

"I suppose I should thank you for that."

"No, no. It was the least I could do. Jennet, I'm sorry things didn't turn out the way we'd hoped." He raked a hand through his hair. "We were young and foolish. I was fourteen and you were sixteen and neither of us knew of the ways of the world, of how powerful suspicion could be."

She adjusted her spectacles on her nose and chuckled sadly. "I thought I had it all planned out. That you would be left to rule in my stead while I could finally be free to see the world. Instead, I locked you into my own fate, sealed with good intentions, but with poor planning. I'm sorry, Jaimie. I would have never have left you in such a predicament if—"

"You tried your best. We both did. I thought of that as the days went by. It was a difficult time, but eventually things came about. The day I turned fifteen, I asked Elspeth to marry me."

"And she did."

"We have four children. She's—" He shook his head, sadness flickering over his face. "She's as beautiful now as the day we married."

"And your father?"

Jaimie gave a rueful grimace that held a hint of anger. "No one can do anything with Father. You, more than anyone, know how that is."

"Yes, I do. Tell me, you didn't happen to save the good whiskey from the stores at Kisimul, did you?"

"Of course we did." Jaimie rose and turned to a small table that was tucked beside the window where a crystal decanter sat. "We saved everything from the castle, even all of the papers your father was so fond of poring over."

"He thought of himself as the keeper of Barra's history."

Jaimie poured two glasses of amber liquid, then paused and added a double measure to one glass. He brought the taller glass to Jane.

At her amused glance, he chuckled and took the seat opposite hers. "You've always handled your whiskey better than any man I knew."

She took a fortifying sip, the whiskey warming her at once. "I'm so glad you saved it."

"Jennet, Kisimul isn't gone for good. It can be rebuilt. Father says the stone is all there. We'd have to replace the large beams, float them here from the mainland, but it could be done."

"You've thought of it."

"Yes, and once our finances come about, I will rebuild her."

Jane looked around the comfortable room, enjoying the warmth of the fireplace. "This is a lovely house."

He glanced about with an indifferent gaze. "It's what Elspeth wanted."

"You love her."

"She is the only reason I agreed to your mad plan to begin with. I never wanted this." He waved at the desk covered with paper. "But she wouldn't have had me if I'd come to her empty-handed. She wouldn't even talk to me until I became the MacNeil of Barra. God knows I don't want it, although Elspeth . . ." He grimaced and took a gulp of his whiskey. "She lives and breathes playing lady of the manor, taking soup and jellies to the poor, sitting in the front pew in church. It means so much to her. But the people of Barra don't like her, and she knows it. How can they when they look at her and all they think of is you?"

"Perhaps, with time, they'll see her differently."

"It's been fourteen years, Jennet. I love Elspeth, but she's not a warm sort of woman. She doesn't encourage trust the way you do. She'll never be accepted here, though I'd never tell her that. I've tried to get her to move, to sell this house and find a smaller one, to make a more pleasant life for us. Somewhere she will be accepted. But every time I say something, she and Father band together, and that's that."

"She and your father? They've made friends, then."

"Father doesn't have friends, just allies."

Jane silently agreed; there was no more ambitious man than David MacNeil. "He reminds me of some of the pharaohs of ancient Egypt who thought that if they'd just declare themselves the center of the universe, that would make it so." At Jaimie's confused expression, she sighed. "Never mind. So your father and Elspeth keep you tied here, though you're not happy."

"I hate it here. We've never been able to escape your death. It cast a long shadow, cousin. So long that I know I'll never outlive it."

Jane didn't know what to say, so she took another sip of the whiskey. Her cousin looked so sad, almost lost. It was a good thing she'd come home, for there was work to be done. As the whiskey warmed her, she began thinking through the possible ways she could help her cousin.

Jaimie stared glumly over his glass at the papers on his desk. "I had no idea how much work it would be, administering to the people of Barra and collecting the rents and paying taxes and— Good God, how did you do it all? You were in charge of everything for a year before you left, and it never seemed to take you half the time it takes me."

"I trained at my father's knee. I suppose I was a fool to think that you, who had only my inexpert tutelage to guide you, could administer the isle the way he did." She swirled the whiskey in her glass. "What a mull I made of things."

"We've both fallen short in many ways. Elspeth—" He stared into his glass. "It pains me to say this, but she never loved me. She married me for the title. It was enough at the time, just to have her. But now . . ." His gaze clouded over, his lips quivering.

"You love her still."

"So much. But it is not enough. She and I will never be what I had hoped." He was silent a moment, but then his gaze turned to Jane. "When I first saw you, I feared that you'd come to take it all back. And maybe that's not such a bad idea."

She sputtered on her whiskey. "What? No, no. Jaimie, I'll make sure things are set to rights before I leave, but I can't stay here. Not after all I've done and seen." She leaned forward and said in an earnest tone, "Jaimie, I've spent the last fourteen years traveling the world and having amazing adventures. I've helped discover ancient societies, spoken to kings and queens from other lands, and held jewels that once rested upon the brow of a pharaoh. While I love Barra and always will, this isn't the life for me."

He looked disappointed, but managed a smile. "It never was, was it?"

"I think even my father was beginning to realize that, before he died." She reached over and took Jaimie's hand. "Do you hate Barra so much? It's a beautiful island and the people are wonderful."

"I don't hate Barra, Jennet. I hate what my life's become here. I always thought Elspeth would come to love me once we were married and had children, but that never happened." He looked utterly beaten. "She abides me, no more."

"I'm sorry."

He gave her hand a squeeze and then released it and picked up his glass. "It's my own fault for thinking childish dreams could become reality if I wished hard enough."

"We all do that at some point."

"Yes. Maybe it's time I stopped." He nodded toward the papers on his desk. "There are other issues, too. There's Father and the finances and what we'll do about the necessary repairs on the crofters' huts and, oh, a million things that I'm not equipped to handle."

The sadness in his voice made Jane sigh. "I'm sorry, but . . . what would you do if you weren't the laird?"

"I don't know. Just . . . not this." He managed a faint smile. "Ignore me. I'm just speaking like a madman."

"Jaimie, this is your life now. Somehow, I don't think you really want it to all go away."

"No. No, I don't. I just wish things were different." Jaimie blew out his breath in a sigh. "This is my life, such as it is."

"You have options. If you don't wish to live here, then talk to Elspeth, convince her to move with you somewhere new. Start over there. You can appoint an estate manager and Elspeth can still be the lady of the manor and—"

"You don't understand. It's not that easy."

"Then explain to me what's really happening here.

Why you don't follow your heart? I can't help you if you don't explain things."

"Help me? Is that what you want to do?"

"Yes."

He gave a mirthless laugh. "You always were a meddlesome brat."

"I still am, I'm afraid."

"So I see. Even though you were only sixteen the day you left—"

"My birthday."

"Yes, it was. After you left, I never once worried about you. I *knew* you'd find your way."

She grinned. "And I did. It helped that I took Mother's jewels with me."

"You sold them all?"

"Every one. I don't miss them a bit, either. They weren't family heirlooms, like the desk there, or the pennant. They were gifts of love from my father and they've more than paid their value in the adventures they gave me. The things I've seen . . . you realize how small you are when you stand in the dust of a lost civilization. And I've stood in many such piles of dust."

Jaimie's eyes gleamed. "I've thought of you so often over the years. I have to admit I was jealous and maybe even resentful. You were out there, living life, and I was here while Father and Elspeth—" He sighed.

"Your father is a bossy soul. But Elspeth? You used to call her your fair flower."

"She was. But after we married . . . I don't know. Things changed. She was happy enough at first, but then Father came back and began to take things—"

"Hold. What do you mean he began to 'take things'?"

Jaimie's scowl returned. "He wished all of the revenues from the licensing from the estates."

"But . . . that's the main revenue!"

"I know."

"You *gave* it to him?"

Jaimie's face darkened. "I didn't have a choice. I'd already made such a mull of things and I-I *needed* him to help. There were so many decisions and no one was nearby to help and—" He shook his head. "My father was the only person who could help, so I let him do so. And in return, he took the licenses."

"But how can you make repairs on the roads or buy new grains for planting or build houses for your tenants?"

"I know that now, but at the time it seemed a fair trade. Later on, when I realized what I'd done and how Barra was harmed, I demanded he return them, but it was too late. I argued at first, but he threatened . . ." He sent her a glance, and then shrugged. "But he was right; I was so overwhelmed with the responsibility. It really was best for everyone concerned."

Jane rubbed her forehead. "It seems I underestimated my dear uncle."

"He's dear only to himself," Jaimie said sharply. "I hate him. When Elspeth saw how Father treats me, she began to do the same, always mocking me and refusing to do as I ask. He's made it worse. I once refused to sign something over to him, a lien of some sort, and he threatened to tell her that I'd only married her for the fine bloodlines she brought to our family."

"You love her. Any fool could see that."

"Not Elspeth. She believes everything Father says. If he told her that, she'd never question it."

"Surely she's noticed how unethical he is."

"He's been very careful to cultivate her, complimenting her while blaming me for the failures of our stay on Barra. She thinks it's because of me that the people here haven't warmed to her."

"Oh, dear."

"Yes. She's decided that her husband is not the man she thought him. Now she can barely stand to be in the same room with me, while I—" His voice broke.

Jane's eyes burned with sympathy. "While you love her still," she said softly. So her uncle had used her cousin's love for his wife to hold them all under his spell. She couldn't wait to give him a piece of her mind.

Jane looked at the papers on the desk. "What's left under your care?"

"This house and the lands from it to the shore."

"And?"

Jaimie shrugged sadly.

Jane leaned back in her chair, tapping her fingers on the damask arm. "So your father has been siphoning off Barra's funds and has Elspeth dancing to his tune. We can't stand for this. Things must change, and soon. We'll just have to find a way to do it. A way to disengage your father from Barra."

Jaimie's expression turned hopeful. "We? You're going to help?"

"Of course I am. I'm not the sort of woman to—"

Jaimie jumped to his feet, scooped her out of her chair, and gave her a tremendous hug. "Och, you wee girl! I'm so glad you're here! I've been alone with this for so long."

Jane, glad her glass was empty, chuckled and returned the hug. "Yes, well, I'm certain we'll find a way out of this mess, though it will mean we must face your father."

Jaimie set Jane back on the floor and regarded her with a less glowing expression as she straightened her spectacles. "That could be difficult. Father's worse than ever."

"Fortunately for us all, so am I. I'm older now and wiser and I have much more experience in dealing with difficult people." She smiled at her cousin. "Are you familiar with Michael Hurst?"

"The explorer who writes the serial in *The Morning Post*? I read it every chance I get."

"He's my employer now. Once I ran out of funds, I became his assistant. I've been working for him for the last four years. It's been remarkable, though he's not the easiest man to deal with."

Jaimie looked deeply envious. "You'll have to tell me your tales."

"I've hundreds." She chuckled. "Still, while I've loved my adventures, it would be wrong to say that I didn't miss Barra, for I have." She looked around the study. "It's nice to be home, at least for a while."

"You're welcome to stay here, if you wish."

"I don't believe Elspeth would like that. She was always a bit territorial."

Jaimie's jaw tightened. "Jennet MacNeil, for so long as you live, you'll always have a bed within the walls of my house."

"Thank you, Jaimie. That's very kind of you." Jane glanced about the room at the furniture that held so many memories. The two wide oak tables that flanked one of the windows used to stand in her dressing room in Kisimul. The low chairs by the fireplace had come straight from her father's study, as had his desk. She looked at the desk now and could imagine her father sitting there. Tears threatened. "I miss him, you know. Even now."

"Och, I'm sorry." Jaimie slipped an arm about her and gave her a swift hug. "He thought the world of you—"

"Jaimie!" came a sharp feminine voice.

Jane and Jaimie sprang apart. Despite the fact that she had no reason to feel guilty, Jane knew her hot face was as red as Jaimie's as they both faced Elspeth, who stood just inside the open door.

Jaimie gulped. "Elspeth, my dear, I was just talking to—" He gestured weakly toward Jane.

Elspeth, who'd looked furious when Jane had first turned around, now appeared shocked. *"Jennet?"*

Elspeth had changed over the years. She was no longer the slender, svelte, lithe girl Jane had met once at a clan gathering. Bearing four children and then being locked away on Barra with its cold winters had left Elspeth well rounded. Jane glanced at Jaimie and saw her cousin staring at his wife as if she were still as beautiful as a nymph.

A pang of envy filled Jane's heart, though she hid it as she dipped a curtsy. "Elspeth. How do you do, cousin?"

Elspeth's startling blue eyes narrowed. "If you've come to reclaim Barra, whatever my lump of a husband may say, we'll not tamely give it up."

"Elspeth," Jaimie said sharply, "there's no need to—"

"There's every need," she spat. "You can't even run the estate the way it should be so that your poor father has to step in all of the time, and now I find you embracing this—this—"

"Oh, no!" Jane inserted hurriedly. "You mistake what you saw. Jaimie was merely expressing his sympathy."

Elspeth didn't appear convinced, though she addressed her husband and not Jane. "It was improper of you to embrace Lady Jennet so."

Seeing Jaimie's miserable expression, Jane continued, "As for my wanting to return to my place on Barra, I left the lairdship to Jaimie and I've no wish for that to change. Not now and not ever."

Elspeth's plump mouth folded with suspicion. "Oh?"

"Aye. I only came to Barra because my employer, Michael Hurst, is on a quest that brought him here. We've come to see the drawings in the caves beyond the cliffs and to look for an ancient artifact that might be hidden somewhere nearby."

"Really?" Jaimie said, interest in his voice. "The same caves we used to play in as children?"

"Yes, though we were fools to do so; they're dangerous. We tried to climb down the path today and the rain caught us." She shook her head. "It was terrifying."

"Aye. I don't allow the children to go there. Youth is foolishness. Still—" Jaimie's eyes twinkled. "We had fun."

Jane had to smile at the mischief in his face. "When we weren't getting scraped and scratch—"

"Stop it, both of you," Elspeth hissed. "Perchance you can explain why I found you in an embrace. Or do I, as a wife, have no right to ask?"

Jaimie hurried to Elspeth's side. "I merely gave her a hug good-bye, for she grew sad thinking of her father.

Much of the furniture here is from his study, you know."
He placed a hand on his wife's arm. "The old laird—"

"I know all about the old laird." Elspeth shot a sullen
glance at Jane and said in a grudging tone, "I suppose
that would make you upset."

"I've had several days of being upset. I didn't realize
the castle had burned until our ship sailed past it."

"Aye," Elspeth said, "'twas necessary to cover your
disappearance. You left us in a horrible state."

"Now that I've returned, I'll do what I can to repair
that harm."

"The best thing you can do is leave before anyone
knows you're here." She turned to Jaimie. "'Tis late. The
children wish to say good night to their father."

Jane sent Jaimie a quick glance. "I'll come back in a
day or so and we'll discuss things," she said.

"'Things'?" Elspeth's gaze shuttled from one to the
other, suspicion bright. "What 'things'?"

"My dear, there's no need for you to worry—" Jaimie
began.

Jane interrupted, "I'm going to go through the
revenues of the island and see what's happened to the
funding."

Jaimie blinked. "Will that help?"

"Perhaps. I grew up monitoring the revenues and
expenses and began recording them when I was ten.
Why do you think so many of the records are in my
hand?" She turned to Elspeth. "I was raised to run this

estate; Jaimie was not. He's doing the best he can." She met Elspeth's gaze directly. "I've no wish to return to my old life, but Kisimul and Barra deserve peace. They were left in the care of the MacNeils and 'tis only to a MacNeil I'd leave her. Jaimie's my cousin and he's the only person worthy of sitting at my father's desk. I do this for him, and not for my own gain."

Elspeth's mouth thinned. "As I said, the only good you can do for us now is to leave before anyone knows you're here."

"I've no intention of staying a second longer than necessary." She forced a smile and turned to Jaimie. "Speaking of which, I'd better get back to the inn before it gets much later."

"I'll escort you to the door," Jaimie mumbled, looking unhappy.

Jane allowed him to do so, though she paused on the portico. "Gather the estate records. I'll come back and we'll see what's been happening to Barra."

Jaimie nodded, though he looked far from happy.

Without another glance back, Jane walked away toward the hillock where Ammon waited with the horses.

CHAPTER 13

From the diary of Michael Hurst:

My visit to Lady MacDonald did not prove as fortuitous as I'd hoped. She'd not only been forewarned by Jane, but the lady also seemed to have her own secrets, all of which were closely guarded. At one point I noted a handsome malacca cane in a stand near the front door, and she practically threw herself between the cane and me and changed the subject in a very heavy-handed manner. As if I cared whether or not she has suitors; I merely wished to know of her childhood in order to find out about Jane's. The entire process was tedious and yielded nothing of value.

It didn't help matters that as soon as I seated myself in her sitting room that I began to sneeze.

I fear I've caught a cold or worse. But that's not the worst of my misfortune; when I returned to the inn, Jane was nowhere to be found. I'm off to look for her now, and if I do not find her soon, then woe betide that blasted woman.

$\mathcal{J}$ane led the way home. It was dark out, but when the clouds broke here and there, the moonlight was bright enough that they kept to the road with little problem.

It was drizzling by the time she and Ammon rode their horses into the stables and dismounted there. Jane noted that Michael's horse was already brushed and put away for the night.

Ammon took the reins from her hand. "I will take care of the horses, miss."

"I can at least brush him—"

Ammon shook his head. "Go. It is late. Mr. Hurst will be worried."

"Mr. Hurst will not be worried. He'll be irritated that I left without leaving him word of my destination."

Ammon's dark eyes met her own. "Was our destination a secret?"

"It could be." She looked up at the servant. "You don't remember exactly where we went, do you?" she asked hopefully.

"I remember everything, miss."

"Oh." She sighed. "If Hurst asks, then you must do as you see fit. I'll probably tell him anyway. He's bound to find out. The isle is so small that if someone on the east side were to drop a pin, it would wake someone on the west."

Ammon smiled. "Yes, miss."

"Thank you for your assistance. You've been quite helpful." She yawned and realized that she was wet and weary and all she wanted was to fall into her own bed. "Have a nice evening."

The servant inclined his head and took the horses to the back of the stables, where he began to unsaddle them.

Jane left, her boots clipping on the cobblestones. She opened the inn door, the hinges creaking horribly as she pushed it closed behind her. She undid her cloak and looked around the common room, where the fire had burned so low that only a sole lamp offered any light.

Michael was nowhere in sight. She'd thought for certain he'd be there, ready to demand where she'd been, but apparently he'd already gone to bed. She didn't blame him. It had been a long, long day.

She hung her wet cloak on a peg, where it hung heavily. Her spectacles were beaded over with moisture. She tried to wipe them, but her clothing was damp as well and did little more than smear the lenses. Grimacing, she tucked them into her pocket and then wearily made her way up the stairs. It would take some time to get ready for bed, for she'd have to spread her clothing before the fire to dry.

She reached the landing and went to Michael's room instead of her own, pressing her ear to the door. She could hear nothing but her own breathing. She sighed and went to her bedchamber, closing the door behind her.

The only light came from the fire someone—probably Mr. Macpherson—had built. She thought about lighting a lamp but decided she was too tired. She'd just peel off her clothes and climb into bed. She removed her spectacles from her pocket and placed them on the table by the bed so she could find them first thing in the morning.

The curtain was open and allowed a sliver of moonlight to slice across the bed. She stepped into the pool of light and untied her gown and dropped it to the floor. As she did so, the events of the day seemed to weigh her down.

Poor Jaimie. He was still so in love with Elspeth. In a way, he was enslaved by that love, making sacrifices to keep it while those same sacrifices destroyed Elspeth's respect. "What a coil," Jane muttered.

The worst part of all was the realization that her uncle was up to his old tricks, and it seemed as if no one had said nay to the man in years. That was bad, for not only had it allowed him to ravage the castle lands of their value, but she had little doubt that he'd also turned into an even larger power-mongering fool than he'd been before.

Fortunately, now she was older than a mere sixteen years of age and, unlike Jaimie, she had no fear of his tricks. But that was for another day.

She hung her wet gown on a peg and undid her chemise, letting it fall to her ankles, the cool evening air making her bare nipples peak. She shivered, hung the chemise beside her gown, and quickly climbed into bed.

As she settled the counterpane, she saw the boot. It sat before the chair that was angled by the fire. It was a man's boot, one she was very familiar with, for she'd moved those boots countless times. It wasn't so much the boot that made her heart thud sickly, but the fact that the only way it could appear as it did, tilted on its heel and leaning back, was if Michael's foot was still in it.

She clutched the sheets before her. "Michael?"

The boot shifted slightly. "Who else?"

His voice, low and smoky, made her skin prickle as if a feather had wafted over it. *For the love of Ra, he was here while I undressed.* "I didn't see you there."

"Apparently not." The boot disappeared as he pulled his feet under him to stand. The old chair creaked noisily.

She swallowed once. "You should have told me you were there."

"And miss the show?" His voice was dark and purred through his lips like silk, soft and yet dangerous.

She could feel his anger. "You're upset."

"Of course I am. I came back to the inn and you were gone. Where were you?"

She wished she could see his face, but all she could see was his broad-shouldered outline before the fire. "It doesn't matter where I went. Now, if you'll excuse me, I'm going to sleep. It's been a long day and—"

He moved a bit more, the moonlight now limning one side of his face until he looked like a glorious statue. "What's wrong, Jane? We've shared rooms before."

"Yes, but I've never undressed in front of you before. That's not acceptable." Still, she couldn't help but wonder what he thought, and then decided she didn't wish to know. She knew she wasn't ugly, but then again, she also knew she wasn't the buxom, curvaceous sort of woman that usually attracted Michael's interest.

Some things were best left unknown. "May I go to sleep now?"

"No. Where were you? I was worried." Michael hated admitting that, but he was still simmering from the way she'd so blithely entered the room and undressed before him. He should have let her know that he was there, and he'd meant to do so. Or he had until she stepped into that silvered pool of light and he'd lost all ability to speak. After that, all he'd been able to do was stare.

"As you can see, I'm perfectly fine."

She *was* perfectly fine, he decided, struggling hard to calm the blood thundering through his head. Nothing made sense right now. Not her actions. Not the happenings of the last few days. Not the way the sight of her, naked and slight under the spill of a silver moon, had inflamed him until he could barely speak.

Her slim, naked beauty infuriated him. Not because he thought her duplicitous, but because he'd been so unbelievably blind. He'd never really looked at her. Not once. Not the way he'd looked at her these last few days as startling revelation after startling revelation had been thrown upon him, not the least of which was the image of her from just moments ago. That image was burning through him now, the slope of her slender waist, the curves of her small breasts, the delicate hollows of her shoulders and neck—all of it indelibly etched into his mind until he wondered if he'd ever be able to look at her again without seeing her thus.

"Michael, please leave. I'm tired." She pushed her hair back so she could see him more clearly, the damp strands clinging to her neck. As she moved, the sheet slipped and hung for one heartrending moment to her breast, curving about her erect nipple, before it fluttered down.

She gasped and caught it before it revealed the round areola, but not before Michael realized that he *had* to taste this woman and press his lips to every inch of her delicious body. She was seductress and mystery, sensuality and innocence. Her long hair—unbound now and damp and curling in the most damnably seductive way—clung to her skin as if mocking him.

"Michael, I know you have a lot of questions, but I'm so tired and—"

Michael crossed to the bed.

She clutched the sheet higher.

"Move over."

She blinked. Once. Twice. Three times. "But—" She opened and closed her mouth, and finally managed to say, "But why?"

He sat on the edge of the bed. "Because I want to do this." He kissed her. And not as if she were Miss Jane Smythe-Haughton, his loyal and enthusiastic assistant, but as if she were what he was only beginning to realize—a flesh-and-blood woman with silken skin, rosebud breasts, and more secrets than he knew what to do with.

Her eyes flew open, the deep velvety brown darkening with surprise, but only for a second. Her expression changed, as quicksilver as she was, into something more. She opened her lips beneath his, clutched his shirt, and tugged him closer.

God, he loved her enthusiasm. He loved that she didn't stand still and wait for life to happen but was constantly surging forward to meet it, just as she was surging forward to meet him now.

He deepened the kiss, looking boldly at her. Her

lashes fluttered and then fell as she gave herself to the kiss, letting go of the sheet in her excitement.

By Ra, but she was magnificent. He broke the kiss to nip at her lips, her chin, and her neck, tasting her silken skin. She gasped and writhed against him.

The sheet was forgotten, and she kicked at it. It had become an impediment, as had his own clothing. Her fingers fumbled at his loosely knotted neckcloth.

He laughed softly and kissed her nose. "Wait one moment." He stood and quickly stripped.

Jane clutched her knees to her chest and watched, her body thrumming with excitement. Michael tugged his shirt over his head, the moonlight tracing every line of his muscled chest and stomach. Her breath quickened and she had to fight the urge to reach out and touch him.

He stripped out of his boots and breeches, kicking them impatiently to the side. She drank in the sight of him greedily. Every muscled sinew of him seemed both new and dearly familiar. He grinned at her perusal. "May I join you?"

She flipped back the sheets in answer.

He chuckled and came to join her in the bed.

Jane slid over and welcomed him.

He laughed at her obvious eagerness and slid in beside her, slipping an arm around her waist and pulling her flush against him.

"Mmm, you're so warm," she said, twining her arms about his neck.

He felt so good and so right, his bare skin against hers, and she knew that no matter what happened that she would never regret this night.

She'd made mistakes in her past, one in particular that she should mention before things progressed further. She owed Michael honesty. As hard as it was, when he bent to kiss her neck, she placed a hand on his chest. "Michael, I . . . I'm not a—"

He placed a finger on her lips. "Jane, please. Just stop talking."

"I don't want you to be disappointed or—"

He kissed her shoulder, his lips warm against her skin and making her gasp. "Sweetheart, I don't know how long your confession might be, but mine would take an hour, and I'd rather spend that time with you."

She had to laugh. "You don't mind that I'm not an innocent?"

"To be honest, I'm delighted." His soft kisses moved to her collarbone, the sensations tingling up her spine.

"Oh . . . really?"

"Really." He nipped at her neck, his warm breath making her breasts ache to be touched.

"So you won't mind if I'm—"

He sighed and lifted his head. "You aren't going to continue until I explain, are you?"

"No."

He lifted himself up on his elbow. "Very well. I've had a virgin or two. That was enough. Then I fell in love with the great adventure." He traced a finger up the slope of one of her breasts. "She is a demanding mistress, and as you've been in my employ for the last four years, you know that leaves very little time for other things. I want an adventure, and you, my love, are just that." He paused, his finger hovering over her nipple, which peaked as if straining toward him. "And you?"

She lifted her brows, though she was panting from the tingle his near touch was causing her. "I thought you didn't want to know."

"I don't. But I can see that you feel the urge to—"

She arched, pressing her breast into his hand.

He closed his eyes, as if soaking in the feel of her.

She slipped an arm about his neck and captured his warm lips with her own.

That was all it took. No more words were necessary as, to her complete delight, Michael once more took over the dance, touching and stroking and tasting until she was writhing beneath him.

Oh, she wanted this. Wanted him. And had for so long. She'd always known he'd be a passionate, focused lover. But she wasn't prepared for the way her body reacted to his touch. How she became bold and demanding, even more than he was. He may have started this interlude, but somewhere along the way, she took control, teasing him until he gasped her name, reveling in the power of making this sensual, strong man reach for her with such desperation in his gaze.

When he finally pinned her to the bed and positioned himself between her thighs, she was more than ready, lifting her legs and locking them about his waist, pulling him inside her, the fullness plunging her into a maelstrom of passion.

Michael captured her lips as she gasped his name, moving with an urgency that matched her own. She lifted to meet him, pressing him to go further, urging him with soft words to take her, all of her. He did so with a flattering alacrity, arching his hips against hers, the excitement building until, with a joint cry, they flew over the edge of passion.

Afterward, he curled around her, his leg over hers, his arms about her. Jane savored the warmth as her breathing finally slowed so that she could once again think and see and hear. The sheets were damp about her, the blanket kicked off long ago, one pillow lodged at the foot of the bed, the other missing completely. But all around her was Michael—her cheek on his shoulder, his chest was pressed to her back, his legs entwined with hers. She'd never felt so peaceful or safe.

She listened as his breathing slowed, and then deepened as he fell asleep. But Jane was wide-awake. This was it, then. She and Michael would never return to their previous comfortable, effective relationship. She was both sad and amazingly sated. How could something that felt so right cause pain? But she knew where this path led. She knew because she'd walked it before, led there by youth and foolishness. This time, she had neither excuse. The bold truth was that she loved him. Had always loved him. And always would.

Her heart ached at the admission. She hadn't been fighting his interest so much as her own, which she'd thought was under control. She sighed softly. *What do I do now? If we continue in this vein, I'll just care more and more. And if we stop—could I stand that, either? He's only become interested in me since he discovered that my past isn't what he'd thought. I know how he is with a mystery—he can't leave it alone until he's worked through all of its secrets. But once he has discovered all that there is to discover, he moves on. I have no reason to think this is any different.*

She closed her eyes, trying not to care but unable to stop the pain her thoughts had caused. In his sleep, Michael sighed and stirred, pulling her closer to him, the gesture unconscious but precious all the same.

I think too much, she told herself. At this moment, warm in his embrace, the feel of him still lingering between her thighs, all she wanted to do was sleep within his arms. *Tomorrow I'll think. But not tonight.*

With that, she put her troubling thoughts away, snuggled deeper in his arms, and immediately fell asleep.

CHAPTER 14

From the diary of Michael Hurst:

There are times when I surprise myself.

The morning sun tickled Michael's nose. He reached up to brush it and heard the door open. Lifting up on one elbow, he was just in time to see Jane slip into the hallway beyond, holding her boots. She shut the door with a quiet click.

She obviously thought him still asleep. He turned onto his back and stretched, enjoying the replete feeling.

His cock stirred at the memory and he gazed down at it where it now strained against the sheet. "Insatiable," he muttered. "Go back to sleep. She's already up and about."

He thought about calling for her to come back to bed—heaven knew the house was small enough that his voice could be heard if he raised it, but as he had the thought, he caught the murmur of voices—Mrs. Macpherson's and a man's voice. *Who is that?* Curiosity had him rising, washing, and dressing as fast as he could. When he was done, he picked up his boots, much as Jane had, and carried them to the top of the stairs.

The voices from the common room rang with perfect clarity. Michael leaned against the wall and listened.

"If ye're certain Mr. Hurst dinna wish fer his breakfast now, I'll put this pan upon a warming stone."

"Thank you," Jane said.

Her voice is tense. Too tense. Michael leaned forward.

Mrs. Macpherson continued. "Lord MacNeil, are ye certain ye dinna wish more eggs, fer I can make them."

"No, thank you, Mrs. Macpherson. I just came to visit our island guest."

"Verrah weel. I'll be in the kitchen if ye need me." Footsteps sounded as the housekeeper left.

"Well, well, well. Jennet."

"Uncle." Her voice was frosty cold.

Michael could imagine the abbreviated curtsy that accompanied it. *What had she called her uncle? Ah, yes, David.*

"Your cousin told me you'd been to visit him," David said. "He also said you were using a false name."

"Jaimie was never one to keep a secret."

"Oh, I had to force it from him."

"Then who told you— Ah. Elspeth."

"He will not remain married long if he doesn't begin to appreciate what he has."

"I see. What do you want, Uncle David?"

Michael wished he could see her face to better gauge her reactions. He stared down the stairs for a moment. An honest man would reveal himself. But an honest man might, by intruding, end this very interesting conversation, and that was the last thing Michael wanted.

It might be rude to listen in on people's conversations—some might call that spying. But he called it good investigative work. As rude as it was to listen in, it was ruder still to keep secrets.

Michael sat down on the top step, cautious not to make a sound, and then bent over to peer into the common chamber.

David MacNeil stood by the fireplace, tall and with broad shoulders, a streak of white at each temple, and a deeply lined face that still managed to look vigorous and healthy. He didn't look as if he belonged on Barra, for he was wearing a multicaped coat left open to reveal a well-made waistcoat, a ruby glimmering in the folds of an intricately tied cravat. He dressed with an elegance that wouldn't have been out of place in the sitting rooms of Edinburgh.

"David, if you've come to tell me that you wish me to leave, then you've wasted your trip. I came for one thing and one thing only. Once I have that, I'll be gone."

His mouth tightened, his smile false. "Ah, my one and only niece. I wish I could say it was nice to see you, but you know the truth of that too much for me to pretend otherwise."

She tsked. "In a temper, are we?"

Michael grinned. *Well done, Jane.*

David's smile slipped. "I'm not in a temper. I'm disappointed, yes. According to the agreement you made with my son—"

"And not with you."

"Whoever you made it with, you weren't supposed to return. *Ever.*"

"Actually, I told him I would return when I turned ninety, so technically, I'm just a little early."

David's smile was long gone.

Jane shrugged. "Fine. I didn't plan to return, but things happened, and well, here I am. I know you won't believe me, but when I left, I thought I'd taken care of things. I'd signed all of my rights to Jaimie and even spent time trying to explain the running of the estate to him, though that doesn't seem to have helped."

"Those documents weren't worth the paper they were written on. You hadn't been gone a day before rumors about your disappearance began to swirl. Jaimie's lucky I was nearby to salvage the situation. Do you *know* what we went through, all those years ago, when you went blithely traipsing off—"

"I do nothing *blithely*. I didn't wish to be married to Jaimie. You knew that."

"Yes, I did. You made it quite plain."

"And you locked me in the dungeon, too, without food or water."

"Only for a few days. You were released." He shrugged. "Besides, you could get out. I saw you myself." A faint smile touched his mouth, the first real one since he'd arrived. "Your friend . . . what was her name? Ah, yes, Lindsee. She brought you food on at least two occasions. I saw her do it."

"You saw . . . You knew I could leave?"

He nodded.

"Then why did you leave me there?"

"I was trying to make a point. I didn't wish you harmed; I just wanted you married."

"To Jaimie."

"Who else should have Barra and Kisimul but a MacNeil? Your father's dearest wish was that you marry Jaimie and keep the lands and castle in the clan."

"He never mentioned that to me."

"Why do you think he invited Jaimie to stay at Kisimul so often? He knew you too well, better than I did, and thought to tempt you into it. My way wasn't as subtle and it failed. As soon as I told you that you were to marry Jaimie, you planted your feet in the dirt like a mule and refused to budge. You never reminded me more of your mother than at that moment."

Michael watched as Jane pressed a hand to her forehead. "Father . . . he really wished me to marry Jaimie? I've always thought you were making that up, trying to trick me into accepting him."

David made a disgusted noise. "Why would I care what you thought? The things Jaimie and I've had to do to cover your actions—"

"No one said you had to burn Kisimul!"

Michael sat up straighter.

David's expression darkened. "The majority of it's made of rock. It can be rebuilt."

"It's over seven *hundred* years old and you toppled it!"

He threw his hand up. "Kisimul was a regrettable decision, but it served. People accepted that you'd died in a fire in the castle you were born in. But now, after all of that, you *dare* come traipsing back. I worked for years to quell rumors about your disappearance. *Years.* People are just now starting to accept Jaimie and Elspeth and then you show up."

"Perhaps they'd accept them more if you weren't bleeding the estate dry."

Michael noted how David paused at that. "You're talking about the licenses," David said.

"What else?" she spat back. "You may wish to pretend that all you do is for the good of the clan, but I know better. Jaimie said he'd signed them over to you. He didn't realize that's where the revenues came from, did he?"

"The revenues are being spent wisely, as they should be. Jaimie's too weak to handle the finances. It's much better to leave them with me. Meanwhile, you have a responsibility to your family name—"

"Don't you *dare* speak to me about my family name!" She stepped forward, anger tight in her entire body. "If my father had known you'd lock me away and try to force me to wed your son, and then steal the funds from the licenses, he would have run you through with his sword, and you know it."

His lips thinned. "Don't press your luck, niece. I had every right to that castle. It should have been mine—"

"My father left it to me."

"He was foolish. To you, a mere female. What about me? The next male issue in line?" His mouth was etched in white. "That castle should have been mine, and yet my beloved cousin—one I dared call 'brother'—made certain it never came my way."

"He feared you'd bleed it dry the way you did the rest of your inheritance."

"What I might or might not have done is of no consequence. The castle and lands should have been mine, damn it." His left hand opened and closed in a fist, his eyes blazing. It was obvious he was struggling to hold his temper, and after a moment, he managed to say in a more normal tone, "But that's all well and good, for I got what I wished for in the end."

"No, you didn't. Jaimie got the lands and the title. All you got were the funds."

David shrugged. "However it is, it's mine and no one will question it . . . until now. Your return is most unfortunate." His black eyes locked on Jane. "Why are you here, Jennet? What do you *really* want?"

Jane clenched her fist, her body trembling with anger. This man—this one man—had caused so much pain in her life. Not just to her, but to Jaimie, and Elspeth, and to all of the people on Barra who suffered because the island's revenues were stripped away and not reinvested in making the lives of the people better by drilling more wells and cutting a better road or helping with their farming. "You've let the people of this island down by stealing their money. That's not what a laird does."

"You don't know what a real laird does. Your father was a fool to give away so much when he—and you—could have been living in far more comfort."

"You don't deserve to speak of my father."

"Perhaps not." David's eyes narrowed. "I have no idea why you came back, but it's time you left."

"Once I and my employer find what we're looking for, I'll happily leave."

"And what *are* you looking for?"

"We're going to the cave on the south shore to see the ancient script on the wall there."

"Why?"

"Because he believes it's—"

A great noise arose as Michael came down the stairs. He was carrying his boots, and his neckcloth was unknotted as if he'd dressed in great haste. "Mrs. Macpherson had better have a large breakfast ready for I could eat a h—" He paused at the bottom step, his gaze finding David. "Oh. We have a visitor. Jane, you didn't tell me."

"Mr. Hurst, this is Lord David MacNeil. He's the laird's father."

David bowed. "I live on Vatersay, an island south of here. I come and visit when I'm needed."

"That's a matter of opinion," she said under her breath before she gestured to Michael. "Mr. Hurst is an explorer. You might have read of his exploits through his serial in *The Morning Post*?"

David's gaze sharpened. "Ah! *That* Michael Hurst. The one who found the gold sarcophagus?"

"Actually, I've found several." Michael waved a hand, as if finding a sarcophagus was as common as finding a copper penny. "Five, I think. Is that right, Jane?"

"Actually, it's seven."

David's brows rose. "Seven? Really?" Doubt hung heavily in both words. "I'm surprised you didn't write about those in your serial."

Michael just shrugged. "It would be boring if I wrote about each and every sarcophagus I happened to trip over. By the way, do you mind . . ." Michael pointed at the boots he still held. "I just rolled out of bed and came in search of nourishment. I didn't realize we had company."

"Of course." David watched as Michael put on his boots. "Having found so many sarcophaguses—"

"Sarcophagi," Jane and Michael corrected simultaneously.

"Yes, sarcophagi, then. You must be fabulously wealthy."

Jane's smile faded. "He only sells the common finds, and then keeps the artifacts that require further study. Most of his finds are consigned to various museums."

David's interest remained locked on Michael. "So there is some such artifact here, on Barra, then?"

Michael shrugged. "I'm sure there are several."

"Valuable ones?"

"Perhaps. The island has been inhabited for centuries, so it's quite possible that you might find any number of artifacts. The older ones are usually made of less precious metals, though you do occasionally find something valuable."

"Interesting," David said.

"Yes, but I doubt that any of them are a sarcophagus." Michael looked regretful. "Those are only found scattered among the sands of Egypt."

David inclined his head. "Of course. I hope you don't mind, but I should be going. I just came to visit Jennet—"

"Jane Smythe-Haughton," Jane corrected.

There was an infinitesimal pause and then David inclined his head. "Miss Smythe-Haughton. Of course. I just came to welcome her to the island. And you, too, Mr. Hurst."

"Very pleasant of you." Michael finished putting on his boots. "It's a lovely island. I was just telling Jane that we should stay an extra week, just to enjoy the sunshine that's finally arrived."

David's lips thinned, but he bowed and picked up his hat and turned toward the door.

He was almost there when Michael called out, "Lord MacNeil?"

David turned on his heel. "Yes?"

Michael walked to the corner of the room and picked up a malacca cane. "I believe this is yours. It's certainly not mine, and I'm the only one tall enough to use it other than you."

David took the cane, though he regarded it with distaste. "I've lately suffered the ill effects of gout, and my physician thinks the cane will help, though I find it nothing more than an inconvenience."

"I'm sorry to hear that. This dreadful climate must be difficult on such a condition."

"So it is. Thank you for returning the cane." David inclined his head. "Good day, sir."

With that, he took himself off. Michael waited until David's horse could be heard trotting smartly across the cobblestones before he turned to Jane. "What in the name of Ra was that?"

"That was David MacNeil."

"I understood that," Michael said dryly. "Who is he in relationship to you— No, wait. Who is he in relationship to Jennet MacNeil?"

"I used to call him 'uncle,' though he's just a distant cousin. He and my father were raised together when David's parents died of the ague."

Jane wished that Michael wasn't standing quite so close. Last night, she'd kissed his collarbone, and she found herself reliving the moment in warm detail.

"You seemed angry at him."

"It was his decision to burn down Kisimul."

"It was burned down *on purpose?*"

"Yes."

"Bloody hell, but why?"

"To kill me." At his incredulous look, she threw up a hand. "No, no. Not the real me. Jennet."

"By Ra, that's barbarous. Parts of that edifice were possibly twelfth-century!" Michael looked as horrified as she felt. "I begin to dislike this Jennet. Trouble seems to follow her wherever she goes."

"I feel much the same way." She forced a smile. "I think I saw Ammon cross the courtyard a while ago. Your coffee should be ready. I'll let him know you're up."

"Please do." Michael turned to the table by the window and took his seat. "While you're there, ask Mrs. Macpherson to bring back those eggs. I'm famished."

Jane had taken a few steps toward the back door, but at that, she paused.

Michael frowned. "Yes?"

"You said to have Mrs. Macpherson bring *back* the eggs." She turned to face him. "You overheard the entire conversation I had with David."

"If you wouldn't be so secretive, I wouldn't be forced to such stratagems."

"Secretive?"

"Oh, yes, *Jennet.*"

She crossed her arms. "Do you or do you not wish for your eggs and coffee?"

"Yes, please." When she didn't move, he sighed. "Yes, please, *Jane*."

"Fine." She turned back toward the door.

"Still," he added, watching her carefully, "I can't help but wonder what Jennet did to deserve to be burned alive in a fire. I suppose I could ask her uncle. I daresay he might have an interesting answer." He tapped his fingers on the tabletop and added in a musing tone, "And if Uncle David didn't have an answer, I wonder if perhaps this Jaimie MacNeil might. Or the lovely Lady MacDonald, who let drop several interesting tidbits just yesterday. Come to think of it, I daresay there are many people on this island who might know the tragic, though fictionalized, story of Jennet MacNeil."

She stood still, her hands fisted at her sides. Finally she turned and glared at him as if he had three heads. "You're not going to stop until I tell you everything, are you?"

"Jane, either you tell me now or you can tell me later, but I *will* find out what happened on this island. And you know that I'm not the type to quit until a job's done." He grinned wickedly. "I believe I proved myself on that point last night."

She flushed and marched to the table and took a seat, all prim business. "It's time. What do you want to know?"

Michael decided he liked both Janes, the wild one in his bed last night, and the prim one who sat with her feet flat on the floor and her hands folded in her lap. "Why have you been hiding your past? And don't say it's because I never asked, because since I realized you'd hidden things, I *have* asked and you *still* won't answer."

"I didn't tell you because I knew that the only way Jaimie would be successful in accepting leadership of Barra was with me gone. People's loyalties run deep."

"As do yours."

Her brow creased, a flicker of sadness in her gaze. "Do they? I feel that I've let Barra down." She adjusted her spectacles more firmly on her nose. "Which is why I'm not leaving until I've settled some things."

"That's noble of you."

"No, it's not. It's necessary. Barra belongs to my family, and this island—Michael, it involves real people, too. This is not some amusing historical mystery you can just poke into and then leave."

"That's not very flattering."

"I don't mean to be judgmental, but ever since we came here, I've realized that what we do—arrive in another country, dig in their past, analyze and judge things—can be impersonal. I don't want that for Barra. This was my life, my family, my island. Whatever has been done, and whatever needs to be done, has to be done by me."

"You have your life cut into little slices, don't you, Jane? And you don't allow them to touch." When she didn't answer, he sighed. "If you feel so strongly, then why did you decide to leave Barra? Was it because of your uncle?"

"I've wanted to leave since I was a child and my father read *Don Quixote* to me. I wanted to wander about the world, ride my mule, joust at windmills, and have adventures." She smiled, both wistful and sad. "When you grow up in a tiny thimble, a dinner plate can seem like an ocean. I wanted to swim in that ocean."

Michael rubbed his chin, considering her words. "I know that feeling."

She put up a hand, and he said roughly, "No, no. I understand. When I was a child, I was ill. And not a little, but all of the time, sometimes for months on end, confined to my bed, unable to rise."

"What was wrong?"

"Weak lungs, or so the doctor said."

"But . . . you're always so healthy."

"I outgrew the illness, whatever it was. When I turned seventeen, I began to get taller, and as I did so, the illness left. I've told you about where I grew up in a big, rambling vicarage with my brothers and sisters. Or it would seem big unless you'd been confined— sentenced—to live within it and never leave."

"You were trapped, too."

"In a place I loved. But not a place I wished to live."

She leaned back in her chair. "You *do* understand."

"Yes. A prison is still a prison, even if it's made of velvet."

She nodded. "I was torn. I loved Barra, but I desperately wished to see the world. To travel. To taste other lives and other places. My father knew that, too. He'd saved for a year to send me to Greece, and had asked my aunt Mary to take me, but then he had his accident and then Mary died a few weeks later." Jane was silent a moment. "I think he thought that trip might cure my wanderlust, but it would have just fanned the flames."

"Once you're bitten, it's difficult to become unbitten. How did David come into this?"

"After Father died, I discovered that he'd left me the lands and title, which infuriated David. It didn't make me happy, either, for it seemed like a death sentence." She waved a hand. "I know, I know. That's a huge overstatement, but I was a youth at the time and yearning to escape. The inheritance felt like a burden. I wouldn't see it that way now, of course, but then . . ." She looked out the window where the sun beamed upon the green grass and the blue, blue sea. "I didn't understand what he gave me."

"When we are children, we act as children."

"Aye. Fortunately for me, as much as I didn't want to rule over Barra, Jaimie did."

"Jaimie is David's son?"

"David's only child, yes." She sent Michael a sharp glance. "You needn't think that Jaimie is like David, for he's not. Jaimie was practically raised here because his mother had died and Father always had a fondness for him. Jaimie and Lindsee and I grew up together."

"Ah. I see."

"Besides, Jaimie didn't just want the title and lands, he *needed* them."

"Why?"

"He wished to marry someone who was interested only in those things. She's with him still. I know because I went to see him. He built a huge manor house on the north edge of the isle."

"Ah, thus the visit from your uncle today."

"I don't think Jaimie told his father I'd been there, but Elspeth, Jaimie's wife, might have." She looked thoughtful for a moment before she gave a wistful sigh. "Jaimie still loves her, you know. After all of these years . . ."

"My parents have been together more than fifty years," Michael said. "People fall in love with each other all of the time."

"Not Jaimie. He loves Elspeth, and he paid the price she demanded, and while she became his wife, it doesn't look as if she's ever loved him. I don't think he realized that the one didn't come with the other." Sadness crossed her face. "When I left this isle, I thought I'd left things in place for it to thrive, for the people—and Jaimie, too—to have good, happy lives. Now I'm not so sure that I didn't just make everyone's life worse. Apparently, it's not as easy to sign away your title and lands as I'd thought, and there are some legal issues involved. But even if the documents had been enough, the fact that I immediately left made it look as if Jaimie had been involved in some sort of trickery. People began to talk. They suspected the worst."

"They thought he'd had you murdered?"

She nodded. "Uncle David returned just as things were getting ugly. He saw what was happening and announced that I was still at Kisimul but had smallpox. That kept everyone away. Then he staged the fire and burned down the castle. I don't agree with sacrificing the castle, but they could see no other way."

"Plus, if there's no roof on it, they don't have to pay rents to the Crown."

She grimaced. "I hadn't thought of that, but you're right. So Kisimul was sacrificed, and my death mourned, which stilled the rumors enough so that no one challenged Jaimie as the legitimate laird."

"Which thrilled your uncle, who has been lining his pockets ever since."

"Yes." She placed her hands flat upon the table. "And now you know all."

His gaze sought hers. She looked worn, as if just by telling the tale, it had drained her. "So now what?"

"So now I must find a way to solve the problems on Barra so that when I next leave, my conscience will be clear."

"You gave up that responsibility once. Why take it on again?"

She smiled, her brown eyes warm. "You wouldn't leave Wythburn Vicarage and its inhabitants in disarray, would you?"

She had him there. "No, I wouldn't. Worse, I couldn't."

"Exactly." She stood, seeming to gather strength as she did so. "We've two things to accomplish today. First, breakfast."

"And then the cave."

"Yes. We'll wait for low tide, face that treacherous path once again, and see what clue was left there."

He nodded. "Fine."

"Good. We're settled, then. While you're eating breakfast, I may ride down the road a bit and see if it's dried out. If it's very wet, we may wish to leave earlier and give ourselves extra time to climb down the path."

"Very well." He watched as she turned from the table.

"Jane?"

She paused. "Yes?" Her eyes were fixed on him, framed by her spectacles and as dark and mysterious as the forest floor.

"About last night. It was—" He lifted a hand and then dropped it back on his knee. "I couldn't have asked for a more—" He gestured toward her. "I was completely—" *Damn it, I'm as tongue-tied as a marble tomb marker.*

Her brows lowered and she leaned forward the tiniest bit. "You were completely what?"

He knew what he wanted to say—that she'd astounded him and driven him mad and how even now his cock was stirring just because he was sitting close to her and how he wanted to carry her back to bed right this second and show her all of the things he was feeling but couldn't say. Instead, he was left saying in a rather deflated tone, "It was very . . . satisfying."

"Satisfying," she repeated in a flat tone. "How lovely."

"Jane, I—" He spread his hands. "It was more than that."

She cocked an eyebrow and crossed her arms over her chest. "Yes?"

He had the impression he was being given one chance—and only one—to right things.

Well, he would right things. This was his opportunity to let her know that their passion had been more than a mere tumble. Years of simply saying what he thought without counting the cost to others stood between him and her smile, if he could only find the words. "Jane, last night was"—he raked a hand through his hair—"nice."

Her expression could only be described as crestfallen.

"No," he hurried to say. "Don't look like that! I didn't mean 'nice.' In fact, it wasn't nice at all."

Her brows lowered. "No?"

"No. I mean, yes! Yes, it was nice, but it was also very, very—" He tried with all of his might to grasp a word that would encompass that heart-pounding exertion that even now was making his balls hum, but to his horror, he heard himself say once again, "—nice. But really, really, *really* nice."

She spun on her heel. "I'll be back at nine. Be ready to ride."

Damn it, I must find the words! Why are the spoken ones so hard to come by? If I were writing a treatise on Amenhotep, this wouldn't be so difficult. He stood. "Jane, wait. I should have said—"

The door slammed behind her.

CHAPTER 15

From the diary of Michael Hurst:

While I was busy rehearsing ways to get out of the verbal hole I dug for myself this morning, Jane went to see about the state of the roads. That was an hour ago and she hasn't yet returned.

If she's not back in ten minutes, I'm taking Ramses and finding her and to hell with trying to say the right thing. This time I'll just show her.

*J*ane pulled Alexandria to a halt and looked up the road at the house that sat basking in the sunshine upon a bluff overlooking the sea. "Heavens," she said aloud, the word whipped away by the wind. She'd thought Eoligary House was impressive, but it lacked the elegance of Lindsee's manor.

Good God. It's a wonder Barra doesn't sink into the sea with two such edifices weighing her down. Jane glanced back down the road she'd just traveled. *Should I have come?* But then she remembered Michael's halting words and she turned Alexandria back down the drive and rode toward the house.

Last night had changed things for both her and Michael. His halting profession of—what had that been? Mere *like?* He'd kept repeating the word as if he were drowning and that was the only word that offered to support his weight upon a troubled sea.

Her cheeks burned at the memory, for it had been more than a little embarrassing to hear a moment she'd thought of as "exquisite" described in such a lackluster fashion.

Of course, she hadn't expected a protestation of love, but she'd thought she'd hear something more than a mere "nice." Now she was confused. She felt something far more than "nice" for Michael Hurst. Her feelings were simple to describe, and were as large and passionate as the man himself. But she didn't dare say those words aloud, not to him, nor to herself, especially after his weak declaration, *if* one could even call it that.

Her heart heavy, she reached the portico of the house and a footman appeared almost instantly, taking the horse's bridle. Jane unhooked her knee from the pommel and allowed another footman to assist her to the ground.

Murmuring her thanks, she looked at the bold house and said under her breath, "Lindsee, you did well."

Not that Jane was surprised. Lindsee had always been focused on having a rosy future, which as a child seemed to involve nothing more than sitting on a large pillow while being fed berries and jam biscuits even during the coldest months of the year.

But as Lindsee grew older, her vision of living well had expanded to include a carriage and six, a dozen servants, including a personal maid (which part Jane was expected to play until the real thing could be arranged), and a large house, all provided by a dashing man of means who would be passionately and completely in love with her.

Lindsee had certainly gotten the house. It was three stories high, with large, wide windows that stared out to the sea. A portico held by graceful columns rose before the huge mahogany doors, encircled by shallow marble steps.

It was, in a word, elegant. It was also rather surprising rising up here, in the same spot that had once held the more modest house Lindsee and her father had once made their home. Jane walked to the door, where a dour-faced butler, obviously ill at ease in his finery, met Jane and then led her into a lovely foyer filled with gilded furnishings and rose-colored rugs. Jane stared about her in bemusement that was only broken when Lindsee, coming down the wide staircase, gave a squeal and ran forward to envelop Jane in a perfumed hug.

Jane stepped back and eyed her friend's gown, a confection of yellow lace and satin. "Did I interrupt something? You look as if you're going to a ball."

Lindsee made a face. "Och, no. If I don't wear a ball gown now and then simply because I can, I'd never wear one." She linked arms with Jane. "I'm so glad you're here. I was hoping you'd come to catch up."

"Yes, well, I have an ulterior motive; Lindsee, I need some advice."

"Oh? About what?"

"Men."

Lindsee nodded wisely and patted Jane's hand. "Then come and have some tea. I can't promise to have any answers, for men are as foolish as they're braw, but I can at least have a good listen."

Moments later, they were perched upon a settee in a rose-and-gold-striped sitting room, sipping tea, the scent of bergamot and mint tickling Jane's nose.

She admired the gold edging on her cup and saucer before she took a sip. "I must say, you've certainly done well for yourself."

Lindsee looked about her with a contented smile. "I do love Dunganon."

"That's a lovely name for a house." She accepted the scone Lindsee handed her. "I don't recall a MacDonald who lived upon Barra."

"That's because he didn't. Ian MacDonald lived in Oban and only came to Barra on his way to Ireland." Lindsee smiled over her cup of tea. "He saw me at the dock in Castlebay and was instantly smitten. I was the same, for he was so tall and elegant."

"And wealthy," Jane added.

"He wore *three* rings and his ship was only one of an entire *fleet* and he owned them *all*."

"I can see that it was love at first sight."

"I loved his wealth immediately," Lindsee agreed without a single flicker of remorse. Her expression softened. "It wasn't until we were married that I fell in love with the man. And oh, I loved him so."

Jane tamped down a very unworthy flicker of envy. "I'm glad you found him."

"As am I. The choices for a husband on Barra are slim. But MacDonald was a very good husband." Lindsee looked about the house and smiled. "He built Dunganon for me. He'd always say, 'My dear, you deserve the best, and the best you shall have.'" She chuckled.

"Which is not always true, but it was nice that he thought so." She looked down at her teacup and her eyes grew wet as she said in a wistful tone, "I miss him still."

Jane patted Lindsee's hand. "I'm sorry I mentioned him."

"No, no. 'Tis good to remember." Lindsee put down her teacup and removed a lace-edged kerchief from a pocket in her gown and began dabbing at her eyes. "Of course, MacDonald spent far too much on the house, though he left me with plenty for the upkeep and gowns and whatnot. Even in death, he's too good to me."

"You found what you'd always wanted."

"As did you. You were forever talking of having adventures. I truly thought I'd never again see you once you left Barra. You could have knocked me over with a feather when I realized it was you after all."

"From what my uncle has said, no one was supposed to know I was alive. I'm surprised you knew I wasn't burned along with the castle."

"Aye, but Jaimie is not one to keep a secret."

"True," Jane said. "I love the man, for he is like a brother to me, but—" She shook her head.

"It's hard to believe his father can be so masculine and in charge, and then Jaimie so weak."

Jane frowned. "You sound as if you admire David."

"I respect him. That's all I can say."

Jane supposed that was fair. "He's definitely a strong sort of man."

"In some ways, he reminds me of your Mr. Hurst."

"Of Hurst? How so?"

"They're both single-minded when they decide they want something and they're set in their ways."

"Hurst is definitely set in his ways." She ran her finger around the edge of her teacup before setting it on the table before them. "He's every bit as stubborn as David, too. Hurst and I came to Barra to find a relic. It's a family heirloom of sorts. There's a clue to its whereabouts in the cave."

Lindsee made a face. "That's a horrible place. I can't believe I allowed you and Jaimie to talk me into going into it."

"We got out fine."

"Yes, but the boat almost washed away. If that had happened—" She shook her head. "It's too dangerous to think about."

"Is the boat still where it used to be?"

"There are two of them now. The men who harvest the kelp use them to visit the cove. Surely you're not going back into that cave."

"We have to. Do you remember the carvings we found?"

"Barely."

"They're the clue we're looking for."

"You're certain that relic is on Barra?"

"We have a map. It's an odd map and you have to open three onyx boxes and lock them together to see it, but it's definitely of Barra."

"Who would have ever thought Barra would hold treasure?" Lindsee took a small bite of a scone. "You mentioned before that this relic was supposedly magic?"

"There are rumors surrounding this amulet. Some of the older records indicate there was something . . . odd about it. Queen Elizabeth grew so fearful of it that she refused to be alone in a room with it. She eventually gifted the amulet to an unsuspecting foreign dignitary to get it out of the country."

"What sort of magic does the amulet hold?"

"Hurst thinks that people believe the amulet could tell the future of the person who holds it."

Lindsee's eyes widened. "Do you think that?"

"I don't believe in things I can't see."

"You can't see love." Lindsee poured more tea in their cups. "And I'm very certain it exists." She paused, looking thoughtful. "It would be a wonderful thing to see one's future. Then you'd know your decisions were right."

"Or wrong."

"Very true. Speaking of men, you said you needed some advice. I take it you're talking about Mr. Hurst." Lindsee picked up her cup, her brown eyes twinkling. "He's quite handsome."

"He's socially unacceptable. He says what he thinks when you don't want him to, and then when you do, he can't make a complete sentence."

"He sounds like a man."

"A stupid man."

"Don't be redundant, dear."

Jane laughed. "Are all men that way?"

"No, but like all women, every man has his own way of telling you what he wants you to know. Some men say it aloud, some men act it, and some men—a very few— are able to do both."

"Hurst can do neither." Although she supposed his lovemaking meant something. *It means he's physically attracted to me, but seeing the dearth of woman on Barra, that's not a huge compliment.*

"He sounds like a difficult man to get to know. How long have you worked for him?"

"Four years."

"And during that time, you've developed feelings for him?"

Jane hesitated, and then nodded.

"And he for you?"

Jane put down her cup, which rattled in the saucer. "Our relationship is not so progressed as you seem to assume. We've only recently— And that just caused more confusion, which—" Jane sighed. "Which is why I'm here. I am in such a quandary."

"I don't know why. It seems as if things are moving along nicely."

"I don't want them to move along."

Lindsee's eyes widened. "No?"

"No." She thought about it for a moment. "I mean, I

wouldn't be adverse to it, but then when it ended— No. I don't wish for it to progress."

"It sounds as if Hurst isn't the only one who isn't very good at expressing himself."

Jane frowned. "Ouch."

"That's always been a difficult thing for you."

"That's not true. I've always known what I wanted."

"You've always known that you wanted to travel. But I never heard you express a desire beyond that." Lindsee took a thoughtful sip of her tea, her gaze resting on her cup. She smiled. "Jane, do you remember all of the tea parties we had when we were children?"

"We had hundreds of them. You'd wear that big hat of my mother's and play like you were the lady of the land. I got rather tired of being your upstairs maid."

Lindsee giggled. "To be honest, you were not a very good maid."

"I didn't like brushing hair," Jane said, curling her nose. "I still don't."

"Not even your own?"

"*Especially* not my own. I do it, of course. But it always tangles and—" She caught Lindsee's interested look and threw up a hand. "Oh, no! Don't even think it!"

Lindsee's gaze narrowed as she looked at Jane. "You'd look lovely with a French knot in the back and curls—"

"No, thank you. I'll do my own hair, if you don't mind."

"Fine, though I don't know why you won't at least try it. You might like it, and that could help with—you know, your problem with Hurst."

Jane set her cup onto the saucer so hard that it rattled. "I don't have a *problem* with Hurst."

"Then why are you here?"

"I just wished for some advice."

"Jane, you're almost thirty and not married." Lindsee patted Jane's hand. "I'd call that a problem."

"Well, it's not. I like being free and unfettered." Or so she'd thought until she'd arrived on Barra with Michael just a few days ago. "Or I think I do. It's not bad, being unmarried. I rather enjoy parts of it, although there are times when—" She frowned. "By Ra, you're right. I don't know what I want anymore."

"Maybe you're changing. There comes a time between every decision where you have your feet in both the past and the future." Lindsee pursed her lips. "This is where that amulet of yours could come in handy; it would let you know what you chose and how it ended up."

"I'm certain that amulet has no more powers than this teacup. But I see your point. Maybe I need to make some decisions before I worry about Hurst."

"It might help you make better decisions if you knew what you wanted. I'm still not certain where your difficulty is; you said he was attractive. Why not allow a relationship to develop?"

"Lindsee, when I left Barra, I took only the few items left to me by my mother. Once those were gone, I had to find work, which I did. Now I make my own way in the world. If I don't work, I don't eat. Getting involved with Hurst means that not only our relationship would change, but also my employment. I know from experience that you can't have them both."

"In all of the years since you left, I never once thought about how you'd make your way, but perhaps I should have." Lindsee looked around at the opulent room where they sat before she turned her dark gaze back to Jane. "I went from my father's house to this one. I can't imagine not living under the protection of a man."

"You're doing it now."

Lindsee flushed. "I won't be alone forever."

"So you'll leave Barra?"

"Never. I'll simply find another husband and bring him here."

"Lindsee, why don't you sell the house and leave?"

"But where would I live?"

"Anywhere you wanted. You could take the funds from the sale of this house, travel a bit, see the world and—"

Lindsee chuckled. "Och, Jennet, 'tis like old times after all. Me, wanting to just drink my tea and enjoy my gown, while you talk of travels afar."

Jane had to laugh. "You're right. It is like old times. I always wanted more for you than Barra."

"And I always wanted you to find peace somewhere, whether it be on Barra or no." Lindsee set her teacup on the table and grasped one of Jane's hands between her own, which twinkled with rings of all sizes and colors. "Jane, I don't know what to tell you about Hurst or your future. I can see that you have bigger concerns than simply grasping the happiness of a moment. But don't throw away the happiness of a moment over something as silly as uncertainty. You'd be better off remembering the MacNeil motto."

"'*Buaidh no bas*,'" Jane said softly. "'Conquer or die.'" It was difficult to face, but perhaps Lindsee was right. Maybe her concern for her future was preventing her from fully grasping the opportunities that were right before her.

Jane glanced at the clock and stood in a rush. "Oh! I have to go. Hurst will be waiting on me. We're to go to the caves today."

Lindsee arose, too. "Of course. I'll walk to the door with you."

Moments later, Jane turned her horse down the road toward the inn and urged Alexandria into a sharp trot. Both the cave with its treacherous path and Michael Hurst awaited her, and she wasn't certain which made her more nervous.

CHAPTER 16

From the diary of Michael Hurst:

I have collected copies of every known reference to the Hurst Amulet. I have maps showing places it was reported to have been; books that describe it in thorough, though probably erroneous, detail; and I've even seen a portrait of Queen Elizabeth wearing the blasted thing. I'm completely certain I'll recognize it when I see it. I hope.

*N*o one said anything about a boat."

Jane turned a startled glance to Michael. "Yes, I did."

He frowned, vaguely remembering it now. "Well, I had forgotten."

"Oh. I'm sorry." She pointed to the boat at their feet. "There's a boat."

"Thank you," he said as gravely as he could.

"With oars."

"So I see."

"It's made of wood," she continued, her voice as helpful as ever.

He scowled. "If you wanted to make me regret my comment, you've succeeded. You may now be silent."

She flashed him a smile, and they set about moving the boat toward the shore.

"Why is this boat here?"

"There's actually two." She nodded farther down the small cove to where another small boat could be seen peeking out from behind some sea oats.

"Two? Surely not many people go into the cave?"

"They're for the men who collect the kelp. They use

them to check the beds located in this bay to determine when they're ready to harvest."

"Ah." They slipped the boat into the water and climbed in. Michael took the oars and rowed them toward the cave mouth. "Our landlady in Oban seemed to think the kelp industry was faltering. What will people on this island do for income if that fails?"

Her brows lowered. "I don't know. Perhaps half of the island's income is from that one industry. It would be difficult to replace."

They were nearing the mouth of the cave. Jane said, "There's an iron ring set into the face of that large rock. We tie the boat to that ring, but make it long, to account for the tide rising."

He did as she asked, and then she climbed out of the boat and made the short leap to the top of the rock. "Follow me."

Michael followed her and looked off the side of the rock. "It's not that deep here."

"No, but the eddy is treacherous. If you had to swim it, you'd be exhausted before you reached shore."

He nodded, liking this day's adventure better than their last. The sun shone brightly, though the wind was chilled. In addition, the climb down the cliff face hadn't been as difficult this time, as the wind and sun had dried the path, though there'd been plenty of difficult moments.

A small ridge connected the rock with the cave. "It's only usable at low tide," Jane remarked.

He looked up at the cave mouth. "The entire thing is underwater when the tide's high?"

"Most of it. There are a few small ledges that stay dry, but it would be an uncomfortable few hours while you waited for the tide to lower."

"It seems like a very small opening for a cave."

"It's more of a tunnel here, but it opens to a larger cavern farther in."

Jane ducked down and led the way into the cave. "This way." Her voice echoed behind her.

"Will we need a torch?" he asked, following her, his shoulders brushing each side of the small opening.

"The main chamber has some natural lighting. Besides, it's too damp to keep a torch lit."

A big drop of water hit his forehead, as if to agree with her.

She paused before him, a misty shape in the growing darkness. "It's only dark for a short distance. Just put your hands on the cave ceiling, so you can judge the height, and go slowly. I'll keep speaking so you can follow the sound of my voice."

"I'll put one hand on the cave ceiling, but the other one I'm putting here." He placed his hand low on her back.

She stiffened.

"It will be safer," he said. "You know the way."

There was a long silence, and then she said, "Fine. Follow me."

With that, she was off and they walked slowly into the darkness. "What shall I talk about?"

"Tell me about growing up on Barra."

"There's not much to tell, but the tunnel's not that long, so . . . fine. Jaimie and Lindsee and I—"

"Lindsee?"

"Lady MacDonald."

"Ah, yes. I visited with her the other day."

"She needs to leave the island," Jane said sharply. "She's wasting away here, waiting to fall in love. That will never happen on Barra."

"I didn't get the impression that she was wasting away at all."

Jane paused, and Michael almost ran into her. "What do you mean by that?" Her voice cracked sharply in the echoing tunnel.

"I meant that she seemed quite content to be here." He frowned down at the blackness around his feet. "There's water in here."

"We're in a cave that is completely submerged at high tide. Of course there's water."

His lips quirked. "I suppose I should have expected that," he said meekly.

She didn't answer, but he felt the faintest tremor in her back, as if she held in a laugh. "Continue with your story," he said. "You were saying something about you, Jaimie, and Lindsee?"

"Ah, yes. When we were young, we would—" She

went on to tell him how the three of them played their way from one edge of the island to the other, pretending to be knights—Lindsee was always the damsel in distress—as they galloped through moors and rolling hills.

As he walked behind her in the darkness, water dripping overhead, his boots wet and icy, he was aware that only his hand was warm where it rested on the small of her back. Because he could, Michael slid his hand ever lower. Just a quarter of an inch, then another quarter of an inch.

Ah. There. Truly, no woman had ever possessed so fine an ass as Jane. It was a petite ass, made for a man's hands, and yet curved enough to provide one with the enjoyment of—

She stopped again and he quickly slid his hand back in place, just on the outside chance she was about to object. Instead, she said, "I feel a bit of a wind. Do you?"

He did, now that he was no longer concentrating on the curve of her rump. "We're near the cavern?"

"I believe so." She started forward, the cave turning sharply to the left. "Ah! Here it is." Her voice echoed oddly.

He found out why a few seconds later as he exited the cave entrance and found himself standing behind Jane in a large room, more of a cathedral, lit by several large crevices in the ceiling where green vegetation peeked through. The walls glistened with dampness and were streaked with red and green mineral deposits.

In the center was a large pool of fresh ocean water, left from the previous tide. A handful of small crabs and fish flopped about, having been swept in and then abandoned. Around the edge was a ledge similar to the one that he'd just stepped on that was just wide enough for one person to walk. "It's beautiful."

His voice bounced around the cavern and returned, seeming far too loud in his own ears. He glanced up and noted that the sandstone cavern was magnificently arched and decorated with dripping spears of rock that appeared to have been thrust from the ground above.

He eyed the spears overhead uneasily. "Those look dangerous."

"They can be. We'll be cautious and stay to the sides of the room."

"Were those here when you played in this cave as a child?"

"I'm sure they were. I'm equally sure that I didn't pay them the least bit of attention."

"How could you not?"

"Because we were looking for pirate treasure."

"Did you find any?"

"No, but that didn't stop us from being certain it was here." She stepped on a small ledge and looked down at the cavern floor.

He followed. "Where's this clue of yours?"

Jane stripped off her gloves, tucked them into her pocket, and pointed up. Way up.

"That ledge up there?"

"I think so. It was so long ago, but . . ." She bit her lip and regarded the ledge for a moment before she nodded. "That's it." She pursed her lips, which made him want to kiss her. "I'm glad you're here. Have I mentioned the snakes?"

His mouth went dry, all thought of kisses gone in a second. "Snakes? It had to be snakes."

She pushed her spectacles farther back on her nose. "Sometimes they climb in through those openings and nest on the ledges, which is what brought us in here to begin with. We were pretending to be dragon hunters and we chased a grass snake through the grass on the cliff and it disappeared in one of those breaks in the cave ceiling. When we peered into the hole, we could see the snake on a ledge."

"So you realized there was a cave here?"

"When you live on a small island you know every nook and cranny, so we knew about the cave; we just didn't realize how large it was. The cave was forbidden, and we'd obeyed, but now we had a reason not to. Chasing dragons is not for the timid."

"Not if you had to climb that rock wall."

"Which *one* of us must climb today. The clue is etched above that top ledge, right where the snake was hiding."

"Bloody hell." He steeled himself. "Let's get this over with. The tide will be changing soon enough."

She led the way around the small ledge. After a moment, she paused. "Have you noticed anything peculiar?"

"Other than the fact that you have an annoying habit of keeping important information to yourself?"

"I can't be expected to remember every little thing." Her boots scraped on the rocks, the faint sound of dripping water loud over the muted roar of the surf beating on the rocks. Finally, she stopped. "There's a way to reach that ledge here, I think." She reached into her pocket and pulled out a short length of rope.

"What's that for?"

"Climbing." She'd already bunched her skirts in one hand, hiked them above her knees, and then used the short rope to tie her skirts to one side of her leg. Her legs were now revealed all the way to above her knees, her sensible boots tightly laced to her ankles.

He grinned appreciatively. "London society would be scandalized."

"London society isn't climbing a rock wall." She turned toward the wall. "Give me a boost."

"What? No. I'm not letting you climb alone."

"I must reach that ledge and copy what's carved on that wall."

"You'll need a notebook and a pencil of some sort—"

She regarded him with a flat stare.

"You already brought them?"

"In my pocket. Now give me a boost and I'll copy the information."

"Jane, I don't—"

"Snakes."

He found himself looking at the ledge, his stomach tight. "How do you know?" He glanced back at her.

She looked him straight in the eyes. "*Big* snakes. Remember that I saw one once."

"When you were a child."

"They breed, so there are probably more now."

He fisted his hands at his side. "I don't care. It's not safe, and I don't want you to risk it."

"I also know the way better than you. I'm also lighter and will put less strain on the footholds. It would be far safer for me, since I'm familiar with the route and know how to climb much better than you—"

"Bloody hell, all right! All right! Go." He cupped his hands, she placed her foot in them, and he gave her a lift up the wall until she was well on her way. He was glad to see that she seemed to know exactly what she was doing. "My own sisters don't argue as much as you do."

A sweetly uttered "Thank you" drifted back to him.

She climbed with a surety that did little to ease his mind, though her footing choices were sure and her progress steady. Finally, she reached the ledge and awkwardly pulled herself around the outcropping.

He scowled. "Be careful. Those rocks are—"

She cried out.

He was halfway up the ledge before he knew what

he was doing. "Bloody hell!" His voice was harsh in the cold. "Is it a snake?"

"No!" She looked back at him over her shoulder. She was flushed, a merry grin upon her face, her eyes alight.

His heart quickened. He knew that look better than life itself. "You found something."

She nodded, her eyes glowing as she moved to stand on the small outcropping. "I'm going to copy it now."

He retreated back to the bottom of the ledge, watching as she began to scribble in her notebook while trying to balance on the outcropping. "For the love of Ra, hold on to something while you're there."

"I can't hold on and write, too."

"Jane, if you don't hold on to something, I'm going to come up there and—"

"Done." She tucked her notebook and pencil in her pocket and began the climb back down.

He watched her, noting how she easily navigated the climb, only slowing when the distance between handholds was almost too far for her. Finally she was within grasp, and he reached up to lift her the last few feet. With a sense of relief, he set her upon the ledge before him. "No snakes, eh?"

"None." She grinned. A thick tendril of hair had fallen from a pin and was now clinging to her cheek and neck, a smudge decorated her pert nose, while a thick wad of spiderweb clung to her shoulder like an epaulette.

He brushed it off, aware of a stab of lust so clear and strong that it took his breath away.

Meanwhile, Jane had tugged her notebook out of her pocket and was staring at it as if mesmerized. "Hurst?"

"Yes?"

"I know where the amulet is."

He froze, his fingers an inch from her shoulder as he locked gazes with her. "Where?"

"Look at the etching. This is a Celtic cross and these—" She stabbed a dirty finger at a series of runes. "These are Nordic runes."

He took the notebook, fished his spectacles out of his pocket, and looked at her drawings. "Jane, didn't you once tell me that there was a Viking grave on that island in the middle of the loch?"

"Yes, at the foot of MacLeod's Tower." She frowned. "The amulet must be in the grave."

"You said the marker had been stolen?"

"Yes, but the grave is still there. Or it was when I left."

Michael removed his spectacles. "I would wager a golden statue of Anubis that someone hid the amulet in that grave and took the marker to keep it from being found."

"Then it's fortunate that I know where the marker used to be."

He held the notebook out so that the sunlight fell across the paper. "These runes are also the same markings as the ones on the onyx boxes. Bloody hell, they're

Nordic. Why didn't I see that? I was so certain they were from Mesopotamia or Romanic or—hell, anything but Nordic."

"Sometimes we see what we want to see. But this"— she tapped the notebook with her finger—"is the end of it. Michael, in only a few hours, we could be holding the Hurst Amulet." Her voice almost purred with pleasure, and Michael found himself leaning toward her. He couldn't imagine another woman who'd so calmly stand before him, their skirts tied to one side, boots muddied, a streak of slime on one elbow, a smudge of unknown origin on their nose, and speak with such enthusiasm about a Nordic grave.

And yet here she was. She understood the excitement of the find, the importance of each artifact and discovery.

More than that, she managed all of that while being supremely unconscious of her beauty. It had been some days now that he'd realized that his indispensable assistant was just that—beautiful. Oh, not in the traditional, boring sense. No, Jane's beauty was her own. It was made up of her no-nonsense gaze, her soft lips, which were all too quick with a sharp word, and her fascinating, never-ceasing-to-amaze-him mind.

He now knew what was wrong with all of the women he'd once known. None of them had a mind as damnably sexy as Jane's. Oh, some of them had been intelligent, but they'd lacked the sparkle, the genuine love of learning, that shone from every smile she'd ever smiled.

And that smile was flashing now. "I can't believe we found it! We're as close to—"

He kissed her. He hadn't meant to, but her enthusiasm and true appreciation for their find got the better of him, and suddenly, he had to taste her. Had to touch her. Had to share her excitement.

She threw herself into the kiss the second his lips touched hers, pressing her body to his. He slipped an arm about her waist and, leaning against the wall behind him, held her to him.

She moaned, her hands tugging, seeking, trying to find purchase in his coat and shirt. She lifted a leg and hooked it about his.

The movement was so sensual, so primal, that he had to clench his jaw against reacting too quickly. He slid a hand to her hip, then to her leg, bared by the tie she'd used to pull her skirts aside.

Her skin was cool beneath his fingertips as he slid his hand up her calf, to her knee, and then her thigh, where he lifted her higher still. She was now pressed against his straining cock, and he thrust his tongue between her lips, demanding more and receiving it.

Jane couldn't think beyond the incredible warmth that seemed to radiate off Michael. His hand where it rested against her thigh, his mouth that covered hers, even his neck where she was clutching him—all of him warmed her despite the chill of the cave. She leaned against him, rubbing her hips on his and enjoying the deep moan that answered her efforts as she—

He straightened, breaking off the kiss with a suddenness that left her clinging to him. She blinked up at him, unable to think, much less stand.

"Water," he said in a grim voice.

"Wha—" She looked down at her feet. Icy water lapped at her toes. "The tide. We must go!"

"Have we waited too long?"

"No. But there's no time to lose." She yanked the tie from her skirts and tucked it into her pocket, and then took out her gloves. "Follow me."

They left the tunnel much the same way they'd entered, Jane in front while Michael followed, one hand upon her waist. The water in the tunnel was up to their ankles by the time they reached the opening of the cave.

Jane ducked out first, Michael behind her.

She started to cross the small ledge to the rock when she came to an abrupt halt.

Michael frowned. "What is it?"

She pointed to where the boat had been. There, hanging on the brass ring, was a piece of rope, neatly sliced as if by the sharpest of knives.

Jane turned a white face to Michael's. "We're stranded."

CHAPTER 17

From the diary of Michael Hurst:

Sometimes, the more you want something, the further away it seems. When those times come, I put my shoulder to the rock and push harder. The meek may inherit the earth, but only after the bold have died and left it to them.

*M*ichael let out a long string of vivid Egyptian curses.

"Who would do this?" she asked.

"I don't know." He looked grimly out at the crashing waves. "We'd never make it if we tried to swim."

"No. And this walkway will be underwater soon." She frowned. "Someone cut the line on that boat to delay us. They know we now have the final key to finding the amulet, and they're trying to slow us down so they can get to it first."

His jaw tightened, but a wave crashing at his feet made him say, "Forget the damn amulet for now. We've got to return to the cave or we'll be in a great deal of trouble."

He was right. She ducked back into the cave, and they made their way back to the cavern and climbed the low ledge that surrounded the pool.

"What will we do?" Jane asked. "We can't just sit here and wait for the next low tide. We've looked too long for that amulet to just sit meekly by while some fool snatches it from beneath our noses."

"I agree. We must find a way out of here." He began to look around the cave, examining every nook and cranny in reach.

Jane watched him a second, her gaze drifting upward to where the largest break in the ceiling gave a tantalizing glimpse of the blue sky. "We could fit through that opening if we could just get there."

Michael's gaze followed hers. "So how do we get there?"

"We'll have to climb." Her gaze narrowed. "There must be a way . . ."

Michael glanced at the half-filled entrance tunnel, his jaw tightening. "Damn it. We don't have a choice; we have to go up. I hope we can reach that opening. I've no desire to spend the next six hours perched on a cave ledge."

"If we could cross from that ledge to that outcropping there"—she pointed—"then we could reach the opening."

"That's a huge gap, but we can try."

The water swirled faster now, the roar of the rising tide growing louder by the second. The icy claw of the surf was already lapping hungrily at their feet.

"Let's go," Jane said. Since she knew the way, she tied her skirts to one side and climbed, Michael following.

Her boots were soaked through, and her toes numb with cold, so she moved slower than when she'd climbed the first time. Her hands ached with cold, and several times when her wet boots slipped on the rock wall, she banged her knees painfully.

Each time, she felt Michael's warm hand closing over

her elbow, or steadying her with a firm pressure on her back, helping her up, urging her on. She was halfway up when she glanced back and saw the water only a few inches below Michael's feet. Startled, she met Michael's gaze before she glanced at the tunnel opening. It was completely underwater, the water churning furiously as it rushed forward.

Jane ignored her cut and bruised hands and scrambled for all she was worth. Finally, they reached the ledge. The water chased after them, reaching its zenith to swirl menacingly inches below.

Michael eyed their destination, a small outcropping directly beneath the opening.

Jane tried to measure the distance, her stomach clenched as she did so. The ledge was at least ten feet away. She'd never make it in her damp skirts. "It's too far."

He sent her an amused look. "Now's not a good time to decide that."

"It looked closer when we were below, but now that we're here—" She shook her head before she looked up at him. "But you could make it."

"Nonsense. We can both do it; I'm sure of it." His calm blue gaze met hers. "I'll go first."

"It's too dangerous. The water's swirling like a spout, and if I fell, it would drag me down and—"

"That's it. I'm declaring myself King of the Ledge."

She blinked. "What?"

"My first law as king is that all of this nay-saying gibberish must stop."

"Common sense is not gibberish. And if you can declare yourself king, than I can declare myself queen, and *my* first law is that all subjects will heed the commands of their queen and I command you to go on without me."

"Oh, I'm more than willing to name you my queen." He shot her a smiling glance that warmed her icy skin with a flush. "Help me take off my coat. I want to be as unencumbered as possible for this leap."

Grumbling, she did as he bid, and when they were done, he took his spectacles from the pocket, tucked them into his breeches pocket, and then tossed the coat into the water.

"Hurst! That's a perfectly good coat!"

"Yes, and I have a perfectly good life. One of those two things is not replaceable." He inched along the ledge until he stood at the very end.

Before she could say a word, he leapt.

Jane's heart froze as she watched him fly through the air, his long arms stretching forward. He landed short, as she'd known he must, his legs dangling into the water. He instantly began to slide down. The water churned white, as if seething to have him. Jane's heart pounded so loudly she could hear it.

Just as she thought he was lost for certain, he caught the edge of the ledge and clung furiously as the water pulled at his booted feet, striving to break his hold on the rock.

"Hurst, don't let go!" she yelled, encouraging, hoping and praying that he would keep his hold on the small ledge.

After an agonizing moment, he began to claw his way up the outcropping, finally pulling himself upright.

She pressed a hand to her chest, as if that alone could return her aching heart to normal. "You scared me to death!"

He grinned and unknotted his neckcloth. He then wound the long piece of muslin about his wrist and made a large knot in the other end.

"What's that for?"

"I'm going to throw this to you and you'll jump. If you don't make it—"

"I'll pull us both into the water. No. I—I'll jump myself." The words were far braver than she felt. The water swirled and roiled below like a living, breathing animal.

"You won't jump until you've caught the end of my cravat."

"Of course," she murmured, no longer listening to him. She straightened her shoulders, took off her spectacles, and tucked them into her skirt pocket.

"Hold while I tighten this now, and I'll toss it to you."

She said a short prayer, and then with all of her strength launched herself toward the outcropping.

As she flew, her gaze locked with Michael's, a shocked look on his face, his knotted neckcloth in his hands. She didn't reach the ledge but fell down, down, down, right into the icy water, the air leaving her lungs as she sank. She fought the water, pushing her head to the icy surface to gasp for air. But her skirts gulped in the weight of the water and began to pull her down again. *No!* She fought with her already tired legs, her aching chest, her exhausted arms. *I will not give up.*

Something white fluttered above her and then dangled in front of her—*Michael's neckcloth.* She grabbed it, digging her fingers into the knot.

"Hold on, Jane," he called, his voice sure and steady. "Just hold on. *Please.*" Slowly, he began to pull her toward him.

Her skirts resisted, tugging and fighting. She wrapped her right hand more firmly about the knot and let go with her left.

"Jane! Don't let go!"

She pulled her spectacles out of her pocket and held them in her mouth, and then reached for her skirt fastening, fumbling in the cold water, fighting against the current.

The fastening suddenly gave, and her skirts broke free. She popped up from the water like a cork in a pond, and Michael's makeshift rope swung her to the cave wall. She banged a knee, but found a foothold, and then a handhold. Hand over hand, fighting the shivering cold, she climbed to the ledge where Michael stood.

Michael leaned over and grabbed the loose bodice of her chemise, hoisting her up as if she were made of air. He set her on the rock ledge and then wrapped her tightly in his arms, burying his face in her neck.

With a hand that shook like a blancmange, Jane took her spectacles from between her teeth. "Th-that w-was c-cold."

"You little fool! The next time we have to jump a ledge, remove those blasted skirts first."

Her teeth were chattering much too hard to answer, rattling like a bag of bones.

He held her closer and rubbed her firmly, forcing the blood back into her skin and veins. "You're colder than a grave."

She might have been, but he burned with his usual warmth, and she burrowed against him, stealing his heat like a thief. He held her to him and rubbed her long enough to still some of her trembling. "We must get you some warm clothes."

"And s-s-save the am-m-mulet."

"Warm clothes first." Michael looked up at the crevice above their heads, and Jane followed his gaze. Through the crooked rocks, she could see the grayish sky now beckoning them forward.

He looked down at her. "Though it goes against

every inclination I possess, I fear I must release you if we're to escape our predicament."

His voice rumbled through his chest and to hers, calming her despite the fear that shivered through her. "Of course." She was rather proud that her voice trembled only the slightest bit. She rubbed her arms. "Sh-should we take that w-way—" She nodded to their left, where a few prominent handholds were visible.

He released her to look at the route she'd suggested, and she instantly missed his warmth.

"That looks like the best way." He yanked his shirt over his head, revealing his powerful arms and shoulders and flat stomach, and then tossed the shirt to her. "Put that on. It's wet, but it will cover your arms, which is better than nothing."

"You'll b-b-be as c-c-cold as I am and—"

"You can't shiver when you climb or you'll fall." He untied the knot in his neckcloth and made a loop. His gaze met hers, warm and brilliant blue, shining with a glint of humor. "If you recognize this knot I just tied, it's because it's the same one I tied in that blasted starched cravat while we were in London shopping for a sponsor."

"Ah. It d-does look familiar. They s-say Brummel's m-most famous knot was c-called the Waterfall. You should n-name this one."

"Oh, I have. I call it Jane's Bacon Saver." He slipped the loop over her wrist. "That, my love, is so that I can catch you if you should fall."

Already warmed by his shirt, she managed a grin. "I w-won't fall. I refuse to d-die clad only in my chemise and b-boots. When I d-die, I shall b-be wearing silk and l-lace. I'm Q-Q-Queen of the Ledge, remember?"

He chuckled and then folded the long sleeves back from her hands so that they were out of her way. "I shouldn't be surprised to discover that you've planned your life down to the final second."

"What you should b-be hoping is that I haven't p-planned *your* final seconds and that they involve a c-cave with a very c-cold tidal pool."

He cupped her cheek. "If there's one thing I do know, it's that you'd choose a far more spectacular way of doing away with me than a mere cave drowning."

"Tr-true."

His expression turned more somber and he slid his thumb over her cheek. "We've got to get you out of here before the cold overtakes you. Are you ready, sweetheart?"

She nodded, swallowing the lump that seemed to have claimed her throat.

"Good. As soon as I begin to climb, you follow. The cravat isn't long enough to allow you to be far behind." He pressed a kiss to her forehead, his breath warm on her skin as he said, "It's going to be fine, Jane. I promise."

He couldn't make that promise—not really. But his wanting to was enough. She managed a smile. "Let's go!"

He reluctantly released her and began to climb the wall, using the route they'd chosen. They inched their way up the slick rock, their hands grasping at every crack and crevice. Jane's knuckles were bloodied and scraped by the time they were halfway up, her nails torn and broken.

She banged her head into an outcropping of rock once, and gasped. Michael halted immediately, but she swallowed the pain and urged him onward. They kept going, on and on. Just as Jane's tired arms protested that she couldn't go any farther, Michael reached the opening. He grabbed the rocky ledge and pulled himself upward onto the grassy bank.

The cravat tightened and tugged at Jane's wrist, threatening to pull her off balance. She instantly undid the loop and let it go.

Sitting in the blessed sunlight, Michael felt the cravat go slack. "Damn it," he muttered. "Stubborn, intractable, foolhardy—"

Her hand appeared over the edge, and he lunged for it, grasping her wrist and helping her from the crevice.

In his eagerness to get her out of the cave, he overdid the pull and fell backward, Jane falling across him again.

Her head lay on his chest, his hands tight about her wrists.

They'd made it. *She is safe. If she'd been injured—* He couldn't bear to think about that.

He released her wrists and slipped his arms about her. "Are you hurt?"

"No, j-just cold."

He held her tighter, rubbing her vigorously, rewarded when her shivers began to abate.

After what seemed to be a ridiculously short amount of time, Jane rolled away from him and got to her feet. She was a mess, her hair fallen and wet, a leaf stuck in it, smudges on her nose and chin, and bloody scrapes on her knuckles and knees. His shirt hung to her knees, so big it looked more like a sheet with arms. Her boots were so wet that he could see water oozing from the leather.

Jane caught his inspection and grimaced, placing a hand on her hair. "I need a comb."

What she really needs is my lips on hers. "We'll be at the inn soon."

She turned toward the faint path and began to walk, Michael following. "We have a problem, Hurst. Whoever cut the line to our boat had to know we could get free as soon as the tide dropped."

He reached forward to move a wet branch from their path, holding it to one side until Jane passed. "And they are trying to slow us down."

"But *not* stop us or they'd have done something far more dire. That can only mean one thing: they're after the amulet, too, and know enough that they only needed a little time to reach it first." She looked at him over her shoulder, her eyes narrowed. "But if they knew about the amulet, then why didn't this person—whoever he or she is—just get it before we arrived?"

Michael thought it through. "Maybe they didn't know what the clue in the cave meant until we came to Barra."

She came to such an abrupt halt that he almost ran into her. "So when we arrived looking for the amulet, the clue suddenly made sense."

"I think so, yes. I haven't mentioned anything specific about our search to anyone, though."

She grimaced. "I have. I told both Jaimie and Lindsee. They've seen the carvings in the cave, too. But . . . Michael, they would never attempt to steal something. They're not like that. But David . . ." Her eyes widened. "It was David. I know it was. He wants the amulet! He's determined to steal everything of value that he can find on Barra. He said as much the last time we spoke. He thinks that anything found here belongs to him."

Michael considered this. "As much as I hate to say it, he's right about one thing: if we find the amulet on Barra, then technically it may belong to the MacNeils."

She stopped and turned to him. "*I'm* a MacNeil, the highest-ranking one, and *I* say that if we find the amulet, then it will be returned to its original family, the Hursts."

He chuckled. "That's kind of you, princess, but I believe your cousin and uncle might have something to say in that matter."

"Leave them to me. I won't let David steal the Hurst Amulet—not when you've searched for it for so long."

"David might not consider it stealing; the amulet is an artifact, and it's been hidden on Barra for centuries. Though I think of it as belonging to my family, someone could challenge it."

"It's the *Hurst* Amulet," she replied in an implacable tone. They reached the horses and she added, "We must hurry to that grave. There's a chance we can catch David red-handed."

"Not if he went directly there after cutting our boat loose."

"But he thinks we're stuck in the cave for several more hours, so in his mind, there's no urgency."

"Amulet or not, we're going to stop by the inn and get you into some dry clothing. I'll not have you catch your death of the ague."

"We don't have time to—"

"It's on the way. Besides, you'd cause a scandal traveling like that." Before she could protest, he added, "Meanwhile, you'll ride in front of me. You won't be as conspicuous as you would be on your own horse." He untied the horses, swung onto Ramses, and tied Alexandria's reins to the back of his saddle.

Then he held down a hand to Jane. "Hurry, Smythe. We've an amulet to find."

She slipped her hand into his, and soon they were galloping to the inn.

CHAPTER 18

From the diary of Michael Hurst:

My sister Triona once asked why I pursued the amulet so single-mindedly, for its value isn't one-tenth of the treasures I normally find in my travels. It's really quite simple: the amulet was stolen from our family. I intend to rectify that wrong by returning it.

Everything and everyone belongs somewhere, and the world is a better place when things are as—and where—they should be.

*A*mmon was standing in front of the inn when they arrived, a saddled horse ready. On seeing them, the servant hurried forward, leading the horse. "Sir! Miss Jane! I—" He saw Jane's attire and skidded to a halt, then quickly turned his back, his ears red.

"We had an accident," Michael said briskly, helping Jane down from the horse before he dismounted. "We were stuck in a cave and Miss Smythe-Haughton's skirts nearly drowned her."

"I'm glad Miss Jane is well. There have been some incidents here, too. I was coming to fetch you."

"What happened?"

"Someone stole the onyx boxes."

Jane, who was hurrying inside, paused. "When?"

"A half hour ago, Mrs. Macpherson went to your bedchambers to put fresh water in the wash pitchers and she found your things strewn about. She came to find me, most upset. I went to set the rooms back in order and I noticed that the boxes were gone."

Jane's eyes blazed, and she turned to Michael. "I will only be a moment."

He gave her a brief nod. "I'm right behind you. I'm just going to find a dry shirt and coat." He turned to Ammon. "Keep your horse. You're coming with us."

"Yes, sir. I shall walk the horses while you change."

"Thank you. We'll need the excavation supplies, a shovel, and the like."

"Yes, sir."

"And ready the pistols."

The servant touched his waist, a smile on his dark face. "They're already loaded."

Michael nodded and went to change.

The boat churned on the loch's blue waters before it landed on the island with a thud, the shadow of MacLeod's Tower blocking the sun for a moment.

Jane gathered her skirts, hopped out, and then grabbed the rope and looped it over a nearby stump.

Michael climbed out and looked back at the Barra shore where Ammon waited with the horses. The servant lifted his arm in acknowledgment.

By the time Michael turned around, Jane was already searching the ground around the bottom of the tower.

Michael joined her. "What are we looking for?"

"It's not quite a pile of rocks."

"'Not quite'? What does *that* mean?"

She gave him a fleeting smile. "It means that there are rocks, but over time, grass has grown over them."

"Ah. We're looking for a mound."

"Exactly, but a knobby one, since the rocks are roughly placed. It's here somewhere, but I don't remember which side of the tower it was on."

"It's a small island; we'll find it."

Moments later, pausing in his search, Michael looked up at the tower. It appeared older than Kisimul and was a different sort of fortification. It wasn't meant to be inhabited but was a watchtower where a guard or two would reside, keeping an eye toward the surrounding countryside, and then give an alarm if intruders came. As such, the tower was narrow, though tall, and consisted of three small rooms stacked one upon the other. "This must have been built to fight off the Vikings."

Jane followed his gaze, the wind stirring her skirts and carrying the faint scent of lavender as it tugged at her freshly pinned hair. Except for a few scrapes on her knuckles, she looked none the worse for wear. "The people of Barra made a valiant effort to resist the Vikings, but they were badly outnumbered and outweaponed. However, do note that the runes we found in the cave were carved alongside a cross. Though the Vikings conquered Barra on the field, the island charmed them, and they adopted many of Barra's ways, including her religion."

"So it became a blending."

"Yes, though at a great cost. Many lives were lost, for the Vikings didn't take the Hebrides one at a time, but rather swooped in with a huge number of ships and warriors and stormed the entire string of islands at once. Thus no one could get provisions or assistance from another isle and some communities had to choose between being starved out of existence or capitulating."

He placed his hand upon the sturdy tower and looked about the small island. "When I first saw this tower, I thought this an odd place for it, far from the shore, but it's actually in the perfect location. It's high enough that a watch stationed on the top floor could see every side of the isle and light a fire to indicate an attack well before any foreign ships could dock."

"It's also hidden. No one would think to look for a tower such as this in the center of the land and not upon the coast." Pride warmed her voice. "Barra's people are very resourceful."

"So I've noticed. There's a—" His gaze locked on an unusual shape to the ground just past Jane. "Is that the grave?" The mound wasn't by the tower at all but to one corner of the island partially hidden by tall grasses.

"That's it!" Her voice rose in excitement as she hurried toward it. "I thought it was beside the tower, but then I was very young when I used to play here."

"You were close enough." He followed her to the mound. It had probably been a large pile of rocks at one time, but as with most relics, bits and pieces of it had disappeared over the years.

"Here's where the gravestone must have been." He pointed to an indentation that was visible only close up. "It must have been huge."

"I can't believe someone stole it," Jane said in a disapproving voice that made him smile.

"I once saw a Roman column worked into a fourteenth-century church as a cornerstone. New civilizations are quick to dismantle old ones. For all we know, that gravestone is now a part of someone's barn."

She shuddered. "That makes me ill to even think about."

"Me, too." He began a close examination of the mound. "It doesn't look as if anyone has disturbed it recently."

"Thank goodness! We're in time after all."

"Perhaps." He wiped his hands on his breeches, his heart pounding. The amulet was close; he could feel it. He'd waited so long for this moment that he couldn't quite grasp it. *The Hurst Amulet will soon be back where it rightfully belongs.* "I'll get the shovel."

Trying to contain his excitement, he brought the shovel from the boat and then reached down to remove some of the grass. "I don't want to dig in a way that could ruin any artifacts that might be with the amulet. Should I begin on the north side, where the headstone was?"

"That would be best. Here, I'll help." She began to pull out large handfuls of grass, clearing the area so he could dig, the scent of fresh grass tickling her nose.

They were making good progress when Michael suddenly stopped.

She looked up at him, the sun behind him obscuring his expression. "What is it?"

He pointed to the ground at his feet. Someone had scraped away a large portion of grass and then replaced it.

Her shoulders sank. "That's fresh."

"Yes, damn it." Michael took the shovel and scraped aside the grass, which she could now see had been scattered over the area, disguising the fresh digging from a casual glance. "Someone's been here very recently. The grass is still green." He bent down. "There's the edge of a boot print here, too, and the wind's barely had an impact on the loose soil."

"Can you tell the size of it?" she asked hopefully.

"No, it's just the edge." He rocked back on his heels. "If the Hurst Amulet was ever here, it's gone now."

The disappointment in Michael's voice echoed inside her. She'd experienced so much loss herself of late: Kisimul was gone, her island uncared-for, her people left to their fate without a strong laird to watch over them, and now this . . . Michael's long-sought-after amulet stolen shortly before they'd arrived.

She looked at his bent head, fighting a desire to

put her arms about him and hug him. *So many things I tried to do have gone astray. I have to fix this, at least, and find some way to—* Her gaze locked on the tower. "Hurst!"

He lifted his head, his expression weary.

"Come with me!" She hiked up her skirts and ran toward the tower.

"What are you doing?"

She could tell from the way his voice was approaching that he was following her. "Just come!" She ducked into the ruined tower, stepping over fallen stones until she stood in the middle of the small room, looking up. When Michael entered, she said, "David stole that amulet while we were at the inn, changing our clothing."

"How do you know that?"

"When we were in the cave, he cut the line on the boat to delay us just so he'd have time to retrieve the amulet, which means he had to row to the mouth of the cave to sabotage our boat, and *then* row back."

Michael leaned on the shovel. "I'm not comfortable with you saying David's our villain without more proof."

"Who else could it be?"

"I'm not saying it wasn't him. But it's not good to make sweeping statements until we have evidence."

"Fine. I'll try not to blame him until we find him with the amulet in his hands. But *whoever* stole our boat most likely *also* stole our maps."

"True."

"And that had to take extra time, so whoever they are, they can't be far from here."

Michael nodded thoughtfully. "That makes sense. So whoever they are, we're right behind them."

"We just need to know which way they're heading. If we can catch them before they leave the island, we can get the amulet back." She pointed to the second floor of the tower over their heads. "Can you lift me? I'll be able to see the whole island from there."

He eyed the broken floor above their heads. "That floor must be a hundred years old, if not more. It can't be safe."

"Wood is brought to Barra by floating it from the mainland through the salt water, so it lasts longer than you might think. Besides, I'm just going to stand on the edges, near that window." When he looked unconvinced, she added, "David's only a few minutes ahead of us, so we have to at least *try*."

Michael's jaw tightened. "I'm probably mad to agree to this, but fine; I'll hoist you up. But you're to take *no* chances. I've had enough frightful moments today." He leaned the shovel against the wall, and then came and put his hands around her waist. With seemingly no effort he lifted her above his head. "Put your foot on my shoulder."

She did so and was soon climbing onto the half of the second floor that was left.

"Be careful where you step."

"I will." She made her way to the window. "I should be able to see from here . . ."

Michael watched as she leaned out the window. "Can you see him?"

"No, the trees are in the way." She peered down at him. "I'm going to the third floor. I'll be able to see the entire island from that height."

"You will do no such thing, blast you. Come down now."

"You, sir, possess a weak spirit." Ignoring Michael's sputter, Jane climbed to the third floor. She was careful not to look directly down, for it suddenly seemed as if the floor—and Michael—were far, far away.

She made her way along the edges of the room and came to the south window, the rough-hewn stone cool under her fingers. The wind whistled loudly, drying her eyes. She squinted against it.

"See anything?"

"No." She gritted her teeth and turned. "I'm going to the west side."

"Jane, no. Just come down now—"

"I'm almost there." She continued to walk along the edge of the rotted flooring, skipping whichever beams wiggled too much for her comfort, until she came to the next window.

She looked out, scanning anxiously.

Below, Michael crossed his arms. "Well?"

Jane didn't answer.

"What is it, blast it?"

"I can see our thief riding on the road to Eoligary House," she said.

He caught a note of something in her voice. "And?"

"It's not David; it's Lindsee." Jane's face appeared in the opening overhead, her eyes wide. "Michael, there's no one else to be seen. *She's* the one who stole the Hurst Amulet."

CHAPTER 19

From the diary of Michael Hurst:

When one is on a quest for an artifact, it's good practice to not get so fixated upon it that you ignore other, more valuable artifacts that you may find along the way. The object of one's quest is not always the true prize.

They pulled their horses to a halt on a small bluff across from Eoligary House. The house was aglow in early evening twilight, the windows glittering like stars.

As they watched, a stable hand led a gray mare to the stables from the front door, as if the rider had just been escorted inside. To one side, a black gelding was tied to a ring, waiting the return of his rider.

Jane frowned. "David's here, too." When Michael didn't answer, she shot him a glance and found him regarding the gelding with a thoughtful look. "Aren't you surprised?"

"Everything surprises me about Barra," he replied in a dry tone. "Ammon will stay here until we leave."

"Very well." She hesitated, and then said, "Michael, whatever happens—whoever is at fault—we'll get the Hurst Amulet back. I promise."

He smiled, his expression inscrutable. "I'm beginning to believe that the Hurst Amulet will be found when it wants to be, and not before. If we find it, we find it."

"And if not?"

"Then it'll be time for me to head off to my next adventure. Now come." With a nudge, he set Ramses cantering toward the house, and she followed, wondering why he hadn't said *we*.

Jane wished that small omission didn't bother her so, but it did. The last few weeks had changed their relationship in ways she'd never even imagined. For the first time since she'd accepted the position of Michael's assistant, she was no longer certain of her place in his life, or even if he wanted her to be a part of it. It was all confusing, painful, and overwhelming.

They reached the courtyard and Michael jumped down and handed Ramses' reins to the waiting groom. Michael then turned to help Jane from her horse.

"What are you doing?" she asked as he swung her into his arms.

"Carrying you," he said, as if it were the most natural thing in the world.

She eyed Michael with a flat gaze. "Please put me down."

He carried her across the courtyard. "The cobblestones are puddled with water."

"It didn't rain today."

"It did yesterday."

"I'm wearing boots."

He glanced at her boots, which were peeking out from her skirts. "Oh. So you are."

"I *always* wear boots. You *know* I always wear boots."

"You could have purchased a new pair of shoes."

"On Barra?"

His lips twitched. "I can see I didn't think that through very well."

His teasing was different now. He used to tease her by mocking her or saying outrageous things or not shaving—anything to prickle her temper. But now he tried to win smiles, and it twisted her heart to think that this, too, would disappear once they left Barra. Isolated, she had his sole attention. But when they returned to the mainland, how would they fare? Could she still be his efficient assistant even if he wished it?

The more difficult question wasn't really that at all . . . she knew she could perform her duties under any circumstances. The real question was whether she wanted to. Would it be enough to just be Hurst's quiet, can-do assistant when she'd had such a rich taste of what it would be like to be more?

It was so tempting to simply lean her cheek on his shoulder and ask him to keep going, to walk past the house and never look back, because once they had the amulet, their quest was over.

He reached the steps and set her down, his hands lingering only slightly, due to the footmen standing under the portico. "There." He nodded to one of the footmen, who opened the door of the great hall.

Michael held out his arm. "Shall we?"

She tucked her hand into place, wishing her heart didn't ache so. "Of course."

Inside, Jane fixed a polite smile on her face and told the butler, "Mr. Hurst and Miss Smythe-Haughton to see Lord MacN—"

Voices raised in anger erupted, and Jane glanced at Jaimie's study, where the voices seemed to come from.

The butler sent a startled glance in the same direction and then said in a rushed voice, "Verrah good, miss. If you'll remove your coats, I'll see you and Mr. Hurst to the small salon to wait—"

A crash sounded.

Every eye in the foyer was now fixed on the double doors.

The butler began to sidle over, as if to cut them off from the study doors.

That's it. Jane whisked past him and walked toward doors. "Thank you, but we'll just join Lord MacNeil in his study."

The butler hurried to intercede, but Michael reached the double doors first, his greatcoat obscuring the room as he threw the doors open. "No need to bother announcing us; we'll do it ourselves." He allowed Jane to slip past him and then shut the doors in the butler's astonished face.

Jane paused just inside the study and took a deep breath. Four people stood in the room. Elspeth was beside the fireplace, dressed in a purple gown that made her pale skin glow. She would have looked attractive except that her mouth was thin with fury, her arms crossed over her plump breasts. She looked as if she were only a spark away from blowing apart.

Across from her stood David. Elegantly attired as ever, he leaned upon his cane and sneered. From the top of his silvered hair to his shiny black boots, he made Jaimie—who was standing behind his desk as if barricaded against a gale force wind—look like a mussed and sweaty farm laborer.

Lindsee, wearing her fashionable blue velvet pelisse, stood in the shadows by the window Jane had climbed in earlier in the week. "You're earlier than we expected."

Jane frowned at her friend. "You expected us?"

Lindsee moved forward and the lamplight caught the dull glimmer of something in her hands—a small, dirty metal box about the size of a book.

Jane's eyes widened. "Is that the—" The word stuck in her throat. She and Michael had searched for the amulet for so long.

Lindsee looked reverently at it. "Yes, this box holds the Hurst Amulet."

Jane was aware of Michael's presence directly behind her, his body tense as if he were prepared to dive for the box.

Jane wet her suddenly dry lips. "Then you've seen the amulet?"

Lindsee nodded, her fingers curling over the metal as if to protect it. "Yes."

Jane frowned. "Lindsee . . . *you* cut the rope on the boat?"

Lindsee's gaze flickered to David.

Jane turned to David.

He bowed, a smirk on his face. "I had that pleasure."

"But . . ." Jane looked from David to Lindsee and then back. "I don't understand. You two are helping one another?"

Lindsee placed her hand over the top of the box, her slender fingers curling over the edge. "David fetched it for me because I asked him to."

The world seemed to swirl around Jane. *I can't believe this. The Lindsee I knew would never have anything to do with David.*

"Lindsee, I don't understand. Why would you ask David to do anything for you?" A suspicion crossed Jane's mind. "Wait a moment. Does David know something about you? Is he blackmailing you into—"

Michael's hand closed over Jane's elbow. "It seems there have been some changes on Barra since you were last here. Unless I'm mistaken, your uncle has been courting Lady MacDonald."

David gave a short laugh. "And here I thought we'd been so discreet."

"I'm sure you were," Michael said. "But I saw a malacca cane in the foyer of Lady MacDonald's house when I went to visit. Then, when you came to visit Jane at the inn, I realized whose it was."

David tapped the cane upon the floor. "I've a bad habit of leaving the blasted thing."

Jane glanced at Michael. "You didn't say a word to me about that."

"It didn't seem important."

But it was. The changes on Barra confused and irritated her. She turned back to Lindsee. "However it came to be in your possession, the amulet belongs to the Hursts."

"Of course." Lindsee walked forward, her box outstretched. "I never intended to keep it."

"Of course not." Jane couldn't keep the sarcastic tone from her voice. "You were only borrowing it."

Lindsee looked down at the box. "Jennet, you told me that the amulet was magical, that some believe that it allows the person who holds it to see into the future." Lindsee leaned forward and pressed the box into Jane's hand. "Forgive me, but I had to know."

"Had to know wha—"

"No!" Elspeth stepped forward. "Lady MacDonald, you cannot give that box to that woman, for it's not yours to give." There was an air of smug triumph in her voice. "My *husband* is the laird of this island. Any treasure found on it is his." Elspeth turned her gaze on Jane. "Isn't that right?"

David gave a low laugh. "She has you there, Jennet. You were raised as the future mistress of Barra, so you know it to be true."

Jane's hands closed over the box. "The amulet belongs to the Hursts and no one else."

"Not if 'twas found on Barra," Elspeth said, sweeping past Lindsee, her plump hand outstretched. "That box belongs to Jaimie now."

Jane sent a beseeching look to Jaimie.

He was still behind his desk, looking as miserable as if someone had thrown him into a sea of sharks.

Elspeth reached for the box, but Jane hugged it tight. "Jaimie, *you* are the laird, so it's *your* decision, not Elspeth's *or* David's! You knew I came to Barra for one reason and one reason only: to help Hurst find his family's amulet. Let Michael take it home, back to his family, where it belon—"

"Jaimie!" Elspeth hurried forward, her silk skirts swishing. "Tell her that she cannot have it! It belongs to us, and to no one else! Your father says it's ours and so it—"

"My father?" Jaimie frowned. "When did he tell you that? Lindsee only just arrived with the amulet; you didn't even know it existed before then. And Father hadn't been here more than a minute prior to that, and not once did we discuss an amulet of any kind."

Elspeth sent David a hurried glance.

"Of course I mentioned the amulet to Elspeth,"

David said in a bored tone. "I knew of it from something Lindsee said to me."

"So you discussed it with Elspeth and not with me." Jaimie's gaze narrowed. "You planned on taking the amulet all along, didn't you? From the moment Lindsee told you about it."

Lindsee's brows lowered. "David?" Her soft voice seemed to cut David, for he flinched.

"You said you didn't wish to keep it," he said.

"I didn't. But it belongs to Mr. Hurst. He should have it. David, I only asked you to find it because I wished to test its powers."

"Powers?" Elspeth's gaze locked on the box in Jane's hands. "What powers does this amulet have?"

Lindsee's expression grew dreamy. "When you hold the amulet, it lets you see the future."

"And?" David asked, his gaze on Lindsee, an avid expression of admiration etched in every line of his face.

She smiled. "I have seen mine."

Jane was astounded at the look on David's face, of the tenderness that shone in his eyes. He was transformed, the cruelty that normally sat upon his face gone.

"*You* should have that amulet," he said to Lindsee. "No other woman is worthy."

"Wait!" Elspeth scowled. "You said it would belong to Jaimie and me, not to this . . . this—"

"Don't." David spoke the word quietly, without a hint of anger.

Elspeth flushed an ugly red.

Lindsee turned to Jane. "David has been asking me to marry him for the last two years."

"Begging is more like it," Jaimie said from his position behind the desk.

His father glared, and Jaimie flushed.

Lindsee placed a hand on the small metal box. "I didn't know how to answer him. But now I do."

Jane placed her hand over her friend's. "Lindsee, don't make a decision based on a mere amulet. What I told you about the amulet being magic . . . it's just rumor. Isn't that true, Michael?"

He nodded. "I'm sorry, but Jane's right. It's far-fetched to think an amulet can allow you to see the future—"

"Och, no. I saw it." Lindsee leaned forward, her eyes wide. "Jennet, I saw it with my own eyes. Take it out of the box and hold it yourself, and you'll see."

A pin could have dropped in the room and echoed in the quiet.

David stepped forward. "Lindsee? What did you see?" There was an anguish in his voice that made Jane look at him wonderingly.

Lindsee straightened and dropped her hands to her sides, a small smile touching her lips. "I saw myself married to you, David, and with two bonny wee bairns on my knee." Lindsee's face was radiant. "Oh, Jennet, my sons will be beautiful. Both of them with hair of black, and blue, blue eyes."

"Lindsee?" David crossed the room to stand beside Lindsee. He looked like a black hawk, silver wings at his temples. "While I love hearing of our sons, I'm far more anxious to meet them in person." He took Lindsee's hand and very slowly pressed a kiss to her fingers.

To Jane's bemusement, Lindsee leaned toward him as if it were the most natural thing in the world and rested her cheek on his shoulder.

Michael said quietly, "The amulet's powers seem a bit stronger than mere rumor."

Elspeth's sharp voice crackled through the room. "This changes nothing. That amulet belongs to Jaimie. Jennet, don't say another word. David said you'd come to this island to steal it from Jaimie, and so you have. Well, I won't stand for it. I say you have to—"

"Hold!" Jaimie frowned at his wife. "You've been speaking to my father about the amulet and yet I've never heard a word of this before now."

She lifted her chin. "*Someone* has to look out for the good of Eoligary House and our family. Can't you see what's happening? She returned to steal the amulet. Once she has that, she'll want more!"

Jaimie's lips thinned, his brows snapping down over his eyes. "You are wrong, Elspeth. Jennet came here to find that amulet and for no other reason. And she's not stealing anything."

"Don't be naïve! She will demand her titles and the lands. We'll lose everything and—"

"Then we'll lose everything, damn you!" Jaimie's voice rang through the room. "They're hers, the title and lands. They always have been."

Elspeth's mouth fell open, her eyes wide.

David scowled. "Elspeth's right, Jaimie. You need to have a care—"

"As for you, old man," Jaimie spat, coming out from behind the desk, his fists clenched. "I am the laird here, not you. And this is *my* household. I've allowed you far too much say in this house and it will stop here and now or—"

"Or what?" David's gaze narrowed.

For an instant Jane thought Jaimie might fold, but instead, he stalked past Elspeth to his father, hands fisted at his sides. "Or else I'll *make* you leave."

"You wouldn't touch me," David sneered. "You wouldn't dare."

Though his lips quivered, Jaimie stood firm. "Father, I love you, but I have put up with your schemes far too often. That ends today. Jennet is my cousin. I sold all I had to marry Elspeth—even my honor. I was mad for her and had to have her. But . . ." He gulped on a sob. "That didn't make it right. All of these years, I've carried that burden. Barra is Jennet's, heart and soul. It always has been."

He turned to Jennet. "Cousin, I can't continue with this. Barra is yours. I'll leave for Edinburgh tomorrow and let the magistrate know you've returned."

"You *fool*," David sneered. "If you give this up, you'll lose everything and *everyone* you hold dear."

Anguish broke across Jaimie's face, but he held his ground. "If Elspeth leaves me for nothing more than a change in title, then I must face the truth: that she doesn't love me"—his voice broke, but he swallowed loudly—"and she never will."

"No woman would stay with such a maw worm," David said, disgust on his face.

"*Hold!*"

All eyes went to Elspeth, who stood stiff and white faced, her gaze locked on David. "Do *not* call him a maw worm. Jaimie is a fine and good man. Better than you!"

David looked impatient. "Stay out of this. Your husband and I have decisions to make—"

"No, Father," Jaimie said. He turned to Elspeth, his eyes bright with unshed tears. "Elspeth, I have something to tell you." He reached for her hands and held them tightly. "From the day we wed, Father has been telling me that you married me for the title, that you'd leave if I didn't do things the way he saw best."

Elspeth blinked. "And you believed him?"

"Aye. You never gave me any reason not to. I know that you don't love me, but I thought that so long as I kept the title, I could keep you."

Eslpeth started to speak, but he shook his head. "Let me finish. I've never loved anyone but you, and I suppose I thought that was enough. That my love was big enough for both of us." His chin quivered. "But I was lying to myself. It's not enough. It never was."

"Your father is right about one thing and one thing only. You are a fool!" Elspeth said. "You decided all of that without consulting me."

Jaimie swiped his eyes with one hand. "Elspeth, I have tried and tried to be the man you wished me to be, someone forceful, but I am who I am. And if that's not enough for you, then—" He dropped her hands, his shoulders slumping.

Jane started to go forward and reach for Jaimie, but Michael's warm fingers curled about her shoulder, and he pulled her back until she was leaning into him.

Elspeth shook her head. "Jaimie, you've never said any of this to me."

"I didn't think you'd want to hear it."

"I wouldn't want to—" She closed her eyes and pressed her fists against them.

Jaimie looked miserable. "Elspeth, please. Don't look like that. Just—"

She dropped her hands. "Is this why you've held yourself from me all of these years? Why you never shared your thoughts, never talked with me about our future, never included me in plans for this house or anything else?" She gestured with empty hands.

Jaimie raked a hand through his hair. "I was trying

to show you I could make decisions. You . . . you would have liked to have done that with me?"

Her lip quivered, her blue eyes glistening with tears. "I'm your wife, you daft fool! Of *course* I wanted to be included in those decisions!"

Jaimie sent an uncertain glance at his father.

"Och, don't you dare look at him!" Elspeth grabbed Jaimie's arm and turned him so that David was well out of sight. "Your father's done enough harm to this marriage as it is."

"I was only—" David began.

"Whist!" Lindsee said absently. "Let them talk."

To Jane's astonishment, David meekly remained silent.

"Such is love," Michael murmured.

Elspeth grabbed two fistfuls of her husband's coat. "Listen to me, you blithering idiot. Your father told you that I only married you because of your title, and he was right. I was a lass of sixteen and knew only what my parents had taught me: that the only thing of value was cold, hard coin."

Jaimie lifted a hand. "Don't say any—"

She gave him a small shake. "No, I'm going to speak and you're going to listen. For once, we're going to talk to each other and not at."

He nodded, his gaze locked on her face, as if he didn't dare look away.

Jane's throat tightened as she saw the anguished love in Jaimie's expression.

Elspeth said, "Your father told you the truth, that I was interested in nothing more than your title and gold. I was happy at first that you never tried to bind yourself to me with useless emotion. But as time passed, as we lived together, I saw you for what you are, and not for what you fear you might be. I saw your gentleness, the way you stood beside me and held my hands during the birth of our children, and how you never raised your voice at me, even when I deserved it." Her voice thickened, and she swallowed before she continued, her eyes growing luminous. "Did your father also tell you how I watched you hold our children with such tenderness, such love? How I saw you kiss their foreheads each and every night, and how I grew so jealous of that loving touch?" Her voice broke, and she whispered, "Something you never gave *me*, your wife?"

Jaimie shook his head in wonderment.

She tugged him closer. "Jaimie, did he tell you how I *dreamed* of the time when you'd sweep me in your arms and declare your love for me and me alone? For if he didn't tell you that, then he didn't tell you everything you needed to know."

Jaimie blinked slowly, as if unable to grasp her words. "You love *me*?"

"Och, you fool!" A sob filled her voice and she shook him harder. "How could I watch you and not love you?

But you never let me close, never told me what you wished, never included me in any decision of any kind. I waited and waited and—" Her voice broke, and with a gulped sob, she turned and ran toward the door.

Jaimie caught her just before she reached it. He slung an arm about her waist and held her to him. "Och, Elspeth, my love, *please* don't cry. I can stand anything but that. You must know that I love you. That I've loved you since I first laid eyes upon you, and I've never stopped loving you since. All of these years, I've held back my feelings because I didn't think you wanted them. And they've burned me from the inside out. I wanted to say something so many times, but you seemed so angry and my father kept saying that you didn't care and would leave and I—"

Elspeth stood on tiptoe and gave him a kiss. It was a short kiss, just her lips pressed to his. But when she finished and dropped back to her heels, Jaimie looked with wonder into her face. "Bloody hell, the time we've wasted," he said.

With a breathless laugh, Elspeth threw her arms about her husband's neck and kissed him again.

Jaimie returned the kiss with the same ardent passion.

A handkerchief was pressed into Jane's hand, and she realized that a tear was running down her cheek. She wiped it away and handed the kerchief back to Michael.

He looked at it for a moment before he took it, folded it in half, and carefully tucked it back into his pocket.

She looked around. "Lindsee and David are gone!"

"They slipped out as soon as it became apparent they were not necessary. Lindsee has David firmly in hand. I get the impression she'll lead him on a merry dance."

"Good. He deserves one." Jane looked down at the box in her hands. "I suppose we've accomplished our goal, too." She handed the box to Michael. "Finally. The Hurst Amulet."

Michael tucked the box into the large pocket of his greatcoat.

"Aren't you going to examine it?"

"Not here." He tucked a hand under her elbow. "Come, princess. It's time to go."

Jane glanced at her cousin, who was now in a passionate embrace with his wife. Her face heated.

"Just so." Michael led her into the hallway, then shut the double doors behind him.

Jane gave a sigh of relief. "That was far more complicated than I expected."

He flicked Jane a humorous glance. "Life always is, isn't it?"

"Indeed. There are still some things I need to talk to Jaimie about—the rents and taxes must be used for the good of all of Barra."

Michael nodded to the footman, who hurried to open the door, and led her outside. "I suspect that once Elspeth is included in the decision making, Barra will profit greatly. She seems the practical sort."

"True," Jane said thoughtfully. "They make a lovely couple, don't they?"

"If Noah'd had your skills in matching the animals on the ark the way you've matched the couples here on Barra, there'd still be unicorns and dragons in this world."

She chuckled. "I didn't organize any of that and you know it." She gazed at his pocket where the outline of the box could be seen. "But maybe something else did."

"I rather doubt it. People see what they wish to."

A groom brought their horses to the step and Michael helped her into the saddle. "We should return to the inn and examine the amulet."

"And then?" The question hung in the air between them, as thick and solid as a wall.

"And then we'll see." Michael climbed onto Ramses and gave her a faint, lopsided smile as he gathered the reins. "Maybe we'll let the amulet do its magic once again."

CHAPTER 20

From the diary of Michael Hurst:

I—no, *we* found the Hurst Amulet and it is all it was promised and far, far more.

I should be satisfied, for this quest was my greatest. Still, there is one more issue to resolve . . . and it might be the most difficult of all.

hey returned to the inn, and Ammon took the horses to the stables.

Michael and Jane found Mrs. Macpherson had prepared a stew for their dinner and was too busy setting the table by the fireplace to notice their impatience.

The box weighed heavily in Michael's pocket. His curiosity was stirred, but he was far more focused on Jane than on the amulet. He had the amulet now and it was his. But Jane? That was a far less certain matter altogether.

As they waited for the landlady to finish, Michael reclined in a chair by the fire while Jane straightened their cloaks on pegs by the door. It was amusing just to watch her. No other woman was as unconscious of her charms as Jane, which made her an even more enjoyable companion. It was also another reason why he needed to keep this newfound desire tamped to a manageable size.

Yet he couldn't help but enjoy her lithe stretch as she reached the top peg, causing the fabric of her gown to press over her small breasts and hips. Instantly, he could picture her naked, the intriguing hollows and dimples that would demand their own exploration, preferably with his tongue—

"Will that be all?" Mrs. Macpherson asked.

"Yes, thank you," Jane said immediately, picking up an apple as she walked past the table. "It was quite kind of you to have dinner ready when we returned. The stew smells delicious."

"I can bring some more bread if ye think—"

"No, no." Jane gently herded the innkeeper toward the door. "There's plenty of bread on the platter."

"Yes, but—"

"Thank you so much. If we need more, we will call for you."

With that, Mrs. Macpherson allowed herself to be escorted out the door.

"Whew," Jane said as she returned, taking a bite of the apple.

"She was determined."

"But so was I." She took another bite, her even teeth sinking into the white flesh with glorious enthusiasm.

He couldn't look away.

"You know what we should do now?" Her voice tripped with energy and excitement.

Fall upon the floor and slake our lust? danced upon the tip of his tongue. With effort, he forced his imagination down and managed a sedate, "Eat?"

She dropped the apple on her plate and pointed to his pocket where he'd tucked the metal box. Slowly, he drew it out. The box was old and battered, made of hammered metal. Dirt traced every nick and dent, and he pulled out his handkerchief to wipe some of the filth away, but then paused.

Jane was leaning over his shoulder. "Wipe it clean. I wish to see if there are any markings on the surface."

He folded the handkerchief and put it back in his pocket, then took one of the napkins Mrs. Macpherson had left with their dinner and used that instead. "There are no markings."

"Which is a great pity. I was hoping for some clues as to how it came to be buried in a Viking grave."

"We may never know the amulet's full journey." He placed the box on the table and wondered that he should be so close to the amulet and yet so loath to even look at it.

He should be panting to open the box, but he wasn't. Instead, he felt a growing desire to put it away.

Why did he feel like that? This was the moment he'd been working toward for so long, and the satisfaction of returning the amulet to the family had been his dream since he'd first learned of it. Why, then, was he hesitating?

His gaze moved from the box to Jane. Her lovely brown eyes met his, and in that second he knew . . . knew what he wanted and why with a clarity that was almost painful. *I don't wish to open the box, because once I do, this is all over—the quest, the adventure, and other things I'm not willing to let go.*

"Open it!" Jane said impatiently, moving to sit beside him.

"I will." He slid the box on the table so that it rested between them. "This is the end of our quest."

Her brightness dampened a bit. After a moment, she said, "Yes. It is the end."

Something about the way she said that made him look at her sharply. "You make that sound permanent."

She waved a hand. "We can talk about that later. Open the box." She reached for it, but he caught her hand and held it.

"No. I don't want to open the box yet. I want to know what you meant by what you just said."

She looked down, her lashes obscuring her expression before she gently tugged her hand free. "Fine. We'll talk about this now." She turned so that she faced him and wet her lips as if nervous. "This is . . . this is all so new for me. For you, too, I think."

"New is sometimes a good thing."

"Perhaps. Things *have* changed. I wasn't going to say this until we were back in London, but I can't go back to just being your assistant."

He didn't have to ask her why; he couldn't imagine her being his assistant again, either. But he didn't know what she should be, or how to address it, or—

She forced a smile. "We will discuss that later. Now, open the blasted box."

His heart weighed in his chest like a block of stone, but he was no match for the sparkle in her eyes as she looked at the box. Over the last few weeks, their relationship had indeed changed . . . or had he changed? He wasn't certain; all he knew was that he was aching to touch her again, to taste her, to bed her until she begged to be allowed to catch her breath. Being enclosed in the small inn had done little to defuse his passions. Looking into her upturned face now, he was aware that the dull ache he'd been experiencing all day was growing with each second.

Damn it, what had happened to the times he used to spend in her company and never notice what she wore or said? The times when they'd spend all twenty-four hours of a day together while they were traveling or setting up a camp, and it caused none of this uncomfortable emotion?

Oblivious to the havoc she was causing, Jane poked at the box. "Open it!"

He leaned forward, still painfully aware of her, of the sweet scent of her hair. He couldn't quite name the scent, but it drove him mad.

She pushed a silky strand of hair from her cheek as a gradual thrumming on the roof told them it was once again raining. She glanced up and frowned. "That may impede us leaving the island."

"I hope so," he murmured, too taken with watching how the rain tracing down the windowpanes threw shadowed lines down Jane's cheek, as if the drops themselves longed to touch her.

Michael marveled at her skin. It wasn't the pale,

creamy color favored by the *ton*, but a warm tan, made for touching and tasting. She had the sort of skin that made one think of summer, sunshine, and sweet peaches.

He wondered if she'd taste like a peach if he kissed her right now. Or at least of the apple she'd just eaten.

His thoughts must have shown, for her eyes widened, her lips parted, her breath came deeper. And then she was leaning toward him, her gaze locked on his mouth, as if she saw nothing but him.

Slowly, she lifted her lips to his. He knew he should stop this, stop her, but he couldn't. He was lost, swept away by desire so strong that a sandstorm couldn't kill it.

He bent toward her, but then she pressed her fingers to his lips and said earnestly, "Michael, I want to kiss you, but first . . . blast it, we *must* open that box!"

Michael had to laugh. But he also understood. "Very well." He pulled the metal box toward him and, reaching in his pocket for his knife, pried off the lid.

Inside was a swath of velvet, the edges frayed. Jane leaned forward, watching as Michael flipped a corner of the velvet out of the way and revealed the Hurst Amulet.

Her breath caught. It was large, about the size of the palm of her hand, and made of heavily chased metals, gold intertwined with silver until it looked like neither. Ancient runes were carved into the amulet, which was studded with precious stones. The crowning jewel was a large piece of amber that glowed as if from within.

Michael left it in the box, but pulled out his spectacles and examined it.

"It's the Hurst Amulet?"

"Yes." He tilted the box so that the amulet caught the light from the fire. "There is a portrait of Queen Elizabeth wearing it, and much of this is the same. This large piece of amber is the exact size and shape, and it's very, very rare. Also, the runes are exactly like the ones in the painting." He set the box down and removed the amulet from the velvet, holding it toward the firelight. "The amber is warm. I can almost . . ." His voice trailed off as he stared at the amber.

"Hurst?"

He continued staring into the amulet, his gaze flickering, as if he were looking at a huge field and not a piece of amber.

She frowned and placed a hand on his arm. "Hurst? Are you—"

He gasped and threw back his head, sucking in air as if he'd been underwater. He practically threw the amulet into the box and slammed the lid closed, pieces of velvet sticking out the sides.

Jane stared at the box, almost mesmerized by the thoughts running through her head. "Did it . . . did it—"

He stood, towering over her a moment, before he scooped her up.

"Wha—" She impulsively grabbed the box, the metal warm in her hands as he turned and carried her toward the stairs. "Michael, what are you—"

"We're going to bed."

"To— But why?"

He glinted down at her, his blue eyes framed by his spectacles, a determined smile on his lips. "Because I'm going to solve this attraction between us once and for all."

"The amulet. It told you—"

"It didn't tell me a damn thing." He'd reached the top of the stairs, and he paused by her bedchamber. "Furthermore, I don't need a damn piece of glass to tell me what I already know."

"But it—"

He kicked her door open.

Her body was already tingling in anticipation. "I'm not saying we shouldn't do this, but what did the amulet—"

He silenced her with a kiss, but not any kiss. He kissed her as if she were air and he were a man drowning. He kissed her as if his entire life depended upon it. And as he laid her upon her bed and removed her clothing, tasting each inch of bared skin as he uncovered it, neither of them noticed when the box fell from her fingers onto the rug.

* * *

Much later, Michael listened to Jane's slow, even breathing as she slept in the crook of his arm, her cheek pressed to his shoulder. She was amazingly beautiful, all delicate planes and astonishingly feminine, tempting in both thought and action. His gaze traced the graceful line of her brow and cheek, down to her determined little chin and on to the tempting hollows of her shoulders.

He'd always seen Jane for what she was to him at any given moment—practical and efficient when she'd been organizing his quests, humorous and lively when she'd been his companion on those quests, and comforting and calming when he faced the uncertainty of each new adventure.

But through it all, she'd always been necessary. He couldn't imagine his life without her, a feeling that had only increased over the last few weeks. And then when he'd held the amulet in his hand . . . he looked at that hand now. It was still warm, and if he closed his eyes, he could still see the amulet's colors swirling.

His chest tightened. When he'd looked into the amber, he'd seen Jane walking away from him. He curled his hand tight, trying to keep the memory from returning, fighting the hollowness the sight had caused. He'd been desperate to erase that horrible feeling, and he'd done so by holding her as tightly and closely as he could.

He opened his hand and smoothed it over the curve of her hip, caressing her silken skin. She stirred, murmuring before she settled back to sleep.

He could not—*would* not—allow the amulet to be right. She was his assistant, his companion, his— He hesitated. She was more than all that, but he couldn't quite define her new role. Friend, of course. Lover, yes. All that, and more.

His palm tingled, as if the amulet wanted to remind him . . . It was then that he knew what he had to do.

Michael ran the tip of his finger over the curve of Jane's thick lashes where they rested on her cheeks.

She batted at him in her sleep and then settled more deeply against him, her cheek warm against his chest.

He did it again, only this time he said softly, "Jane?"

Her lashes fluttered, but she didn't move.

He leaned forward and said a bit louder, "Jane, my love. Wake up."

She slowly opened her eyes, their velvet brown settling about him like a warm cloak as she smiled sleepily. "Good morning."

"Actually, it's good evening."

"Ah, I remember now." She lifted on her elbows and stretched. "Our stew will be cold." Her firm breasts pressed against the sheet.

He cleared his throat. "Damn the stew. Jane?"

"Yes?" she said, yawning.

"You're dismissed."

Her smile vanished, and she sat up so quickly that her hair fell into her face. She brushed it away with an impatient flick. "You're dismissing me after we just—" Color flooded across her.

"Yes. As you have so rightly pointed out, things have changed between us. Ammon will be a better assistant for me now. And I know that he'd enjoy the challenge."

She clutched the sheet to her, her face a study of bewilderment.

He added in a thoughtful tone, "I'll have to hire a new valet, though. I'm hoping I can find a married man."

She rubbed her forehead, confusion darkening her eyes. "I don't— Michael, why must you find a married man?"

"Because if I can find a decent valet who is married, then perhaps his wife will make a decent maid for mine."

"For your . . . wife?"

"Yes. And that will make our traveling all the easier." Her gaze locked with his. "Wife?" she said again.

He pulled her into his lap, tucking the sheet about them both. She didn't try to leave, which he took for a good sign.

Instead, her breath came out in a long, slow sigh. "Wife. I-I never thought—"

"Wife or concubine. To be honest, I don't care which, though I know my parents would prefer the former. They're sticklers, especially my father. Vicars are like that."

She didn't crack a smile. "But you . . . you don't care?"

He captured her chin and lifted her face to his. "Jennet MacNeil, or Jane Smythe-Haughton, or Scottish princess, whatever you want to call yourself, all I care about is spending the rest of my life with you. And I'll do whatever it takes to make that happen."

Her eyes grew moist and she bit her lip. "So I get to choose between concubine and wife?"

"Yes. I must say, being a husband appeals to me more. There are certain"—his gaze brushed over her slender form—"benefits to that position. Benefits that I relish."

Delightful color warmed her skin, staining her cheeks a lovely pink. "I don't know what to say."

"You don't have to say a thing except yes. You don't have to do anything, either, for I'm quite willing to plan it all."

"You?"

"Yes, me."

"You'd plan all of it? Even the wedding?"

"Why not?"

"You don't even like to plan your own breakfast."

He grinned. "You mean more to me than bacon."

"More than *bacon*? I'm honored."

"You should be, my foolish pea brain."

"Foolish—oh! Foppish nitwit."

"Lazy slugabed." He grasped her hand and nipped on the tip of a finger.

She shivered. "Rude sapsku— Oh!"

He'd sucked gently on her finger and then said in a loving tone, "Most beautiful of all Scottish princesses."

"That's not fair. You changed things right in the middle."

"Get used to it."

She smiled, her face alight with happiness. "I'll do my best."

His heart rose, too. "Last night, you said that once my quest was over, then so were we. That you couldn't return to our past way of life. Neither can I, Jane. So while you were sleeping, I've been thinking—and one thing kept occurring to me: I can't live without you."

Jane didn't know what to say. "I thought you'd grow bored with me once you'd finished this quest."

"I can't believe I'm hearing so much balderdash from such lush lips." He gave her a lopsided smile that made her heart tighten. "Jane, if I spent a century with you, I'd never get bored. You're quicksilver and sensible wool. You ensnared me with one, and then wrapped me in the other. I'm beyond smitten."

"Beyond smitten. I don't suppose you'd call that love, would you?"

"I might," he teased.

She splayed her hand and rubbed his jaw. "Do you love me enough to always shave?"

"Don't press your luck."

"Do you love me enough to tell me what you saw in the amulet?"

His brow lowered, his expression serious. "I suppose you should know that." He captured her hand and held it to his chest. "I saw *you.*"

"And?"

"You were going away."

Her gaze locked with his and she could feel the thudding of his heart. "Then the amulet didn't say we were to be together."

His hand tightened over hers. "*I* say we will be together. That will be enough for both you and the amulet."

"But how do you know?"

He gestured to the side of the bed. "Look at it and see."

She pulled her hand from his and leaned over the side of the bed and saw the box on the rug. She leaned down and picked it up. She met Michael's gaze. "Are you sure?"

His smile couldn't have been more confident. "Hold it."

She opened the box, removed the velvet, and grasped the amulet.

The second it touched her skin, the amber began to swirl. Her hand grew warm, and even the metal around the amulet seemed to vibrate and become alive.

Inside the amber she could make out shapes. It was her . . . walking away as Michael had said.

An ineffable sadness engulfed her at the sight, sinking into her soul, and she could taste the bitterness of the tears that shone on her face.

Jane wanted to drop the amulet, to throw it away, but Michael's warm hand closed over hers and held it in place. "Look into the amulet, Jane. *Keep looking.*"

Though it pained her like a hot coal pressed to bare skin, she fixed her gaze on the amulet. To the image of herself, heartbroken and weeping, walking away, leaving forever. Just as she reached the further reaches of the amulet, Michael appeared. Tall and broad shouldered, he ran after her.

Jane gasped and peered closer, watching as he caught up to her, grasped her wrist, and pulled her to him—

She blinked, realizing that she was no longer looking into the amulet, but into Michael's eyes.

He smiled. "See?" He took the amulet, placed it back in the box, and shut the lid. "Satisfied?"

She nodded mutely, realizing her cheeks were wet with tears. "Did you *feel* that when you saw me leave in the amber?"

He nodded. "I'll never let you leave like that. Ever."

Her heart lightened. "You came after me."

"Of course I did," he said, as if he already knew that.

She thought she detected a hint of relief in his voice. "Well?"

"Well what?"

She sighed. "Hurst, you haven't asked me to marry you yet. You just *told* me."

"That's because the marriage is a mere formality. So long as you are mine and no one else's, then you may pick your title—wife, concubine, sultana, queen, partner of my ventures, even dancer, though your talents in that area are—"

She placed a finger over his mouth. "Don't."

He chuckled, caught her hand, and pressed a kiss in the palm. "Jane, you've but to say what you want, and I will make it so."

"And if I want to be all of those things?"

He drew her close, his gaze the most serious she'd ever seen it. "There's only one woman who could handle all of those. And that, my love, is you."

Tears made her blink and she threw her arms about his neck. "Then I'll take them all, Hurst. Every last one. And while I'm at it, I'll take you, too."

"All of me?"

She grinned and rolled to one side, pulling him with her. "Oh, yes. All of you. Because all of you, my love, is your very best part."

EPILOGUE

A line of coaches pulled up to the wharf where ships bobbed dockside. The wind tried to tear at the rolled-up sails and had to settle for moaning through the riggings and slapping the flags against the masts. White-capped waves raced below the white cliffs of Dover and tried to yank the ships free of their bonds.

Michael climbed out of the coach and looked at the largest ship. "Right on time."

"What is?" Jane asked, sticking her head out the coach door.

He held out a hand to assist her in alighting. "My brother, William. He and his wife, Marcail, are to sail with us as far as France. From there, another ship will take us to Egypt."

Ammon came forward, quietly speaking with Turner about the horses, and then ordering the footmen to remove certain bags from the coaches. He bowed to Michael. "I shall see to the loading of our supplies."

"Good man. I believe Jane is making a list of what we'll need to purchase once we reach Egypt. You might want to add to it before we arrive."

"Very good, sir." Ammon bowed to Jane, who stood beside Michael with one hand upon her bonnet to keep the wind from stealing it away.

She watched Ammon move aside to count the trunks being piled beside the coaches. "He seems to like his new position."

"Very much. I hope he doesn't frighten Marcail."

"From what I've read of your sister-in-law, it will take more than a massive Egyptian to frighten her. I do wish you'd told me she was going to be with us, though. I would have dressed in something a bit more presentable."

"I didn't know it until last night, when I received Mary's letter."

Michael put his arm about Jane and walked with her toward the ship. "Apparently Father and Mother are in Greece and plan on staying there for the next four months. And Mary and her husband are on their way to Portland for some auction, accompanied by my brother Robert, the antiquarian, who is now purchasing objects for the British Museum's collection."

"I hope the museum appreciated *your* donation."

"They'll take good care of the amulet. It will never go missing again. As Robert says, it is the perfect place for our family heirloom."

Jane nodded her approval. "Your brother Robert is a very intelligent man."

"So he likes to tell his lovely wife, Moira." Michael scanned the ship and saw William in conversation with a sailor-looking type. "Let me see, what else was in that letter? Oh, yes. My sister Caitlyn and her ever-increasing brood of children are accompanying her husband to Italy, and they hope we'll visit them at the villa they've let for the summer."

"How lovely." Jane looked impressed. "That was all in one letter?"

"Yes. And Mary wonders why I don't always read every word. It was pages and pages long. I fell asleep twice before I finished it."

Jane chuckled. "When did you receive this letter?"

"One of the footmen delivered it to our suite."

"I never heard him."

"You were asleep. Weary from our rather tiring, er, activities."

She blushed and Michael gave her a wolfish grin. "We *are* newly married. It's only right to celebrate that fully."

Jane's shy smile made him feel ten feet tall. "Did Mary tell you anything else?"

"Yes. You, my dear, are to become an aunt twice over come May."

"Mary's with child?"

"No, my sister Triona is."

"How lovely! But . . . you said 'twice over'?"

"Yes, Triona is having twins."

Jane's eyes widened behind her spectacles. "Twins?"

He shrugged. "Triona and Caitlyn are twins. There are a lot of them in my family, you know."

Jane blinked. "No, I didn't know. Twins. I can't imagine."

"Neither can I." He paused at the foot of the gang-plank and pulled her close, tugging her cloak tighter about her neck. "But then, I also never imagined I'd end up married to a sharp-witted harridan who holds my heart in the palm of her hand."

"Harridan?" Jane smiled and leaned toward him. "Rude curmudgeon."

"Silly gapeseed."

"Foolish jackanapes."

He lifted her hand and kissed the wedding ring on her slender finger. "Bossy wife."

Her lips parted in a sweet smile. "Yes, I am. And don't forget it." She twinkled up at him and then, just as he decided she needed another kiss, she turned and lifted a hand in greeting to his brother William, who stood at the head of the gangplank, grinning down at them.

Reluctantly, Michael loosened his hold on Jane and watched her go to meet his brother, charming him within moments. Michael grinned; he knew just how that felt.

Before he joined them he turned his face into the wind, tasting the excitement that always came at the start of a new adventure. With Jane, there would be more moments for kisses, discoveries, and smiles, and much more, too.

He'd make sure of it.

Smiling, he followed Jane up the gangplank and into their next great adventure.

Turn the page for a sneak peek
at the first delightful novel
in *New York Times* bestselling author
Karen Hawkins's
new Duchess Diaries series

Coming soon from Pocket Books

*T*here you are."

Rose stiffened at the sound of the low, masculine voice. She knew that voice—far better than she wanted to.

She swallowed hard as she slipped her arm through a rung of the library ladder and slowly turned toward the man she never thought she'd see again.

Lord Alton Sinclair, known to the *ton* as Lord Sin, stood in the doorway. His broad shoulders were outlined in stark relief by his perfectly fitting dark blue coat, his legs encased in tan breeches tucked into black Hessian boots that had been shined to a mirrorlike polish.

It had been four years, two months, and three days since she'd last seen him, and the fact that she knew that down to the day made her face heat. His dark blond hair was longer now and his expression more marred by dissipation. Only his sherry-brown eyes looked exactly as they had when she'd last seen him—blazing with anger.

Rose forced her lips into a stiff smile. "Lord Sinclair, how . . . pleasant to see you. I didn't know you'd be here."

His smile was that of a cat who had cornered a mouse. "Of course I'm here. My aunt invited you at my express request."

Rose eyed him warily; she was glad she was up here, away from the simmering storm of a man who was crossing the room toward her. She tried for a casual tone. "I hope you're well. It's been a very long time since we last met."

"Four years. Four very *trying* years."

His smoldering anger was so clear, she had to fight an overwhelming urge to climb farther up the ladder. "I'm sorry to hear that you've had a difficult time."

"You had to know it wasn't easy."

Her brows knit in puzzlement. "I should have? Why?"

His mouth was a hard, straight line, his eyes blazing hot. "Don't play the innocent with me. I *know* you."

Good heavens, what is this all about? Though they'd hadn't parted on good terms, she'd caused herself a good deal of embarrassment, but not him.

He was immune to scandal. Despite his reputation, he was welcome in all the best homes and ballrooms. Handsome, wealthy bachelors were in high demand, and much could be forgiven the one who was the handsomest and wealthiest of all.

He now stood at the foot of the ladder, one large hand resting on a rung by her foot, and her heart sped up uncomfortably. What did he intend to—

He stepped onto the lowest rung, his expression stern and unyielding as he blocked her exit. "You made me the laughingstock of London." Anger crackled through his voice.

As he began to climb toward her, Rose's breath

shortened. "How so? I behaved inappropriately, but you did nothing to earn censure. I've often wished I could take back my actions that night, and—"

"You humiliated me in front of the biggest gossips of the *ton*, and then you fled. You should have stayed to make a public statement to clear the air instead of leaving town like a coward, never to be seen again, which damned me all the more."

She blinked. "But I left because I didn't wish to cause you any more trouble. I thought that was the best way."

"It was the *worst* way." He leaned forward, his chest pressing against her knees, and she felt like a butterfly pinned in a display box. "People gossiped about what they'd seen, and made up what they hadn't. Within a fortnight the story went from my attempting to kiss you to a full-blown attempted seduction. A forceful one, too."

Rose was shocked. "But that's not what happened!"

"Oh, it gets worse. Supposedly your gown was torn, the pins pulled from your hair, one of your shoes lost when you'd tried to flee. After that, no gentleman dared leave his precious daughter alone with me, a man so depraved that he attacked an innocent."

Rose pressed a trembling hand to her lips. "But not a single word of that is true! I wasn't harmed at all!"

He eyed her coldly. "Which you *could* have told everyone, had you not fled and left me to deal with the vicious rumors."

Guilt settled into her stomach like a lead weight. "Oh, dear. I had no idea that people would make up such lies. My aunt was insistent that I leave town until the talk died down, and my only intent was to minimize the damage I'd—"

He climbed to the next rung, his chest now against her thighs.

A wild tingle raced through her, as intoxicating as champagne. Oh, no—this was exactly the feeling that had gotten her into trouble four years ago.

"I hold your aunt responsible as well as you. If she'd had you on a much-needed leash, nothing would have happened to begin with."

Rose's temper flared. "While I understand your desire to blame others for that unfortunate night, allow me to point out that your reputation was hardly unsullied to begin with. Don't pin your or my weaknesses on my aunt."

"Before you came along, people merely spoke of me as a rakehell. No one thought me a seducer of innocents until *you* made me appear so."

Rose's eyes narrowed. "I realize now that I should have stayed in town to help weather the scandal storm that brewed afterward. And I've already apologized sincerely. There's nothing more to be done about it."

His brown eyes snapped fire. "So little, so late." He climbed another rung, his broad chest brushing her hips in an alarmingly intimate way.

Rose's traitorous body tingled again, and she took a nervous step up the ladder, but Sin followed.

"The world thinks that I attempted to deflower you, my little Rose-of-many-thorns. But that's not what happened, is it? I wasn't the seducer in that little scene, was I?" Sin's arms were now on either side of her shoulders, his chest nearly pressed to hers. "Admit it, Miss Balfour. I didn't pursue you at all. *You* pursued *me*."

She tried to swallow, but couldn't. He was right. She'd been fascinated with Sin from the moment he'd walked into her aunt's ballroom, looking as dark, dangerous, and handsome as a villain in a novel. Despite Aunt Fiona's dire warnings, she'd instantly been smitten.

From that moment on, she did whatever she could to attach herself to him at every event they attended. To give him credit, he'd studiously avoided her, making her even more determined to gain his attention. After weeks of being shunned, she'd tricked Sin into accompanying her into the garden at Lady MacAllister's ball by pretending to feel faint. The second they were alone, she'd brazenly thrown her arms around his neck and kissed him.

A maelstrom of physical responses had roared through her when her lips met his, shocking and frightening her. Panicked, she'd put her hands on his chest and shoved him away.

The force of her push had sent Sin stumbling backward, and he'd tripped over the edge of a fountain and fallen in. Appalled, she'd screamed for help, bringing others running.

Now Rose could see how it all must have looked. And clearly the other guests had quickly made their own deductions on finding Edinburgh's most notorious rakehell in a fountain, and one of the year's newest debutante's shaken and red-faced.

The memories were suddenly as fresh as if they'd happened only yesterday. Rose gazed into Sin's eyes, their streaks of gold giving him a faintly lionlike appearance. "Lord Sinclair, I'm so *very* sorry that people shunned you."

He scowled. "It was even worse than that—I was mocked as well."

She looked at him, confused.

"Since the fountain incident, I am now called Lord *Fin.*"

Rose blinked. Then, from deep inside her, a giggle arose.

Lord Fin glared all the more, which made her laugh even harder. She just couldn't help it.

"Miss Balfour," Sin snapped between clenched teeth, "if you do not stop laughing this instant, I will not be responsible for my actions."

His blazing eyes told her that he meant it, which sobered her laughter. She pressed a hand to her lips and took a deep breath. "I'm very sorry to hear that. I had no idea . . ." Another giggle snuck out.

Sin couldn't believe she had the audacity to stand

there and laugh in his face. "Beware who you laugh at, Miss Balfour. It can come back to haunt you."

But rather than looking intimidated, she just looked irritated. "Oh, please, stop being so dramatic."

"You nearly ruined me!"

"Not on purpose."

"I'm not so sure of that. You were angry that I didn't respond to your juvenile attempts to seduce me," he charged.

"For the love of—" She cast her eyes heavenward. "I was only sixteen, much too inexperienced for such stratagems."

He continued to glower at her.

"Fine!" She threw up a hand in resignation. "If you aren't going to believe me, then yes, I did it on purpose. I deliberately embarrassed you because you fully deserved it." She lifted a brow. "Are you happy now?"

He should have been, but she'd robbed him of that satisfaction by taking such an attitude. He narrowed his gaze on her. "You're being deliberately difficult."

"*I'm* being difficult—of all the nerve! I even admitted to something I didn't do just to make you happy! Are you going to hold me accountable for every little thing that's happened since that night? Perhaps you'd also like to blame me for your notorious temper, though you had that long before I met you. Or perhaps you have an allergy to shellfish that you'd like to blame on me? Or a tendency to snore? I'm sure *that* is my fault, too."

Sin ground his teeth. "You are pushing me, which is most unwise."

"I'm not pushing you; I'm *arguing* with you. But perhaps you prefer biddable women." She folded her hands demurely, saying in a high voice, "Yes, Lord Sinclair. Whatever you say, Lord Sinclair." She tittered in a way that made his teeth ache. "Oh, Lord Sinclair, you're *so* funny! I vow, you're the smartest peer in—"

"*Stop that.* I had a purpose in bringing you to my aunt's house, Miss Balfour. A very specific one."

A look of wariness finally entered her blue eyes. "What purpose is that?"

He smiled then, his body holding hers captive against the ladder, his lips so close to her rosy ones. "If I'm to be condemned for seducing you, then I should be granted all the pleasures of that seduction—not just the pains."

She blinked, realization slowly settling in her eyes. "The . . . the pleasures? What do you mean?"

He chuckled with satisfaction. "I mean exactly what you think I mean. This time there will be a *real* seduction. And it will involve far more than a kiss."

Sin saw the flicker of fear he expected, but it was swiftly replaced with outrage. Her delicate jaw firmed and her chin rose as she said in a lofty tone, "That is a ridiculous idea."

"We shall see how ridiculous it is. You are here for two weeks, and I shall make it my first priority to seduce you."

"It was foolish of you to warn me," she said sweetly. "I shall not succumb to your blandishments."

"Oh?" He trailed his fingers down the silk of her cheek. "Are you *sure*?"

She stiffened, her eyes sliding closed. He could see the wild beating of her heart in the hollow of her throat, and the sight sent his own blood thrumming through his veins.

He leaned close to whisper in her shell-pink ear, "You see how it is between us? How a simple touch sets your skin afire? How will you possibly resist that?"

She slowly opened her eyes, her gaze steadier than he'd expected. "I shall be on my guard now. Your plan won't work."

"Won't it, my bonny Rose?" He captured one of her silken curls and slowly ran it through his fingers, noting how her gaze darkened and her breath quickened when the backs of his fingers brushed her warm skin.

He chuckled softly. "I don't think you can resist me, my sweet. That kiss at the fountain showed me that you possess a passionate nature that is barely in control. It won't take much to set that ablaze." He released her curl and traced the line of her throat to her ear. "And this time, run though you might, you will not escape."

Fantasy.
Temptation.
Adventure.

**Visit PocketAfterDark.com,
an all-new website just for Urban
Fantasy and Romance Readers!**

- Exclusive access to the hottest
urban fantasy and romance titles!

- Read and share reviews on
the latest books!

- Live chats with your favorite
romance authors!

- Vote in online polls!

 www.PocketAfterDark.com

26119